Forbidden Key

Forbidden Key
A French Gothic Tale

Joan Friday

The Fairy Tale Series
by Joan Friday:

My Sister, My Soul: An Arabian Nights Tale
The Plans of Morgiana: An Arabian Nights Tale
Forbidden Key: A French Gothic Tale

Copyright © 2021 Joan F. McKechnie
All Rights Reserved
ISBN-13: 9798490425625
Cover Image by Reinhold Silbemann
Cover Design by John McKechnie

For John, David, and Christopher

Table of Contents

Prologue

She raced back through the empty halls of the chateau, her mind numb from the horror of what she had seen. Why was there no one around, no one to hear her screams? He must have planned it this way.

She had to hide from him somewhere, anywhere. The staircase rose up in front of her. Perhaps she could get to her rooms and lock the doors.

When she reached the bottom step and lifted the hem of her skirts, she felt the key still in her hand. Sobbing, she flung it away and ran up the stairs. But the mistake had cost her precious moments and she could hear his footsteps right behind her.

Somehow she made it up the first flight of steps to the landing. He was right at her heels. She could feel his breath. The huge window loomed up before her.

If only she could fly.

3

Marie

Chapter One

"Such a tragedy," said Widow Dubois as she pawed through the early melons at our market stand. "Poor Count de Roesch, to have his new bride fall from a window like that. And so soon after his third one died." She smiled in triumph as she held up a melon. "Does your father think I'll pay full price for this? It's marred. Half is what I'll give you." She pulled out a small purse from inside her blouse.

It was hardly a mar at all, anyone else would have overlooked it. But I knew my father would tell me to have mercy on her. "All right, half my price." I took the coin and put it in my pouch.

Widow Dubois leaned forward. "There's talk, you know. I heard it when I took a new maid's dress up the hill. There's talk about all of them." She was a seamstress and one of the few villagers who went up the twisting drive to the chateau on the hill.

"That's just servant's gossip," I said.

"I'm only repeating what I heard." She straightened up. "The count has already sent for glass cutters to fix the window. All different colors, it was."

I saw her gnarled fingers picking at her basket and thought how difficult it must be for her to hold a sewing needle. "You can have a second melon at the same price, if you'd like." She held up the largest one, dropped it in her basket, and gave me another coin.

Her beady eyes swept over the rest of the fruits and vegetables I had for sale. "That's all I'll give you at half price," I said, perhaps a little harshly. She clucked and moved to the next stall, the melons rolling in her basket.

I looked down the row. All the stalls except ours were full of food to sell. We didn't have as much as we usually did this time of year, not with Papa sick and unable to help in the fields. But he'd be better soon. I started rearranging the melons which were left.

Just as I sold another one the count's large black carriage came down from the chateau. I wondered where he would be going so soon after burying his wife. Most people would stay home and mourn. The carriage came so close I could see my reflection in its shiny sides. The curtains moved as it passed my stand and I lowered my gaze in respect.

It stopped near the end of the stalls and the count descended. He was easy to spot in the village, not only because of his expensive clothes but because of his intense black flowing hair and beard. He lifted his walking stick and called to a man inside one of the stalls.

A second man climbed down from the carriage. It was his servant, Monsieur Martel. He went up behind the count and seemed to listen intently to the conversation that had started. I was staring at him and didn't realize when someone came up and stopped at my elbow.

"Hello, Marie." It was Thomas, the village wheelwright.

I gave a quick smile and looked back down the stalls. "Count de Roesch just went by," I said. "I wonder why he's not staying home."

Thomas spat on the ground.

"You shouldn't be disrespectful," I said. "He *did* just lose his wife." Thomas could annoy me faster than anyone except my sister.

"I feel sorry for the wife but not for him. You don't care about him either, no one really does. Don't pretend, I know what you think." He picked up a melon. "It's marred."

"It isn't," I said, snatching it from him. "And don't say no one cares, he might hear. The village needs his charity."

"You know they say there's a curse up on that hill."

"Only the gypsies," I replied, putting the melon back.

8

He ignored my comment. "And I'm sure he knows what the villagers say about him. Martel, his ferret of a servant, sneaks around and listens to people talk. I don't think anything happens here he doesn't know about."

"That's the one I don't trust," I said. "Martel's too sly. You can see it in his eyes."

Thomas looked up the street. "Anne's coming. I thought it was your day at the market."

"It is," I replied.

My sister threaded her way through the stalls, slipping past knots of haggling townspeople. Anne was three years older than me. She had been working our fields with Maman when I left for the market and she hadn't even brushed the dirt off her skirts.

The count's carriage caught my eye again as it pulled away. I tried to imagine what he had felt, burying his fourth wife, and wondered what the new priest had said to console him. That priest was so awkward. I doubted he'd even know what to say.

Someone shook my arm. "Marie, you're not listening to me." It was Anne.

"I'm sorry. I was thinking about the countess's funeral. I wish Father Samuel was still here, the new priest blinks too much. Every time he talks he squeezes his eyes shut. Have you seen that?"

"Did you hear what I said to you?"

"No, what?"

Anne's vivid green eyes bored into mine. "Maman wants to know how Papa was when you left."

Tightness wrapped around my chest. "He was sleeping. I woke him and asked him if he wanted water or help getting to the chamber pot, but he said no and went back to sleep."

"We couldn't wake him when we got back. You need to come home."

The tightness turned into a vise.

I heard her voice from far away. "Thomas, close the stall for us, would you?"

If she hadn't been holding my arm, I think I would have collapsed. It must have been my fault they couldn't wake him. I was the last one with him. Maybe I should have gotten him

9

something to eat or helped him sit up. I could have sent for a neighbor or had Maman come back sooner. I shouldn't have left him. I should have seen something was wrong and fixed it.

I stumbled on the cobblestones and Anne pulled me closer. She was walking too fast. I could hardly keep up.

We couldn't go on without Papa. I had prayed for his sickness to be healed, maybe I should have given something to the new priest so he would pray for Papa. Father Samuel wouldn't have taken anything from us. He would have prayed with us by Papa's bedside, holding our hands. He should be here. Everything would be all right if he was here.

Somehow we made it to our family's cottage at the edge of the village. I could hear Maman sobbing as we went up the path. The only time I'd heard her cry like that was when our younger brother died of the fever when he was little.

The vise in my chest was smothering me.

We went through the doorway. I couldn't see Papa for the people standing around his bed.

"Make way," said Anne as she steered me through the parting crowd. I saw Maman on a stool next to the bed. She was draped across Papa's chest, her head buried in her arms.

I forced myself to look at his face, although I already knew. My Papa was dead.

10

Chapter Two

I don't remember much of what happened right after Papa died. Anne told me later Maman cried and moaned and even tried to stop the village men from putting Papa's body in the casket. All I knew was they carried him out lying in a hard wooden box and I didn't want him to go.

He was buried in the churchyard near the elm tree. He told us once he liked that tree and Anne thought of it in time to ask for a spot under its branches. Papa was admired in the village and the men who dug the grave were pleased to put him, they said, where he'd see the tree.

Except he couldn't see any more.

Father Gregory, the new priest, said prayers at the graveside. I hated him being there and wanted our comforting Father Samuel back. Maman stood by the casket. Anne and Adam, Anne's beau, were next to her.

Just before the casket was lowered, Count de Roesch's carriage pulled up. He stepped down, came into the churchyard, and stood right next to Maman. His presence felt like an intrusion. When I looked up at him he seemed to be watching me and his dark eyes glittered when they met mine. But I looked back down at the ground and told myself it was grief causing me to see things.

Maman and Anne cried. The village women cried, too. But my eyes were dry as I watched the men throw dirt on Papa's casket.

Later that day when Anne put food in front of me and told me to eat, it was too much effort to raise the spoon. All I wanted to

11

do was sleep. The next day I couldn't eat either. Anne looked worried and told me to go back to bed.

The third day after Papa was buried Adam came over and talked quietly with Anne. Then she went outside and Adam sat next to me at the table.

"Look at me, Marie."

I did, feeling dry and hollow inside. I hoped he wouldn't ask me questions. I had no words to give him.

But he didn't. "You need to listen to me," he said. "You can't sit inside and stare. You have to go out to the fields and pick your crops and sell them at the market. And you'll have to cook, you and Anne, until your mother is stronger. The village wives can't keep feeding you. I'll help you and Anne however I can, you know that. But you have to start doing things again. Your Papa wouldn't want you to grieve for him like this and go hungry."

I watched his face as he spoke and thought vaguely of how lucky Anne was to have him as her beau. Adam was a good man.

"Anne needs you too, don't make her carry this alone," he said, his voice wavering, and that made something inside me break.

I finally cried for Papa. Adam held my hand awkwardly until I pulled it away to cover my face. I cried until I had no strength and could hardly draw in a breath.

Then Anne came in and walked over to where we were sitting. "Is she back, Adam?"

"She is."

She put her arms around me. I laid my head on her shoulder and pulled in deep, shuddering breaths. "Thank you," she said to him. "I can't bear losing everyone at once." She kissed my forehead. "Now will you eat?"

"Yes," I replied, exhausted.

She brought some bread and cheese and they both sat with me while I ate it. Then Adam said, "I have to go back to the mill. Will she be all right?"

"We'll be fine," Anne said.

"Good, then." He rose from the bench. "I don't think you've heard me say it yet, Marie, but I'm sorry that your Papa..." his voice trailed off.

"She knows, Adam," Anne said.

12

I tried to smile and he patted my shoulder. He kissed Anne's cheek and went out the door.

Then I saw Maman sitting in the shadows near the fireplace and realized I hadn't heard her speak for days. "Why is she rocking?"

"She's been doing that since Papa's funeral," said Anne. "At least she's eating. From time to time she cries, but she won't talk."

I knelt down by her stool and took her hands. "Maman?"

She didn't answer.

"Maman, do you hear me?"

She watched the fire and rocked on the stool.

"I've tried, Marie, she doesn't talk at all," said Anne. "Widow DuBois said it's her way of grieving. She said she's seen it before and when Maman's ready, she'll come out of it. We're to make sure she eats and drinks, that's all."

I sat back on my heels and stared into the fire. Papa was gone. Maman was, too. I felt like my world had fallen into an abyss.

Maman finally spoke late one night. The three of us climbed into the bed and settled under the covers. The embers from the banked fire barely lit the room. I closed my eyes and was drifting off when I heard her voice.

"He promised he'd never leave me." The fire hissed softly. "I left everything for him. He said we would always be together."

I felt for her hand under the covers. "We're here, Maman."

"You'll leave me, too."

"No, Maman, we won't, I promise," said Anne.

"Promises mean nothing. I married for love and a promise and it wasn't enough."

We didn't answer. In the silence the embers' glow dimmed even more. After a few minutes Maman's breathing grew deep and even, but I stayed awake far into the night.

That was the end of her silence. But she was different, and it was hard getting used to her changed ways. She rarely smiled and when she spoke her voice was flat. When Widow Dubois heard how Maman was, she clucked and said, "You'll get her back.

13

Sometimes it takes longer, that's all." She had been right about Maman talking again so I took comfort in her words.

It was hard to work in the fields and pick everything for the market stand now that so much was coming ripe. We couldn't get all the work done without Papa and we had no money to hire workers. And Maman seemed too fragile to leave alone.

So sometimes I picked the crops and carried buckets of water to the fields all day while Anne stayed home with Maman and did the chores. Then we'd switch. On market days one of us would be at the stall in the morning and go to the fields later. The other would tend Maman.

But we needed Papa's strong back and quick hands. Even with all our hard work the crops spoiled in the fields and we had very little money. At least this time of year we had food from the fields. I tried not to think about the coming winter. And Anne still needed a dowry to marry Adam.

Then taxes were due and we couldn't pay them.

I was home the morning M. Martel, Count de Roesch's servant, came from the chateau. He entered as if he owned the cottage and looked around disapprovingly.

"Your taxes are past due, my dear," he said.

"Decent people knock before they enter," I said.

He narrowed his eyes at me. "Decent people pay their taxes before I need to come and collect," he said, looking like the devil with his short, pointed beard. He took a paper from his jacket. "Here's the bill."

I took it, making sure I didn't touch his hand. "This is more than last year's," I said with dismay. "We can't pay it."

"Arrangements will have to be made with the count if there's a problem," he said.

"Why is it more?"

"That I can't say. I only deliver the statements to those who don't pay in time."

I stood with the paper in my hand, not knowing what to do. Maman had been out back gathering eggs and she entered the door with a basket over her arm.

"Good morning, M. Martel."

14

"Good morning, Madame," he said, finally removing his hat and bowing graciously. I felt like spitting on his polished shoes. "Count de Roesch sends his greetings to you and wishes you to know that he is available to help someone of gentle birth such as you."

Maman brightened at his comment. "Please give the count my thanks for his kind thoughts." It made me sick to hear them talk like that.

"I regret that I have to leave you with something as disagreeable as a tax bill, but even with your husband's illness taxes still must be paid," he said.

"Oh. Yes." My mother paused, frowning. "May I see the bill?"

I handed it to her.

Her eyes widened. "This is a large bill."

"Count de Roesch extends his apologies and suggests that perhaps something may be worked out."

"Such as?" I said sharply.

"Hush, Marie." Maman put a hand on my arm.

He bowed again. "He requests the presence of you and your daughters to dine with him tomorrow evening to discuss it."

"Please tell Count de Roesch we accept his gracious invitation with pleasure." Maman looked happier than she had since before Papa had gotten ill. How could she betray him like this?

"He'll send the carriage for you an hour before sundown." Martel bowed again and left.

"He's sickening, talking like that to you," I said as the carriage pulled away.

"Marie, don't be rude," said Maman. "He's done nothing wrong. I'm sure your father meant to pay this. It must have been an oversight."

"I don't trust that man, Maman. Or the count. We shouldn't go."

"The count is acting as a gentleman should toward a lady, and M. Martel is his messenger. I'm sorry you don't understand, but it's because you've lived here in the village all your life."

And then, for the first time since Papa died, I saw Maman smiling to herself.

15

Chapter Three

My parents had done the unthinkable. My mother had married Papa against her wealthy family's wishes. As the youngest son of a youngest son, any land or title had long ago passed my father's line, and my mother's parents thought him beneath her. As if that wasn't enough, he also had a cousin who had stolen a large sum of money and then disappeared. My father never knew him, but it still made him worse in her parents' eyes. They forbade her to have anything to do with him or his family.

And Papa's parents expected him to enter the priesthood. When he told them he wanted to marry Maman instead, they forbade him to have anything more to do with her, too.

So my parents eloped and their families disowned them.

Almost penniless, my papa hid their background, borrowed what he needed to buy the land, learned how to work it, and paid off the debt in seven years. By the time a traveling priest told Father Samuel and Widow Dubois who Papa and Maman really were, they had become part of the village. Knowing their background elevated their status in the neighbors' eyes, which Papa never liked. But he accepted their opinion of him graciously and no one ever challenged his right to the farm.

Until now.

"We can't pay that bill, Thomas," I said. "What are we going to do? Papa poured his life into this land. It's all we have left of him. And I don't want to go up there for dinner."

16

Thomas had stopped by shortly after Martel left and we were leaning against the garden wall in front of the cottage. He flicked away a bee. "I don't blame you but your mother's already accepted, whether it was wise or not. At least you'll get a good meal out of it."

"I won't eat."

"Marie, don't be like that. Martel probably won't even be there, if that's why. And you don't have to charm the count, you only have to be there with your mother and Anne. Your mother will be doing all the talking anyway. She seems pleased about it."

"She is. She was singing after he left."

"She hasn't been like that since your Papa was sick."

I sighed. "I know, but it's different. *She's* different. It's hard to explain. It's like the Maman I know is down inside her and there's someone else on the surface. She never cared about her background before, she wouldn't even talk about how she grew up. Papa was all that mattered."

"She doesn't have him anymore," Thomas said. "Maybe those things have become important again."

"Why?"

He shrugged. "I don't know. Maybe the future frightens her."

"But we're still here."

"Sometimes people don't act like themselves when something bad happens to them. I did that when my parents died, remember? I was angry all the time. I fought with you every day."

"Yes, but I knew you'd come back."

"She will, too."

"That's what Widow DuBois keeps saying."

"Well, listen to her," said Thomas. "She knows a lot about people." He pushed himself off the wall. "I have to go back to the shop. Things will work out, Marie. They always do." I watched him stride away and felt like my comfort was leaving.

Several doves flew into the holes under the eaves above me. We had a small dovecote at the front of the house, the only one in the village, tucked under the roof. I listened quietly to their gentle cooing and watched one fly down to the ground and search for a piece of grain. I wanted to stay out here where it was peaceful. If I went inside and Maman was singing again I'd scream.

17

Then Anne came in from the fields, dirty and haggard-looking. All we had inside was some thin soup warming in the kettle. For the first time I thought of the food that would be at the meal tomorrow night at the chateau. Thomas was right, we'd get a generous dinner there.

Anne disappeared into the cottage. I followed her in.

"And we're going tomorrow," I heard Maman say. "We will, of course, have to wear our best clothes, which aren't good enough at all, but I'm sure Count de Roesch will understand our hard times. Not like when I was younger, mind you, when I could have new dresses for anything important. My mother was always careful to have her girls look their best for any available young man, and of course we must do the same."

Anne was standing in the middle of the room, her mouth hanging open. When she saw me she turned her back on Maman and said, "What is she talking about? She hasn't stopped twittering since I came in. What's happened?"

"Taxes, that's what," I said, pointing to the paper on the table. She looked at it and drew in her breath.

"So much! How can he do that? He knows we can't pay."

"Don't worry, the count has something to tell us," I said dryly. "That's why we're going up to the chateau tomorrow evening for dinner."

"Dinner? Why would he want us for that?"

"Because of our background," said Maman. "Things will be fine, girls, you'll see." She started humming and Anne's mouth dropped open again.

Maman patted Anne's shoulder as she went to the table. "He'll tell us all about it tomorrow. He'll take care of us, girls. And remember, you must look your best."

"He could take care of us by not charging taxes this year," said Anne. "He's got plenty of money, he doesn't need more from us."

"We don't need to discuss this any further," said Maman. "Let's have our soup."

I ladled soup into bowls for the three of us and brought it to the table, my feeling of unease growing as I saw Maman's bright eyes.

Then I realized what she'd been hinting.

18

"What do you mean we need to look our best? We're not going up there to entice him, Maman. Anne has Adam and I would never marry someone like him."

She didn't answer me and my chest tightened.

Anne's spoon stopped halfway to her mouth. "Maman, if that's what you're thinking we won't go." She put down her spoon. Anne was rarely angry and Maman seemed to fade as Anne glared at her.

"We're just going for dinner, girls," she said, her voice sounding strained, and I knew she was lying.

There was silence. I was no longer hungry. I went to the fireplace and dumped the rest of my soup back into the pot. Anne did the same.

Maman spoke again. "Perhaps I can find a sash for your dress, Anne. I have a few things put away —"

"I'll wear my own clothes tomorrow," Anne said. "I'm going back to the fields."

Maman didn't answer as Anne went through the doorway.

"I have a lovely dress I haven't worn, even to church," she began, smiling at me.

"I won't wear it, Maman. I'm going to go help Anne."

"What about the work here?"

"You can do it. Or leave it. We'll do it later." I heard her start to protest but I went through the doorway and ran up to Anne, who was marching along the path.

"She wants one of us to catch his eye," I said when I got next to her.

"I know. It makes me feel sick."

"Me, too." I saw a figure on the path ahead. "Who's that?"

Anne shaded her eyes. "Our new priest."

"What's he doing on the field path? And why don't you ever say his name?"

She shrugged. "I don't like him."

"Shh, he'll hear," I said.

He came up to us, folded his fat hands together, and gave a little bow. "Hello, girls. A warm day. Coming back from the village?"

19

I thought it a stupid question since that was the only place the path went, but tried to be cordial anyway. "Yes, from our mid-day meal."

"Did you have a visitor this morning?"

"M. Martel from the chateau," I replied.

"I heard he was taking some tax letters out," he said, wiping his hands on his robe and then stroking his crucifix.

"Please excuse us, Father Gregory," Anne said, "but we have to get back to the fields."

"Yes, yes, good day," he said, giving a quick little bow again.

"There, I said his name," Anne said as soon as we were out of his hearing. "He's so strange, not like a priest at all. I wonder what he was doing out here."

"Maybe he was trying to find someone."

"Who?"

"Probably Martel," I said, "and he got lost." I looked back and saw him staring after us. He turned quickly and walked toward the village. "He was watching us!"

Anne glanced back. "He isn't now."

"He makes me think of a fat rabbit," I said. "I wish Father Samuel was still here."

"Well, he's not," said Anne, and we both fell silent. He was the only one who had gone up to the chateau when the count's second wife died of plague. He paid dearly for his Christian service, he caught the plague and died there several days later.

"Don't you miss him?" I finally said.

"Yes, I do. But I can't talk about it now, not so soon after Papa died."

I took her hand. I hadn't done that since we were young and I was surprised she didn't shake me off.

We came to the edge of the field and looked out over the spoiling crops. "Where's the bucket?" I said. "I'll water, you can pick." She pointed to the bucket half-hidden in the weeds and moved to the first row.

We worked hard until sundown and when we got home, Maman was already asleep.

"She went to bed so we couldn't say anything to her," I said.

"I'm too tired to think about it," said Anne as she pulled off her boots.

She fell asleep almost instantly. I lay next to her, angry at Maman, angry at the count, angry at life. Everything was so difficult. If we were rich like the count, Papa wouldn't have gotten sick, the crops wouldn't be rotting, and we could pay the taxes.

The curse wasn't up on the hill. It was here. It was a curse to be poor.

Chapter Four

The morning dawned gray with the type of heavy drizzle that hangs on all day. It matched my mood and I clunked the wooden breakfast bowls down on the table.

"Careful, Marie," Anne said softly.

I clunked down Maman's bowl the hardest. Some of her curds landed on the table.

"Marie! You must be careful. A lady doesn't spill her food," Maman said sharply.

"I'm not a lady. You and Papa left all that. He was a farmer. I'm his daughter."

At the mention of Papa she stopped for a moment. Then she said, "Tonight will be different. I'll bring that dress of mine out of the trunk —"

"And I told you I'm not wearing it. Neither is Anne. Our dresses are fine."

Her shoulders slumped, but then she sat up straighter. "Then I'll wear it. I'm sure it still fits. I suppose you girls will look acceptable in your dresses, he knows we've fallen on hard times since your father grew ill." Her voice faded.

I wished she'd think of Papa more, even if it made her sad. The rain came down harder and I felt worse. If I came up with an errand to do, I could visit Thomas in his shop. "Anything you'd like me to get in the village?"

Maman gave me a dark look. "We have extra things to do here."

22

"What?"

"We have to press our dresses, and you can't be out in the mud. You only have one pair of boots each, and they mustn't be dirty."

"You only have one pair too, and someone has to feed the animals. Besides, Count de Roesch knows we've fallen on hard times," I said, echoing her. "That's why we're going up there, remember? I'm sure he'll overlook some dirt."

I was surprised Anne didn't shush me for being rude to Maman. I went outside to feed the animals, making sure to step firmly in the mud, and went back inside in a fouler mood than when I had left.

But when I came through the door, I stopped and stared. Maman had pulled out her old trunk and removed the tray from the top. I had seen some of her things in the tray before, papers that stated who she was, lineage charts, some scarves and handkerchiefs that she brought to church, but nothing from under the tray.

I never imagined Maman owned anything as beautiful as the gown that lay across our rough wooden table. It was green silk, the kind of light green you see from the first early spring plants. Long sleeves came down to tight bands at the wrist. The high-necked bodice was tightly tailored silk, the very top was sheer lace, and I glimpsed a dark green underskirt.

Maman was sitting on the bench holding a green velvet hat. Attached to the side was a large feather that long ago must have been white but was now yellowed and crushed.

Then I realized she was crying. I sat on the bench next to her. "What's wrong?"

"The dress doesn't fit her anymore," said Anne. "It's too small."

"It was my favorite out of all the dresses I ever had," Maman said. "That's why I saved it. And now it can't be used." She started crying again, the hat dropping to the floor when she put both her hands to her face.

I picked it up and turned it around. "It would match your eyes," I said to Anne.

"If you're trying to get me to wear it, don't bother. Maman already tried." She turned away.

23

Maman stopped crying. "You could wear the dress, Marie," she said eagerly. "You're willowy, just like I was. It would look beautiful on you."

"My eyes aren't as green as Anne's."

"It will pull out the color in them, you'll see."

I touched the dress. The silk was smooth and my rough, calloused palm caught on it.

"No, Maman, I'm not meant to wear clothes like these. I'll wear my own dress. Let's put it back in the trunk."

"We'll leave it out for now," Maman said with that strange light in her eyes again. "There's time enough to put it away later."

I went to the fireplace and tossed another piece of wood on the fire. It wasn't for coldness in the house, though. The temptation to wear that dress was strong and a chill was growing inside me.

The carriage pulled up long before we had been told to expect it. I watched Martel step down and was delighted to see his spotless shoe land in a mud puddle. He grimaced and pulled it up, then noticed me at the door. Immediately he smiled and bowed.

"Good afternoon," he said.

"You're too early."

A shadow of annoyance passed over his face. "Count de Roesch extends his greetings and would like to give a small token of his esteem to your mother, your sister, and you before tonight's dinner."

"Don't waste talk like that on me. It's my mother who's impressed with it."

He looked like it was painful to keep smiling. "I certainly wouldn't want to upset you, my dear. Is your mother at home?"

He walked up the path as he spoke. Before I could answer he pushed by me and went through the door.

"Good afternoon, Madame," he said, sweeping off his hat and bowing deeply to my mother. "Count de Roesch extends his greetings to you and your daughters. Knowing of your difficulties he hopes that, although it is out of the ordinary, you would

24

consider it proper to accept a small token from him before the coming evening."

"Oh?" she said uncertainly.

Martel went to the door and clapped his hands. Three servants from the chateau stepped down from the carriage, each carrying a large bundle which they tried to shield from the raindrops. They hurried up the path and into the cottage. Maman's eyes grew larger as they lay the muslin bundles on our table.

"Just a token, Madame, nothing more. He hopes this brings pleasure to you and your daughters." And with another bow he went out the door with the servants and the carriage pulled away.

"Quickly, Marie, get scissors. Careful now, don't cut what's inside by mistake," Maman said.

I got scissors from Anne's sewing basket and cut the strings on the first bundle. Maman unrolled the muslin wrappings and a sapphire blue velvet bodice appeared, the material much richer than Maman's dress from the trunk. She lifted it by the shoulders and the rest of it unfolded; velvet and satin sleeves and a long, gathered skirt. Underneath the folded dress was a pair of soft white leather shoes.

There was a note pinned to the bodice. "Lady Catherine" was all it said.

"It's for me." Maman almost breathed the words.

"But you're not called Lady Catherine."

"I was once."

I touched the velvet. It was smoother than forest moss. I was afraid to stroke the satin, remembering how my rough hand had caught at Maman's dress. I picked up one of the shoes. "I've never felt such soft leather before."

"I used to always have shoes like these," she said, smiling as she ran her fingers along the side of the other shoe. "And look, here's a hat that matches the dress." She pulled out a small hat with a plume on it.

"The feather's white, Maman. That's what your feather looked like once, isn't it?"

"Yes, a long time ago."

25

We sat and stared, entranced by the richness of the gown, until I remembered the other packages. "Do you think there's one for me and one for Anne?"

"I'm sure there is."

I'd never shared excitement with Maman like this. We sat together on the bench and giggled like young girls as I cut the string and she unrolled the muslin. A dark green bodice with matching lace edging appeared. On the note was written "Lady Anne."

As we shook it open a matching hat fell from the folds. Underneath the dress was another pair of shoes.

"Green leather, Maman."

"Yes, they can dye it to match the dress. Oh, this will look lovely on Anne."

"What will?" Anne's voice cut through our excitement. "What's this? Another of your dresses, Maman?" She sounded angry.

"No, Anne, not Maman's," I said, still looking at the dress. "It came from the chateau. Count de Roesch sent it for you to wear tonight. Look, Maman's is blue like her eyes, and yours is green. Do you think he knew your eyes are green? And he's called Maman Lady Catherine, and your note said Lady Anne. We haven't opened mine yet."

I reached for the third bundle, then realized Anne hadn't replied. I put down the scissors and looked at her.

She was furious.

"What are you doing, Marie? Don't you see what's happening? Maman, we're not nobility. You and Papa left all that and I refuse to pretend you didn't. I won't put up with this. I'm not going tonight."

Maman rose from the bench with a fury on her face that more than matched Anne's. "You *will* go tonight, Anne," she said quietly, "and you will *not* disobey me. You will wear what the count has sent and you will be cordial to him at his table. And there will be no further discussion on this matter."

I'd never seen her like that and it frightened me. Anne looked unsure but she tried to challenge Maman again.

"This won't work, Maman."

26

"We have been invited to attend a dinner by the Count de Roesch. I have accepted his invitation and we are going. Do you understand?"

They stood facing each other across the room. Then the fire sputtered and Anne took a deep breath.

"I'll go tonight, Maman, and I'll wear the dress because you've said I must. But only this once. Don't ask me to do this again, or I'll leave our house and live somewhere else."

Maman looked triumphant. "One day at a time, Anne," she said, and turned back to me. "Let's see what the count has sent for Lady Marie to wear."

Chapter Five

The carriage came back for us an hour before sunset, just as the rain finally stopped. Maman went out the door first, her head held high and the white plume on her hat waving slightly as she walked. She held the edges of her dress above the mud on the path, stepping carefully and giving the coachman her hand to help her into the carriage. Anne went next and let her dress drag on the ground as she walked. The bottom edges were coated with mud almost as soon as she stepped out the door. I thought of her beautiful matching green slippers, surely soaked from the puddles before she reached the carriage.

I wanted to follow Anne's lead, to scorn the dress and the coming dinner as she did. But to my shame, I couldn't.

I waited until Anne swung herself up into the carriage. Then I rubbed my hands down the rich, ruby-red velvet of my dress one more time, lifted the skirt, and stepped through the door. I tried to place my black leather shoes where I could see stones showing through the puddles on the wet garden path. I forgot about the hat and it tumbled off into a muddy puddle.

"Oh, no, I've ruined it."

Anne snorted.

"Don't worry, dear, it will dry quickly," said Maman. I climbed into the carriage and she took my hat. "Can you clean this?" She handed it to the coachman. He took a spotless white cloth out of his pocket, carefully removed the mud, and gave it back to Maman. She reshaped it and put it on my head.

28

"Thank goodness yours didn't have a feather," said Maman. "We couldn't have rescued that. We should have proper hat pins."

"Why do you care about these clothes?" Anne said to me. "You're only wearing them for one night." A look from Maman silenced her.

We rode through the village and turned at the large stone posts. Winding up the chateau's drive, the three of us were quiet. Through the carriage window I watched the forest pass and wished Anne wasn't angry. It spoiled the excitement of being in the chateau's private park.

I had been in its woods before. Thomas and I sneaked in several times when we were younger. Once we'd even gone all the way to the edge of the forest by the chateau and stared at the dark windows. It seemed a cold and forbidding place, and I'd pulled on Thomas's hand and told him I wanted to go home. He laughed and teased me, but he took me home.

The silence grew in the carriage and I could feel Anne's anger in the air. I cleared my throat and said, "I don't like him either, Anne."

She didn't answer me.

"Aren't you at least curious about the inside of his chateau?"

"No."

I felt the smooth velvet of my gown again. "We'll get a good dinner."

"I'd rather starve." She looked out the window, back toward the village.

"I don't think Adam's angry with you."

"Oh, Marie, be quiet."

I gave up and looked out the window again. The trees crowded the drive and at times their branches met overhead. In the late afternoon light it was already getting dark as we drove underneath them. It made me feel the same way I had long ago, only this time Thomas wasn't with me to laugh and take me home.

We went into the courtyard with a clatter of hooves and wheels. The house was larger than I remembered and the gray stones and dark windows made it seem cold and stark. The carriage pulled around to the front door. The coachman opened the carriage door and stepped back.

29

"He should help us out," grumbled Maman, and then Martel's pinched face and pointed beard appeared in the opening. He held out his hand to Maman. She took it and stepped down from the coach, smiling back at us when he told her how lovely she looked.

When he reached for Anne's hand she ignored him, held onto the side of the opening, and stepped down by herself. I decided I would do the same.

Except when I took hold of the door frame, he pulled my hand off the carriage and held it. "Don't touch me," I snapped. He smiled, bowed, and stepped back, letting go of my hand.

I hated him.

It was hard to come down from the carriage with such full skirts swirling around me and the material caught on the doorframe. It was the coachman who unhooked it, and he took my hand and helped me the rest of the way down.

Martel was already trying to impress Maman with the history of the chateau. I didn't listen. I thought of Papa and knew that seeing us here would sadden him.

We walked through the front door into a vast entry hall. A wide staircase rose up across the hall leading to a landing which had a large, multi-colored glass window. I wondered if it was the window the countess had fallen through.

At the landing the staircase split, winging back with matching stairs going up to the next floor on either side. The ceiling soared high above us. Hallways on the ground floor lined both sides of the staircase. There were rooms off each side of the entry hall. I'd never seen so much space inside a building before. Even the church seemed small compared to this.

Martel led us through the huge main hall to the doorway of a large room on the right which had a roaring fire in the grate. Then he stood next to Maman and announced her in a loud voice. "The Lady Catherine."

Count de Roesch rose from a seat across the room and came to the door. "Ah, Lady Catherine. I'm so pleased you and your daughters were able to come tonight. You are a vision in blue, a reminder of the sky."

I was disgusted with Maman, who twittered and babbled at him as I hid behind Anne's shoulder. How could she do this to Papa?

30

After the count kissed Maman's hand, Martel announced Anne. The count reached for her hand. Anne looked uncertain for a moment and then gave it to him. He swept her arm out to the side as he looked at her.

"A dress in green that's as deep as a primordial forest, Lady Anne. It becomes you." He kissed her hand, too, and I saw her wipe it on her skirt as she joined Maman.

Then he turned to me.

"And Lady Marie," said Martel.

The count smiled as he took my hand. "Blood red becomes you, Lady Marie," he said, and kissed my hand.

"She has a temper to match," I heard Martel say under his breath to the count. I thought I saw the count's eyes glitter as they had in the graveyard.

"Your comfort is my wish, Lady Marie," said the count to me. "I'm looking forward to your company tonight.

"I have one more guest tonight, Lady Catherine. Father Gregory, come greet the ladies."

I hadn't noticed him. He got up from a chair by the fire, adjusted his robe, and came to us.

"Good evening. Such a delight, yes, this is wonderful, isn't it?" he said, addressing his comments to Maman.

"Oh, yes, Count de Roesch is a wonderful host. He supplied our garments, did you know? These beautiful dresses, I haven't worn anything like this in years."

She babbled on, and I watched Father Gregory. His hands were folded and he leaned his heavy body forward slightly as Maman spoke. The perfect listener, I thought, although somehow it seemed that he wasn't really listening.

I felt a hand take my arm and thought it was Anne. But when I turned it was the count and he was much too close.

"Come near the fire, my dear. The evening is chilly."

I stepped back but he held onto my arm. I looked around for Anne. She was staring at a large portrait of a woman hanging near the fireplace.

The count let go of my arm and went to her side. "That was my first wife. Her name was Élise. I met her in the city. We moved

31

here soon after we wed." He gave a sad sigh. "We were quite happy. It was very difficult when she was taken from me."

I didn't believe him. I wasn't sure why, his voice sounded grieved but he didn't seem sad. Then I realized it was his eyes. They were too sharp and alert.

Maman shook her head. "So sad."

"Yes. It was the fever that took her. Then plague took my second sweet wife. She died after I had a visit from a ship's captain, and I always wondered if he brought it with him. That's why I have no more outside visitors here."

"The same plague took Father Samuel," said Father Gregory. He stroked his crucifix and blinked. I thought again how unlike a man of God he seemed.

"Come sit by the fire, Lady Catherine," the count said, moving over to my mother. She was running her hand along a high, polished table.

"Oh, Count de Roesch, it's been so long since I have been in such fine surroundings," said Maman. "When I was growing up, my father had a table just like this one."

"It is yours. I'll have it moved down to your home in the morning."

I heard Anne's quick intake of breath just before Maman spoke. "Oh, Count, how generous," Maman said. "But I can't take it, we can't repay a gift like this. It's really too generous."

"I have no intention of letting you pay me back," he said.

"Thank you, Count. You don't know how refreshing it is to be in your company." Maman beamed at us.

"We couldn't accept such a gift," I began, but he broke in.

"The gift is not for you, Lady Marie, it is for your mother, in honor of her childhood. And she has already accepted it."

Anne sank down into a finely upholstered velvet chair, watching Maman carefully. "Are you feeling well, Maman?" she asked.

"Why of course, my dear."

But then I saw her eyes were too bright, almost feverish. "Are you sure?" I said.

"Yes, Marie. Really, girls, you must stop worrying."

32

The count took her hand and wrapped it around his arm, moving her to the couch. "Your mother is only happy, is that not so, Lady Catherine?" He sat her down and took a seat opposite her. She talked and smiled like a silly girl and it made me ill. Had she forgotten Papa already?

They seemed engrossed in each other so I sat in another chair near Anne. "You'd think she's the one trying to catch his eye," I whispered to her.

"I've never seen her like this. It's shameful, and so soon after Papa died." Anne looked around the room. "I wish we could leave."

My stomach growled. "I want to eat first," I said. "Don't be angry, Anne. I want a good meal, like Thomas said."

"Thomas wouldn't want Maman acting like that."

"Why would it matter what Thomas thinks?"

"Marie, sometimes you're just plain stupid." She got up from the chair and went to a window. I followed her.

"What do you mean I'm stupid?"

"Nothing. Here comes a servant."

Dinner was announced, and we followed Maman and the count into the dining room. There was a long, polished, wooden table that could have easily seated twenty people. Five chairs were pulled up at one end. Maman sat at the count's right hand, Anne at his left, Father Gregory sat with Maman, and I was next to Anne.

The tableware wasn't made of wood or pewter, as it was at our house. The knives, forks and spoons were silver. And the plates were beautiful white and green porcelain.

Right after we sat down they brought in the food. I'd never seen so much, all of it arranged perfectly on the platters. Maman nodded at the servant standing by her chair.

I couldn't help it, my mouth watered as I watched him heap food on her plate. I thought they'd never get to me. Roast pheasant, venison, rice, vegetables, breads – I wanted it all. I didn't realize my empty stomach was hurting until I smelled the food on my plate. I was famished and had to sit on my hands so I could wait until the count began to eat before I lifted my fork.

33

As soon as he began I started eating. I was aware of his voice, but didn't listen to him. All I wanted to do was taste everything.

Suddenly my stomach was uncomfortably full, long before I wanted to stop eating. I put down my fork and felt like crying. All that wonderful food and I couldn't eat any more.

The count chuckled. "My dear Lady Marie, there is plenty of food here. Give yourself a few minutes, you'll be able to eat again." He smiled at me and for the first time I thought he looked kind.

"I'm sorry, Count. My manners are lacking, I know. I've been so hungry for so long, and to see all this food, I couldn't help myself."

"When you eat a good meal after a time of going without," he said, "you must eat slowly."

I looked at the others. Maman was eating daintily, taking small pieces of the food on her plate. Father Gregory was clumsy with his knife and chewed with his mouth opening wide with each bite. Anne's food was untouched and the count noticed the same moment I did.

"Please, Lady Anne, enjoy your meal. I'm sure Adam would want you to eat tonight."

Anne gave a start at Adam's name and I wondered how the count knew about him. Then I thought of Martel creeping around the village. Of course he would know.

Anne slowly picked up her fork, speared a piece of pheasant, and tasted it. Once she was eating, the count spoke to me again.

"How are your crops?"

It was an uncomfortable question. "Not doing as well as they should be."

"I know it's hard for your family to farm the fields with your father gone. Women such as you shouldn't be doing farm work. I'll send down two of my men to work your fields until harvest. Then I'll make arrangements to reap the crops."

"Thank you, Count," I said, caught off guard by his concern and uncertain of how to react. "That is very kind of you. It has been worrying us, how we'd get along at the harvest."

He nodded to me and turned to Maman, once again engaging her in conversation. I felt dismissed.

34

"What should we do?" I whispered to Anne.

"Let him help, I suppose," she whispered back. "I don't know what else we can do. We're not able to do it ourselves, and the men in the village can't harvest for us. It's too much to ask of them."

I didn't like receiving his help, but I was relieved to have someone else take care of Papa's fields. I gave silent thanks, picked up my fork, and ate more of the count's heavenly food.

Chapter Six

It was a glorious evening. We spent hours over dinner. I suspected it was the count's intention to give us time to eat it without becoming ill. We had a light dessert because, he said, anything more would not agree with us. After dinner he took us to the music room where musicians played for us.

Then, much later than I'd realized, he stood, thanked us for coming, and called for the carriage to take us home. And just before he closed the carriage door, he leaned in, told us he had a delightful time, and said we must come again.

The carriage floated down the road to our cottage. My stomach was still full from the lavish dinner and I could hear the beautiful music in my head. The coachman helped us down and we went inside. In the dim light of the fire we undressed and laid our gowns carefully across the table. Then we crawled into bed, hardly saying a word to each other.

It was when I was drifting off to sleep that I remembered something he'd said.

"Maman, he told us his first wife died from fever."

"Yes. Go to sleep," she said.

"But she died of consumption. It was his third wife that died of fever."

"How could he get that wrong?" said Anne.

"It doesn't matter, girls." Maman sounded drowsy. "He just confused them."

36

"And Maman, he didn't say what the arrangements would be for our taxes," I said.

"It's all right," she said. "Please, go to sleep."

"Wasn't that why we went up to dinner?" said Anne, sounding wide awake. "I forgot, with all that food. We still owe him more than we can possibly pay."

"Don't worry, girls," Maman said. "We'll discuss it with him next time."

"Next time?" I said.

"Yes, he said we'd come again, remember? Now go to sleep."

"Maman," said Anne, "I told you tonight would be the only time I'd go up."

"Don't ruin the evening, Anne," Maman said. "I'm much too tired to talk now."

It was only a few moments before Maman was snoring. Anne's even breathing started a few minutes later. But I lay awake until dawn thinking about the chateau up on the hill.

The fields will need both of us," Anne said in the morning. "The rains yesterday will make everything messier today."

"Just a minute," I said, "I'm not done washing the bowls."

But the sound of a heavy cart brought me to Anne's side at the door. Two men jumped down from a farm wagon and came to us.

"Count de Roesch sent us to work your fields," one of them said. "Yours are down the path?" He pointed behind the house.

"Yes," Anne answered. "But what —"

"Remember last night, Anne?" I said. "The count told us he'd send two of his men."

They got back on the cart and took it around behind the cottage to the fields. Just before they pulled out of sight, Adam walked up the garden path.

"Who are they?"

"The count sent them for our fields," Anne answered.

"What did he say about the taxes?"

"Nothing," I said. "I remembered last night after we got home, but it was too late."

37

"He wants us to come back," Anne said, "but I told Maman I won't go again. I don't like it up there."

"Oh, Anne, it was a wonderful dinner," I said. "Adam, you should have seen it. So much food I couldn't eat everything on my plate. He told me to go slowly so I did, but I still couldn't eat it all."

"Did you eat?" he asked Anne.

"Yes, but not much. I wasn't hungry, really. Marie ate like a pig."

"I did not!"

"I'm glad you got a good meal," Adam said. "But why did he send men for the fields?"

Anne shrugged. "He said we shouldn't be doing it."

"Well," said Adam, scratching his neck, "he helped the Bruns once, when M. Brun hurt his leg and couldn't plant."

Anne took his arm. "I don't want to go back up there, Adam." She glanced at me and said, "I don't like how he looks at Marie and me. And how familiar he is with Maman."

"What do you mean, how he looks at us?" I said.

"You saw it, didn't you?"

"Well, maybe, when we first got there. But not at the table or after dinner. He was nice then."

"There's something in his eyes, Adam. It worries me."

"Maybe he won't invite you," said Adam. "That might just be talk, him saying he wants you to come back. Wait and see. The important thing is your taxes. He didn't say anything about that?"

Anne shook her head.

"Well, you'll have to wait then. Here, I've brought you some flour. Can you use it?"

"Oh, yes," said Anne, and they went into the cottage together.

I walked down the front path. There were still some puddles from yesterday and I stepped around them carefully. I remembered how the dress felt swirling around my legs the night before and wished I could wear it again.

My morning chores were done, the animals fed, the house swept, the dresses from last night wrapped back in the muslin. If I went inside Maman would find mending for me to do, and I hated mending.

38

I left quietly and hurried down the road before she could call me back.

Ours was a small village but large enough for a market that pulled in people from the smaller villages nearby. We didn't have all the shops that the larger towns had, but we did have a butcher, a blacksmith, a carpenter, Thomas's wheel shop, and Adam's mill at the edge of the village. Produce was sold on market days in the center of town, and a tinker came through twice a year. Sometimes a peddler brought his wagon through. And when the gypsies camped nearby, they did odd jobs and repairs.

Thomas's shop was almost exactly in the center of the village. I peeked in and saw him working. "Want a visitor?"

He stood up and wiped his hands on his pants. "How was your evening?"

"It was wonderful! His chateau is beautiful inside. He's giving one of his tables to Maman just because she liked it. And he sent lovely dresses for us to wear, because he knew we didn't have anything nice. You should have seen me in the dress he sent – red velvet! It made me feel so rich!" I took a step in and twirled around. "And the dining table! I've never seen so much food. There was pheasant and venison and rice and –"

"Sounds like he impressed someone."

"Anne didn't like him, but he mostly talked to Maman, so I didn't mind him." I took another step in. "And he sent workers to our fields today. He said Anne and I shouldn't be out there, and they'd work it instead."

"You sound quite taken with him," Thomas said.

"Are you angry?"

"No, Marie, not really. What does Anne think of the field workers?"

"Oh, I don't know, she said thank you to the count last night, so I suppose she likes it. She's telling Adam all about it now. I left before Maman found more chores for me. I shouldn't have to do chores, the count said so. He thinks we should have help for that."

He picked up one of his tools. "Well, I don't have servants to do my work. There's a man coming for this wheel at mid-day and I'm not done with it." He bent back over the wheel.

"Are you sure you're not angry with me?" I asked him.

39

"Why would I be angry? I have to finish this, Marie." He turned his head and spoke over his shoulder. "Don't go past the village on the chateau end. The gypsies are camped out there."

Annoyed at his dismissal, I went back out into the sunlight. I was tempted to walk to the gypsy camp just to spite him. But even though Papa had always been friendly with them they made me nervous, so I heeded his warning and turned the other way.

I knew I should go back to the cottage, there was always something to be done there. I couldn't make myself hurry, though. My feet dragged as I went through the village. I wanted to find someone to talk to, but everyone was busy. Some of the village women worked in their cottage gardens, children scampering around their legs. Mme Brun hung her wash. I watched old M. Lambert, bent and tired, patching the side of his cottage. Then I thought of the chateau. It would be lovely to live like the Count de Roesch and never have to work.

I meandered back, daydreaming, until I saw the chateau's carriage at our cottage. In front of it was a large cart. I picked up my skirts and ran the rest of the way. Just as I reached the gate Martel came out our front door.

"Good morning," he said with a sharp bow. Then he climbed into the carriage and both the carriage and cart pulled away.

When I went inside I saw the table Maman had admired in the chateau last night. She, Anne, and Adam were standing by it.

"He remembered," Maman said, running her hand along it as she had last night. "It's just like the one we had. I think it should go here, don't you, Anne?"

"But the bed goes there."

"That can go on the far wall."

"It's making things crowded in here," Anne said, her hands on her hips.

Maman ignored her. "Adam, drag the bed over by the chest, would you?" He moved it across the room. "See, it fits," she said, "We don't even have to move the chest."

"You haven't told Marie the rest," said Anne.

"The rest of what?" I asked.

40

"The count has invited us up again tomorrow night to dine with him. And he said he has a solution for our tax problem," Maman said.

"I already told you I'm not going, Maman," Anne said.

"Just once more. It won't look right if we don't all go."

Anne looked up at Adam. That was annoying. She wasn't even betrothed to him yet.

"Anne," said Maman, "it's really best for all of us if you go."

"I suppose once more won't hurt, Anne," Adam finally said. "I don't know how you can turn him down politely." But he didn't look convinced, and neither did she.

I tried hard not to smile. I'd get to wear my lovely red gown again. I thought of the soft chairs, warm fires, and piles of food. I had to swallow the sudden saliva in my mouth when I remembered the taste of all that tender meat. I could even tolerate Martel again if it meant another glorious night at the chateau. And the count would fix the taxes so we could keep Papa's farm.

Everything would work out, I just knew it.

41

Chapter Seven

What I couldn't understand was why the invitation made Thomas angry.

"You were just up there." He flung a rabbit on the table, a gift for our dinner. "Why are you going up again?"

I looked at the rabbit he'd brought. Usually it would make my mouth water to see meat on our table, we had it so seldom. But it looked a sorry meal with the promise of another lavish dinner tomorrow at the chateau.

"I'm sure this time it's for the taxes," said Maman. "We'll have stew tonight with your rabbit, why don't you stay?"

"No, I've got more work at the shop." And he stomped out the door.

"What's the matter with him?" I said.

"Oh, Marie," said Anne, and she picked up the rabbit and went outside to skin it.

"Never mind, dear," said Maman. "He'll get over it. Help me cut up some vegetables for the stew."

We were quiet, working together, and then I said, "Do you think he'll send more dresses?"

"He may."

"What if he doesn't?"

"We'll wear the same ones. They're much better than any we have."

"I wouldn't mind wearing the same dress."

Maman smiled. "We'll see," she said softly.

42

Anne came back in and I cut up the meat and put it in the pot.

"Is Adam coming back?" Maman asked Anne.

"No."

"We'll have plenty, then." Maman stirred the pot and Anne set the table. I sat in the chair by the fire and thought of the music room at the chateau.

Dinner was quiet that night, and we went to bed early.

I was feeding the chickens the next morning when the chateau carriage pulled up. I peeked around the side of the cottage and watched Martel step down. How I wished there was a puddle for his shoe again. But when a servant stepped out with a muslin package over his arm, I threw down the rest of the feed and ran for the door.

Once again, three servants brought three muslin packages inside while Martel stood in the center of the room as if he owned our cottage.

"Oh, how exciting!" Maman said. "Tell the count we are overwhelmed with his kindness."

Martel bowed. The servants took the dresses we had already worn and followed him out to the carriage.

"I'm not wearing his clothes again." Anne stood by the fireplace with her hands firmly on her hips. "I'll go to the meal, but I'm wearing my own dress."

Maman didn't say anything and Anne stalked out of the cottage.

"What should we do?" I asked Maman. "If she doesn't wear what he's provided it will insult him."

"He'll be gracious about it. And Anne may change her mind."

But she didn't. She spent the day working out in the fields, even though the chateau work cart came again with the same two men. When I brought her and the men a mid-day meal she was in one field and they were in another. She saw me but didn't come over. I left the meals on a wall under a tree and went home.

When it was time to leave for the chateau that evening, Anne just washed up and cleaned the dirt spots off her dress. Maman and I wore the new gowns. Maman's was a dusky dark gray silk

43

and mine a royal blue. We left the dress that said "Lady Anne" folded up on the table.

"Anne, look, I have satin shoes. Are you sure you don't want to wear what he sent for you?" I said.

"I'll go as myself. I'll not pretend I'm someone else."

Maman's hand on my arm stopped me from saying more. We waited for the carriage in silence. There were no puddles to step through when we walked down the path, the sky was clear and there was a warm breeze in the evening air.

But this time it was Martel by the carriage door, not the coachman. "Lady Catherine," he said as he helped her up. He tried to take Anne's hand, but she gathered her skirts and climbed in without his help.

"And Lady Marie."

I didn't like touching him but I didn't want my dress to get mussed. His hand was too warm and soft and I dropped it as soon as I had my balance in the carriage. I was glad he sat up front with the driver.

We rode in silence. Anne's face was stone, and I knew she was angry. Maman smiled and her fingers stroked her dress. I thought it looked silly until I realized I was doing the same thing with my dress.

Count de Roesch was waiting at the massive doorway when we pulled up. The carriage door opened and I saw with relief it was the coachman helping us down. Touching Martel once in an evening was enough for me.

"Good evening, Ladies," said the count, spreading his arms open. "It is an honor to have dinner with such lovely companions again."

Maman twittered something and Anne ignored him. I looked at him in awe. He seemed larger tonight. His clothes were much fancier than they had been the previous time and his hands flashed with diamonds.

He complimented Maman on her gown and she thanked him, sounding thrilled. I held my breath as Anne stepped down, but he didn't seem surprised at all. He took her hand and said, "Ah, Lady Anne, the practical one. Welcome again," and bent over her hand.

When he took my hand, he seemed to hold it tighter than necessary.

"Lady Marie. Did this gown meet your expectations?" I nodded, unsure how to answer. He bent over my hand longer than he had Maman's or Anne's.

The count himself ushered us into a smaller room this evening, warmer and more intimate than the large one where we had gone before. There was a harpsichord, several sofas and chairs, and a small table. Maman went immediately to the harpsichord.

"Oh, I haven't seen such a beautiful instrument since I was young. My father had one and we all played it."

"Lady Catherine, you have an open invitation to come play it any time you wish. Do your daughters play?"

She ran her hands along the keyboard, sending notes into the air. "No, they don't. We have no instrument, of course."

"They may learn here. I will employ a music teacher for them."

"No, thank you, Count," Anne said in an icy tone. "I have no need to play a harpsichord. And neither does Marie."

The count looked at her, smiling, and she glared back at him. After several seconds, her gaze dropped.

Maman began to ask him about the chateau and he turned his attention to her. I went over to Anne.

"Why are you being rude?"

"I told you, I don't want to be here. And I don't trust him. It's like he's playing a game. I'm sure he has something planned we won't like."

I arranged my skirt. "Why do you think that?"

"Because he's like a cat playing with a mouse." She glanced around the room. "At least we don't have the new priest here tonight. I don't think I could bear both of them again."

We stood quietly until the count waved us toward the chairs. He and Maman sat on one of the sofas and continued to talk. I didn't join in, I stroked the skirt of my dress and thought what a beautiful gown it was.

A servant called us to dinner. I ate more slowly than last time and was delighted to find I could put more in my stomach. The count and Maman seemed to have no trouble at all with their plates, and Anne ate more than last time, too.

45

When dessert was finished he said to Maman, "Let's retire to the large salon. I have something interesting for you to consider." He pulled back her chair and gave her his arm. We followed them back into the room.

He led Maman to the sofa. "Please take a seat," he said to Anne and me, indicating the chairs near her.

This was it. Our taxes. I sat down and leaned forward. He went to the fireplace and put his arm along the mantel.

"Lady Catherine, I have heard of your story from others and have always thought you deserved more. Not a different husband, since you loved him and he was well thought of in the village. But an easier life.

"Now he is gone, and you are not able to work your farm. Your taxes are due and because of unforeseen circumstances of mine, I've had to raise them. It grieved me to do so, and I hoped you would be able to pay, but I see now that is impossible. However, I think I have a solution."

He came toward our chairs.

"You have two lovely daughters. With your circumstances, their future outlook is a bleak one. They have no father. They have no money for a dowry. They have no relatives who can help them. Perhaps in one of them is our answer."

"What do you mean?" Maman asked.

"I am a lonely man. I have had several wives, all of whom met with unfortunate and untimely deaths. I have grieved deeply for each of them, but I still wish my loneliness was gone. It can be, if one of your daughters would give me her hand in marriage."

"No!" shouted Anne like a crack of thunder, and it startled me so much I fell part way off the chair. "I will *not* be part of this, and neither will Marie. Maman, tell him no."

"In that case," he said gently, his voice sounding sad, "I will have to take your farm."

46

Chapter Eight

I had been through this before. The feeling that everything was unreal, a dream was swirling around me, and surely I would awaken.

Except that now, as when Papa died, it wasn't a dream.

We didn't move. The fire sputtered, and still we sat. The count went to the couch and took Maman's hand. "You can see how this would be our answer. One of your daughters would be my wife, I would not require taxes from you since you would be family, and you would once again have the finer things that you have for so long been denied. I will be content with either daughter, they are both exceptional young women."

Maman didn't answer him. He turned his gaze on Anne and then me. I felt frozen.

He looked back at Maman and let go of her hand. "Of course, I didn't expect an agreement tonight. I would like to give your daughters a chance to see how enjoyable it would be as my wife. I'm extending an invitation to you three, and one or two of their friends, to stay at one of my other chateaus with me for a week. I will also invite some young people whom I know and give you a reception. It will be a delightful time, I assure you. Perhaps when the week is over your daughters will see me in a different light."

In spite of my shock, I was intrigued with the idea of spending a week in another of his chateaus. He seemed to sense my interest and smiled encouragingly at me.

47

"The chateau is even larger than this one, Lady Marie. I'm sure you'll enjoy it. Anything you wish for while you're there, if it is within my power, you will have."

Maman cleared her throat. "That is very gracious of you, Count, but —"

"I realize it is a surprise to all of you, Lady Catherine. I won't press for an answer tonight. Please think on it and I will contact you later this week."

"We are not a business arrangement, Count," said Anne.

"Of course you are not, my dear. That is why I'm offering time with me at my other chateau, then I will let you decide. I would never insist on it if you didn't desire it.

"But you cannot deny that it would be a wonderful way for one of you to rescue your family and your father's farm."

"Not charging us taxes would do the same thing," said Anne coldly.

I marveled at her bravery but hoped she didn't anger him. He had the power to ruin us. I looked at him. To my amazement, he was smiling. "That wouldn't be fair to the rest of the village. Surely you can see I can't show favoritism like that — unless there is a marriage involved, of course.

"I will give you some time to think about my offer, Lady Catherine. For now, I thank you for your company. I enjoyed my evening and hope you feel the same."

He called for the carriage and escorted us to the door. Then he told us again what wonderful company we were and how much we would enjoy a week at his other chateau. He bowed, the perfect host, and withdrew as we climbed in the carriage.

"We're not going to —"

"Hush, Anne, until we're home," Maman said, and we rode down the hill in silence.

After the carriage left, Anne planted herself in the middle of the room. "We're not going to marry him, Maman. Papa would never have agreed to this. He'd rather lose the farm."

"Papa isn't here. If he was, we'd be able to pay the taxes," Maman said.

"Has anyone else had their taxes raised?" I asked.

48

"Yes, everyone," Anne said. "I heard Mme Bois talking about it. But they can pay. It's harder, but they're doing it. Besides, it doesn't matter. If the count tells us that's what our taxes are, we have to pay them. It's maddening, because he has so much, but there's nothing we can do."

I was quiet, trying to sort through what had happened. I slowly took off my gown and stepped out of the shoes. I knew it would be the last time I would ever wear anything that fine. But then I slipped my old dress over my head and smoothed down the fabric, and felt comfort in its patches and worn spots.

"I'm not going to marry him," I said.

"Neither one of us will," Anne said. "We have to figure out something else. Or we have to move."

Maman gave a sob and put her hands to her face. Anne put her arm around her. "This will work out, Maman. I'll talk with Adam, maybe he'll have an idea. Or Thomas."

I had hardly thought about Thomas since the day before. He already had a hard time getting by, I didn't see what he could do.

"We should go to bed," said Anne. "We're tired and we'll think better tomorrow." She turned down the bed covers and we crawled in.

The next thing I knew it was morning. As I woke I was dreaming of slowly stepping down the staircase in the chateau, swathed in silk and velvet.

When I opened my eyes I realized one side of the bed was cold. Maman was up and out of the house already. But instead of rising I lay next to Anne and tried to think. If we said no to the count's invitation it would insult him and he would take the farm. If we said yes, he would think one of us would marry him and we wouldn't. I turned it over and over in my mind, trying to come up with a solution. There was nothing.

Anne stirred. "You awake?"

"Yes," I said. "I've been thinking."

"Me too." She propped herself up on one elbow and faced me. "Maybe we should go, just to give us some time. Maybe if he gets to know us a little more he'll like us and won't take the farm, even though we won't marry him." She sighed. "Oh, that sounds so…"

"Deceitful?"

"Yes, that's it. Pretending to think about his offer and knowing we'll refuse it." She dropped back down on the bed.

"Well, I don't think it's deceitful. We've already told him we're not going to marry him and he told us to come anyway. I don't know what else to do."

We lay there silently for a while, then Anne said, "We should go."

"I think so, too," I answered.

Then Maman came in. "Awake, girls? The chickens have been fed. Anne, can you take care of the goats? Marie, stir the fire while I start breakfast."

I groaned and rolled out of bed. How nice it would be to have someone else build up the fire and do the chores. I got dressed, pulled on my boots, stirred the fire, and went outside for more wood.

I was on my way to help Anne when she came out of the shed. "Who will you invite?" she said.

"What?"

"To come with us, remember? The count said we could invite a couple of friends. Who will it be?"

"You're really going to ask someone to come with us?" I said.

"We might as well, since he told us to bring someone. I'll bring Adam."

"I don't think the count meant to bring a beau with us."

She tossed her head. "I don't care. I decided while I was milking the goats that I'd only go if Adam came, too. That way I'd feel like we were safe."

"Safe? Safe from what?"

"From his attentions," she said.

"It won't help *me* if you bring Adam. It'll make things worse."

"You can bring Thomas," Anne said.

"I can't bring Thomas, he has his business to do. Adam's father can run the mill, but it's only Thomas in his shop."

Anne smiled. "I think that would fix the count, if we both brought a beau."

"Thomas isn't my beau."

"Well, not officially."

"Anne, we're just friends."

50

"Oh, fine, he's just your friend." She paused. "Who will you bring, then?"

"Maybe Jacqui."

She nodded. "It would be good for her to have some fun."

"That's what I thought. I'm going to find her. I'll meet you at the market stall later."

Jacqui wasn't at her cottage and she wasn't at the butcher's, where her mother had sent her. But I knew where she'd be.

I found her sitting by the bridge near the mill where her brother had been killed two years ago in a wagon accident. I sat next to her and we watched the water for a while. Then she said, "Did you bring something to the mill?"

"No, I was looking for you."

She nodded and drew her legs up, resting her chin on her knees. "I feel closer to him here."

"I know." We sat quietly for several more minutes. Then I said, "Can you come with me somewhere?"

"First I have to go to the butcher. My maman is waiting for the meat. I've probably been here too long already."

"She wasn't upset when I talked with her. She knows you take extra time down here. But I didn't mean come with me today. It's a few days from now, and it'll be for a week."

She looked at me in surprise. "A week! Where are you going?"

"The count has invited Anne and me to another of his chateaus and said we could invite a guest. Anne's taking Adam and I want you to come."

"Why don't you want Thomas?"

"Why does everyone think I should take him? I want you to come."

"I wouldn't know how to act," she said uncertainly. "I've never even been up the chateau's drive." She paused. "But if you really want me, I'll go. I'll have to ask Maman, because I won't be home for chores. I've never been away from the village, Marie. Do you think it's proper for us to be with him?"

"We'll have a chaperone, my maman is coming." I stood up. "Let's get your meat and go to your house," I said, and pulled her up.

51

After everything had been explained and Jacqui had permission to come, I made one more stop before I went to the market. I knew Thomas wouldn't be annoyed with me anymore, that never lasted with us. And I wanted to tell him where I was going instead of letting him hear it through someone else.

"How was your dinner with the great Count de Roesch this time?" he asked as soon as I settled onto my stool.

"The dinner was fine. He had a surprise."

He stopped his work. "What?"

"He wants us to go to another chateau of his for a week so we can get to know him better. He's giving a reception for us, too."

"A reception?"

"Yes. And Maman's going, too. He told Anne and me to bring a guest. Anne's bringing Adam and I'm bringing Jacqui."

He put down his tool and leaned on the wheel. "He wants something, Marie."

"Yes, I know. He wants me or Anne to marry him."

"Marry him?"

"Last night he told Maman if one of us would be his wife, he wouldn't require taxes from her. He said it would solve everything for us."

"But Anne's got Adam, and you're..." He gripped the wheel tighter.

"Anne said right out she wouldn't marry him because of Adam. And I won't marry him either."

"Marie, you shouldn't go."

"He's talking about taking our farm if one of us won't marry him."

"He said that?"

"Yes."

He was quiet for a while, leaning on the wheel. "What did your Maman say then?"

"I don't remember exactly. But we're not going to marry him. We'll just go for the week." I kicked at the hem of my dress. "I don't think I'll ever marry anyone."

"You should marry because you want to," Thomas said, "not because you have to."

52

"Maman told us marriages are arranged with nobility. The daughters marry whoever the parents pick. She was different. I'm glad."

He ran his fingers along the edge of the wheel, watching me. "You need to be careful, you and Anne. He's a powerful man."

"Well, he can't force us against our will."

"No, he couldn't do that. He's sly, though. Be careful."

"Don't worry, I know."

He kept looking at me as if he wanted to say more, but I jumped off the stool. "I'm going to market. Anne's bringing some vegetables to sell, she'll expect me there." I was already out the door when I heard his goodbye.

At the end of the day I closed up the stall, put what hadn't sold in a basket, and went home. As I came up the path, I heard Anne's raised voice.

"You don't know him, Adam. You haven't been there when he looks at me or Marie with that light in his eyes." I stepped inside.

She leaned against Adam. "I'm sorry. We'll talk about it later."

"Maybe I can come up with the money," Adam said.

"Not what he's asking," she replied.

He kissed her cheek and patted my shoulder as he went out the door.

Anne waited until he left. "It's not natural, Maman, the way he looks at Marie and me."

"We're going," said Maman. "I sent word up to the chateau today when they came to get the gowns."

"Don't forget his first three wives died from illness," said Anne, "and the last one killed herself."

"Oh, that's just village gossip," Maman said. "There's no curse, if that's what you're saying."

"There's something not right up there, Maman. Four wives, all dead. And you want one of us to be the fifth?"

"I certainly don't believe that means you'll die, if that's what you're saying." She started to cry. "You girls think I'm awful, but I'm not. I want what's best for you. We're about to lose everything we have. Don't you think I want you provided for? We don't know, really, what he wants. Perhaps he just wishes some

53

entertainment, and then he'll fix everything for us. Maybe it's just loneliness, like he said.

"We have nowhere to go. I can't go back to my family and we have no money to move to another village. What will we do if he takes the farm? Go to the city? We don't know anyone there." She brushed her tears away. "Perhaps we can ask for employment at one of his other chateaus. I could cook, you girls could help me or be maids."

"I don't want to cook and clean for him," I said. "I want to work Papa's farm."

"Please, girls, just do this. We can't anger him, not now. Maybe while we're there we can find an answer."

"We won't marry him," said Anne.

Maman gave a deep sigh. She looked so tired. "No more arguing," she said. "I've had enough. Let's eat supper."

I ladled out the stew and looked at the meager pieces of meat floating in the broth. It was impossible not to think of the count's table and the platters piled high with food. Knowing I would eat at his table for an entire week made me smile and I had to turn my face so Anne wouldn't see.

Chapter Nine

The next day I left the cottage just after breakfast to see Thomas. When I went in his shop he was kneeling over some strips of wood. He stood up when he saw me.

"Hello, Marie." The lines of concentration on his face faded as he spoke to me. "It's early. You're not in the fields today?"

"I don't have to go, the workers came from the chateau." I pulled out my stool from the corner. Thomas made it for me when I complained there was nowhere for me to sit in his shop. I brushed off the seat and climbed onto it. He told me he made it high so my dress wouldn't get dirty from the shop floor, but I knew really it was because I loved to swing my feet.

I perched on the stool and leaned forward, cupping my chin in my hand, and watched him go back to work. We sometimes spent an hour or two like that, either talking or sharing a comfortable silence, broken from time to time when he asked me to get a tool for him. Today we talked.

"Maman sent word to the chateau that we're going."

"I heard."

"I wish there were more people from the village coming. It would be more fun with you there."

"I wasn't invited. Besides, there's no one to step in and do my work. I can't close the shop and leave. I have people from other villages coming to me for business and if I'm gone, they'll find another place to go. My shop's starting to be profitable, and soon I'll be able to afford..." he looked at me with a half-smile, "more.

55

I don't have time to play." He reached for a rag and wiped his hands, watching me steadily. "I'm not worried about Anne, she'll have Adam there. But I am worried about you. Don't go anywhere alone with him. Don't trust him, Marie."

"I know that. I didn't come here for you to tell me what to do." I jumped down from the stool and left without saying goodbye.

I entered the cottage in a sour mood. "I'm glad you're back," Maman said when I flopped down on the bed. "I have something for Adam. He gave us some flour and I've made bread. There's a basket on the table with two loaves for him. Take it to him at the mill. And don't muss the bed cover."

I got up, took the basket, and stomped out the door. No one was pleasant with me today. I walked along the dirt road to the mill. There was a bird singing from the branches of a tree up ahead and I felt like throwing a stone at it. As I drew near the mill, I heard the flowing sound of creek water. It usually calmed me, but not today.

No one was outside the mill. The door opened easily, swinging on its hinges. Adam was filling sacks with flour in the shadowy coolness inside.

"Bread from Maman." I held out the basket.

"Thank her for me." He brushed his hands on his apron and took it. "Been in the village today?"

"Yes. I stopped in Thomas's shop, but he was busy."

He put the basket down in the corner. "You argued with him, didn't you?"

"He's so exasperating. I don't even want to talk to him."

"Marie, I've never heard you say that about him."

"He told me I shouldn't trust the count. I've hardly spoken to the man, and he makes it sound as if I've done something wrong."

"He doesn't think that, it just worries him."

"He's not really worried. All he cares about is his shop." Suddenly I felt like crying and looked away from Adam so he wouldn't see my eyes filling with tears.

"Marie —"

"Don't forget to take the bread home tonight, Adam."

"I won't. Don't be angry with Thomas."

"It doesn't matter."

56

He seemed to want to say more but I shook my head. He went back to his work and I left the mill.

I felt totally out of sorts. And it was all Thomas's fault.

Two days later, Count de Roesch sent a carriage to take us to the other chateau. We were picked up right at our doors. I was still annoyed with Thomas and didn't speak to him again before we left.

He hadn't sent any fancy clothes for us this time. Maman had tried to talk me into wearing her dress from the chest. I was sorely tempted, remembering the beautiful color and how rich it had felt, but Anne said of course I wouldn't and that was the end of it.

It took most of the day to get there over roads and through forests I'd never seen before. I was content to look out the windows as the fields and trees passed by. After the first hour, everyone else was quiet, too.

We stopped for a light meal by the edge of a bridge and then went on our way again. It was late afternoon when we rode through a village, past two large stone columns, and onto the private drive of the chateau. We wound through a forest, skirting a pond and going over a small bridge along the way.

This chateau's park didn't feel dark and dense like the one near our village. Even though it was late in the day the woods were bright with light and dancing leaves. I wondered at the difference.

The carriage finally pulled up to a chateau even larger than the one by our village. The walls were clean, white stone. Dozens of windows reflected a dazzling late-day sun. Wide marble stairs led up to the front door which was flanked by massive white pillars. It seemed magical.

Then I saw Martel at the top of the steps, his hands folded together, watching our arrival. I looked away.

The coachman helped us out. After I brushed off my skirt, I was startled by Martel's voice at my shoulder. "We're so glad you have arrived safely, ladies and gentleman. The Count de Roesch will greet you later, after you have refreshed yourselves from the journey. You'll meet his other guests at that time, also."

He took Maman's arm and led her up the stairs. Anne, Adam, Jacqui and I followed right behind her. I caught my breath when I got a glimpse of the grandness of the chateau through the wide front doors.

We entered and stood in a large entry hall. Polished planks of dark wood stretched in front of us to a grand staircase. Half-way up, the stairway split into two matching staircases, each one doubling back, as the staircase did at his other chateau. The ceiling soared above us and made me dizzy when I looked up. Rooms opened out on either side of the entrance hall, and wide hallways ran along both sides of the staircase. Everything was bigger than at his other chateau, and it was overwhelming.

Then the servants took us upstairs to our rooms. Maman, Anne, and I had a suite. It was an apartment with two enormous bedrooms and a sitting room in the middle. Maman was in one bedroom and Anne and I shared the other. Each one had a large bed, two small chairs, bureaus, wardrobes, and washstands. The sitting room had tables, velvet chairs, and two velvet sofas. Several tapestries hung on the walls and heavy rugs covered most of the floors. Unlit fires lay in the grates. Draperies framed the open windows and moved gently in the breezes.

Our luggage, which consisted of one small bag each, was carried into the rooms and laid on our beds. I felt poor and out-of-place and wished I still had one of the dresses the count had provided for us at his dinners.

Anne and I stood by the silk-covered bed, not knowing what to touch. A maid came in with a pitcher of water and glasses and put them on a small bedside table. Then she went over to the two large carved wardrobes. "Count de Roesch would like you to consider these your garments," she said, and opened the doors.

I heard Anne gasp and I think I did the same. Both of the wardrobes were full of gowns, cloaks, shoes, and hats.

"This one, Lady Marie, is for you," she said, her hand on one of the wardrobes, "and the other is for Lady Anne."

"Does our mother have one, too?" Anne asked.

"Yes, she is fully supplied. You will find underclothes and night clothes there in the bureaus. Your guests, too, will find several changes of clothes in their rooms. Count de Roesch hopes it meets with your approval. If there is more that you want, for yourselves or your guests, you have only to ask. We have instructions to supply you with anything you wish. Is there anything more you want now?"

"No, I don't think so," I said.

"Then the count suggests that you rest from your travels, and he will send for you later." She smiled, gave a curtsy, and left.

Anne and I went to Maman's room. Another maid was leaving her room. Maman was standing by her wardrobe, touching the skirts of the dresses hanging there for her.

"We have new clothing, too," I said.

"It's hard to believe," said Maman. "I thought he might provide a dress or two, but this is far more."

Anne peered into Maman's wardrobe. "So much."

"I think we may have misjudged him, girls," said Maman.

"I don't know." Anne looked uncertain.

I opened one of Maman's bureau drawers. "Oh, look – there are jewels!"

Maman and Anne came over as I pulled out a necklace from a cloth wrapping. Maman took it and said, "Emeralds and diamonds." She opened another packet. "And these are topaz earrings. How beautiful." She opened another and more jewels sparkled. "I've never seen such jewelry. These are worth a fortune."

"What's the red stone on those earrings?" I asked.

"Those are rubies." She lifted up the earrings. "They have diamonds, too."

I ran back to my room and opened the bureau. Several cloth packets were in the top drawer. My fingers shook as I opened them.

"Oh, I have them too! Diamonds and emeralds, and lots of rubies. Anne, come see what you have!"

"They're not ours, Marie, we can't keep them," I heard her say, but I ignored her.

They came through the doorway and Anne opened her drawer. There was a note lying on top of several packets.

"What does it say?" Maman asked.

Anne picked it up and read, "'Please enjoy these while you are at my chateau. I hope they bring you pleasure.'"

She put the note down on her bureau and I looked at it. He had signed it 'Count de Roesch' with a fancy flourish on the R.

Anne slowly opened her packets. "So many jewels." She pulled out a necklace and earrings made of diamonds and black stones.

"Onyx," Maman said. Then Anne held up a green pendant. "Jade. My father had a jade and diamond ring, I'd forgotten. He always wore it. A large green stone on a band of double diamonds. He said one day it would be my brother's." She sat on our bed and looked as if she would cry. "I haven't thought of that for so many years."

"Maman, don't be sad," I said. "I'm sure that's not what the count wants."

She dabbed at her eyes with her sleeve. "You're right, Marie. What we should do now is rest and he'll call for us when he's ready."

She kissed us, went back to her room, and closed the door. After looking through the wardrobes and bureaus, Anne and I took off our dresses and pulled down the covers.

"Linen sheets, Anne. And it's so soft. We've never slept in such a bed."

"I'm so tired I could sleep on a rock." She climbed onto one side of the high bed and I climbed up the other. We fell asleep almost immediately.

Much too soon, the maid was standing by the end of the bed. "Count de Roesch will send for you shortly," she said. "You'll hear the dinner bell. I'll help you dress and style your hair."

I rose slowly from the bed, wishing I didn't have to leave it, and Anne and I went to our wardrobes to choose our gowns for the first evening.

60

Chapter Ten

We met up with Jacqui and Adam at the foot of the staircase after the dinner bell rang. I hardly recognized them. Jacqui was wearing a beautiful gown and had ribbons twisted through her hair. Adam was wearing a well-cut coat, waistcoat, knee breeches, hose, and shoes. Neither of them had jewels.

Jacqui looked delighted. Adam looked uncomfortable.

"Some man tried to help me dress," Adam said. "I didn't let him near me."

I giggled. "Your hose would have been straighter."

He tugged at his trousers. "You should see the room I'm in. It's huge. It's got two big chairs, a table, and a big bed with linen sheets."

"Ours has them, too," I said. "Are you sharing your room?"

"I think so," he answered. "Someone's trunk was there, but no one came in. Are you?"

"Yes," said Anne. "Marie's with me. Maman has her own room, but they're connected. We have a sitting room, then the two bedrooms."

"Oh, this is wonderful," said Jacqui. "When will we see the count?"

"He's supposed to be greeting us at dinner," I answered.

But when we were ushered into the dining room, he wasn't there. "Count de Roesch will be with you shortly," said the butler. He withdrew and left us in the long dining hall.

There were more guests at the other end of the room, eight young men and women our age. They were dressed in elegant clothes and looked very comfortable wearing them. They looked past us as the door opened again.

The butler stood to the side of the door and said, "Your host, the Count de Roesch."

He came through the door, looking splendid in black velvet and white satin. "Good evening, ladies and gentlemen. I trust everything is acceptable for my guests of honor?"

Anne and I nodded. Maman extended her hand. "Everything is beautiful, Count," she said. He took her hand and bowed over it.

Servants came from the doorways and pulled the chairs back from the table. I was surprised at how many there were but they all seemed busy, scurrying in and out of the room, bringing trays of food for us, filling our glasses.

The count introduced us to his other guests as we sat. They were from other chateaus in the region and I forgot their names almost as soon as he said them. I felt isolated and sat quietly while the chatter at the table seemed to rise up and swallow me. The count spoke mostly with Maman, seated at his right hand. I was sitting next to her. Adam was next to Anne, across from me, and when we sat down, he pulled his chair closer to hers.

"Lady Marie, you aren't conversing." The count seemed concerned, and leaned forward. "Are your rooms satisfactory?"

"The rooms are beautiful. And we found the jewels."

"I hope you enjoy them."

"Oh, yes, but —"

He put up his hand and said, "No protests. Enjoy them."

His smile seemed genuine and his voice sounded warm and friendly. He wasn't acting like a man who would take Papa's farm away from us.

"There is something wrong," he said.

"No, it's just, you're being so kind, Count."

"I'm glad you can see this side of me, Lady Marie. That's why I brought you and Lady Anne here. I'm not unapproachable, although I may seem that way to the village." He was right, that's how he did seem. And he *was* a different person here.

62

He leaned back in his chair. "Let me know if there is anything you wish, Lady Marie. Anything at all." He turned to Maman, who thanked him profusely for the rooms.

I kept my head down and studied him through my lashes. Perhaps I had been too harsh in my judgment of him. There was nothing unkind about him as he laughed with Maman. I looked at his velvet coat and beautiful silk shirt. I had never seen anyone dressed in such fine clothes. His glance caught mine and I smiled shyly at him.

"Have you seen the river?" he asked me.

"No, I haven't look out the windows."

"It's a beautiful waterway. We have a private canal which passes near the back of the house. It makes river access quite simple, and I have several boats. If you would like, you and Lady Anne and the rest of the guests could go on a river outing tomorrow. My boatmen can handle everything and you can spend the afternoon on the water."

Maman said, "That would be a glorious way to spend the day, Count. Don't you think, Marie? Anne?"

"Yes," I replied. "It sounds lovely."

"I would like you to have an enjoyable stay here, Lady Marie. If there is anything else you want to do, all you have to do is mention it and I will make arrangements."

He picked up a small bell by his plate and rang it. When everyone's attention was on him, he rose and said, "Tomorrow there will be an outing on the river. Boats will be provided and a picnic will be taken for a light meal along the banks. My boatmen know some excellent spots. I'm sure you will enjoy it.

"I regret that I will not be able to accompany you, business takes me to another town in the morning and I will be there until later in the day. I'll look forward to hearing about your adventures in the evening at dinner.

"Tonight there will be musicians for your pleasure and in two evenings I will host a ball for you."

He sat down, nodding and smiling as several people thanked him. Then he leaned toward me and said, "And perhaps at the end of your week you would enjoy a masquerade ball?"

"Masquerade?" I said stupidly, as if I didn't know what it was.

63

"Yes," he said, still leaning forward. "Costumes will be provided, of course."

"Oh," said Maman, "I used to love costume balls."

"It is up to Lady Marie," he said.

"And Lady Anne," I answered.

"Of course." He turned to Anne, who had been listening. "And Lady Anne. I'm sure you would find it enjoyable."

Anne looked unsure, and said, "Whatever you wish, Count."

He leaned back in his chair and said, "Yes, we'll have a masquerade ball."

And although he had said it was up to me, I knew it was already decided.

After dinner we went to the music room. It was a large room with green walls and white and gold trim. There was a small raised platform where a group of musicians waited for us. They were quite skilled with their instruments and the evening passed with beautiful music and spirited conversation between pieces. The count sat between Anne and me and I noticed that he spoke more to me with each break in the music.

Along with sharing witty remarks with his guests from the other chateaus he asked what I had enjoyed at dinner, what I thought of the music, and if I liked the chateau. He told me a funny story about one of the musicians finding a mouse in his instrument. And when I stifled a yawn, he stopped the concert.

"There is coffee in the other room," he said to me as we rose from our chairs. "And you won't have to sit still for so long."

He and I led the line of guests to the salon. After he made sure Maman, Anne, and I had been served, he left us to speak with the other guests. I always knew where he was because laughter seemed to follow him, both his and those who were listening to him.

I grew bored with Anne and Adam, who were sitting quietly and occasionally whispering together, and went over to one of the windows. The moonlight was bright outside. I was usually in bed by now. For some reason, I thought of Thomas and how we never walked together any more.

"Are you enjoying your evening, Lady Marie?"

64

I jumped. I hadn't noticed the count approaching me.

He chuckled. "I didn't mean to surprise you, my dear," he said as he put his hand on my arm. I let it stay there.

"The musicians were wonderful, Count de Roesch. Thank you so much for having us here."

"You're welcome. I saw you frowning, and wanted to make sure you were pleased with the evening."

"The evening is lovely. I was just thinking of someone back at the village who always has so much work to do now. He says he's building up his business."

"Well, perhaps your friend doesn't know how to have fun. It's a shame, but there are people who wish to do nothing but work. They may be successful, but it does make it hard for their family, don't you think?"

I looked into his eyes and was surprised to see concern there. "Yes," I said, "I suppose it would."

"Think of the poor woman who marries him. She'll be spending her time alone while he works." Then he smiled. "But here, we enjoy ourselves. Your mother told me you and Lady Anne both like to read. Let me show you some of my books."

The count led me to the far side of the room and opened a door. Before us was a large library with bookshelves on two walls stretching up to the ceiling. There were three velvet chairs, a couch, and a polished table with two more chairs. Large windows lined one wall. A fire in the grate threw dancing shadows into the room.

"These are just a few of my books," he said, ushering me in. "I have a library in each of my houses."

"I've never seen so many books," I said. "How can one read so much?"

"Many are reference books for information, such as this one." He pulled a book off a shelf and opened it. "This is about medicinal plants and what they treat."

I took it from him and leafed through the pages. "And poisonous ones," I said, looking at the headings.

He took it back and replaced it on the shelf. "Yes, often what can cure can also kill. One needs to be careful." He reached for my hand and pulled it through his arm. "You are welcome in here

65

any time. Your sister and mother are, also. My home is yours." He covered my hand with his.

"Adam is very attentive to your sister," he said as we walked toward the door.

"They've talked of marriage," I said, uncomfortable about discussing Anne with him.

"Yes, I know."

I stopped. "You do?"

He smiled. "Knowing what is happening in the village is part of my responsibility, Marie. I don't just run the chateaus and give parties."

I mulled that over. "You feel responsible for the village?"

"Of course. We're like a family, are we not? All of us pull together when something is wrong. We share each other's burdens."

"But you're not of the village."

"But I am," he said. "Without the village, what would I have?"

"Everything."

"Not for long. Where would I get workers for my fields and vineyards? Or most of the staff for my chateaus? And how would I pay my taxes?"

I turned to him in surprise. "You pay taxes?"

"Of course. To the king."

This was a new thought. "Did he raise your taxes too?"

"Yes. I wouldn't force more money from the villagers out of cruelty."

So there had been a reason.

"Sit with me, Marie." He led me over to the couch. "I think you have the wrong view of me." We sat down. He seemed too near and I moved away several inches.

"I know there is talk in the village about my wives," he said. His shoulders sagged and he rubbed his face. When he took his hand down, it was shaking. "Please believe me, I cared deeply for each of my wives. There may be things said about me —" His voice broke, and he stared at the rug.

I had no idea how to respond. I waited, wishing I was in the other room.

66

He drew in a deep breath. "I lived far from your village when I was younger, but I always felt a pull back to that chateau. I know my father rarely went there, much of it was in disrepair when I arrived. Then, when I married, I brought my first wife there. She was the one who insisted the large ballroom be restored as soon as possible." He smiled sadly. "She loved entertaining." Then he whispered, "That is why I stopped. I couldn't bear lavish parties without her at my side."

"I'm so sorry, Count," I said softly.

He shifted his body slightly closer to me. "Then to watch my second one die such a terrible death. I thought I couldn't go on."

I didn't know what to say. My image of the count was crumbling and I didn't know what to put in its place.

"And then I found my third wife. I thought she could help me forget the pain I had gone through. But she was taken from me, too."

The fire had gone down, and he rose from the couch and went to the stack of logs. I watched him put two more on the grate. He seemed so ordinary, doing something like that. When he came back, he sat closer.

"And then I met my fourth wife. She was a gentle girl and loved being with me. She was just beginning to learn how to be a countess when –" He stopped and rubbed his face again. "No wonder they say things about me."

"You mustn't think that way, Count."

"Their deaths haunt me," he said. He stared across the room as if lost in memories. Then he sighed deeply and said, "I shouldn't be telling you this. It's something I am meant to carry myself."

"Sometimes it helps to share a burden," I said.

He looked at me with a sad smile. "Not this. But let's return to the others. I don't want them to think I'm neglecting them."

We rose and walked back out to the other room.

"Oh, Marie, there you are. Count, you mustn't take her away," said Maman.

The count gave a slight bow. "Everyone wants to be with the charming Lady Marie, including her host. Excuse me for keeping her to myself. I'll whisk her away some other time."

67

He bowed again and moved away. I closed the library door, wondering what to do with my new knowledge of the count.

I tried to speak with the other young people there, but they all seemed to know each other and had little interest in us. I gave up and sat with Maman and Jacqui. Although the count didn't speak to me the rest of the night, several times I saw him looking at me across the room.

He excused himself before the rest of us went to bed, saying he would see us tomorrow. He kissed my mother's hand and bowed over both Anne's and mine, and then withdrew.

Not too long after the count said goodnight, Martel appeared at the doorway. "It is time to bring the evening to a close," he said. "You will find everything you need in your rooms."

He watched over us while we went to the hallway. I didn't like him there and made sure my skirt didn't brush against him as I went by. Then several servants led us all back to our rooms.

When Anne and I got to our bedroom, we were surprised to see sleeping gowns laid out on the bed. "They're made of silk," Anne said. "I wonder what Maman's is like."

"It's silk, just like yours," she said from the doorway. "Aren't they beautiful?"

I touched mine softly. "I'm afraid to put it on," I said. "My hands catch on everything."

"I have something for that," said the maid who was helping me undress. She reached into the bureau drawer and pulled out a bottle. "This is cream to soften your hands." She poured some of it onto my palm and I rubbed my hands together. "It will heal your skin," she said. "All the roughness will be gone in two weeks."

I stroked the silk nightgown and my fingers slid along, scarcely catching at all. "They don't even feel like my hands anymore."

She slipped the bottle back into the bureau drawer. "The Ladies Catherine and Anne have some in their bureaus, too."

Maman disappeared back into her room and returned a few moments later, rubbing her hands together. "It does feel lovely. Anne, try yours."

"My hands are fine, they don't need to change. If they get soft, they'll hurt until the calluses are back."

68

"I wish you weren't like this," I said. "Can't you just pretend we don't have to go back and work?"

"But we do. I don't want to pretend."

"It doesn't matter, Marie," said Maman. "Get some sleep, you'll have a big day on the river tomorrow. Goodnight, girls." She kissed us both and went back to her room.

Anne and I crawled in between the soft linen sheets. I was so tired, I didn't even say goodnight to her before I was lost in a dream.

I was dancing with the count at a ball. He spoke softly to me and I laughed. But when I tipped my head back to see his face it was Thomas, and there were tears on his cheeks.

Chapter Eleven

"Good morning," said the maid as she opened the drapes. Morning sunlight spilled into our room. "It's a lovely day for boating. Count de Roesch sends his regrets that he will not see you this morning, he has already left the chateau. Breakfast will be in half an hour."

I sat up and rubbed my eyes. "How late is it?"

"It's almost mid-morning. You and your guests have slept in."

Anne groaned and pulled the covers over her head. "I don't want to go boating today."

"Oh, Anne, you have to."

"Adam can't swim well."

"He doesn't have to swim, he'll be sitting in a boat." I pulled the covers down from her face. "We have to get dressed or we'll be late for breakfast."

She groaned again, but she got up. Two maids came in and pulled out dresses for us to wear. Both were beautiful embroidered linen; mine was white and Anne's was a soft gray. They were light in weight and would be cool in the warm sun.

Maman came in while the maids were helping us dress. "I'll spend the day in the library. This is for you and his other young guests, not someone old like me," she said, and wouldn't change her mind.

We finished dressing, had breakfast downstairs, and went out to the entrance hall where Martel was waiting. "The carriages will be here shortly," he said, bowing.

70

He really did look like a weasel. I moved away from him.

Then three carriages pulled up. "We could have walked," I said to Maman as she kissed us goodbye on the steps. "Jacqui said she can see the canal from her bedroom window."

"Nonsense," said Maman. "It's proper to be taken in a carriage. And you'll be tired at the end of the day. Have a wonderful time. I want to hear all about it when you get back."

"The boathouse is directly below the chateau," the footman said to me as he helped us into the carriage. "It's only a few minutes' ride."

"Which is why we could have walked," I grumbled to Anne, who didn't answer. She sat with Adam, opposite Jacqui and me in the carriage. Neither of them looked as if they were planning on enjoying the day.

Three wide-bottomed boats with large canopies stretched across the backs waited in the water for us. A small dock led out to them. There were two men with oars in each boat and another man sitting in the rear at the tiller.

"They don't look very big," Jacqui said, looking doubtfully at the boats.

"They're big enough for us," I said. "Look at the seats. You can sit in the sun in the front or under the canopy in the back."

"But what if they turn over?"

"They won't. Let's get in."

The boatmen helped us into the vessels. Jacqui and I shared a boat with Adam and Anne. All of us sat under the canopy out of the sun.

"This is the most fun I've ever had in my life," said Jacqui, giggling, her eyes shining as we floated out of the canal into the river. Her giddiness made me think more kindly of the count. I hadn't seen her that happy since before her brother's accident.

"You're lucky, Marie," she said, holding tightly to the side of the boat. "I wish the count looked at me the way he does at you. He knows Anne is almost promised to Adam. I think he did this all for you."

The kindly feeling I had about him faded. "He did it for both of us." I looked out over the water and no one spoke. Then I said,

71

"What do you think of this chateau? It's even bigger than the one at our village."

"You have to come and see my room. It's beautiful," said Jacqui, evidently not noticing the awkward silence, "and it's huge, almost as big as our whole cottage. Come tonight, when we go up after dinner. I've never had so many gowns. Five of them! They're velvet and linen and satin!"

"You can wear the fanciest one tomorrow night," I said. "Remember, the count is giving a ball for us."

"Oh, I haven't forgotten!" she said. "We can act proper and dance in a real ballroom instead of on the village green. I think the count is wonderful for doing so much, don't you?"

I paused. Why should I feel a touch of unease? The memory of his threat to take the farm seemed so far away here. "Yes, he's being very kind."

"And especially kind to you," she said.

When I didn't answer, Anne took my hand. "Look, we're ahead of the others. They've made it a race. They're trying to get in front of us."

I was grateful to her for stepping in. I squeezed her hand as we watched the other boats struggle to pull abreast of ours. The oarsmen had a good-natured race and when we finally went ashore for the picnic, we were far upriver from the chateau.

The boatmen doubled as servers and spread several large tablecloths on the riverbank. The ground was flat and had a stand of trees where we sat in the shade. Basket after basket came out of the boats and the boatmen piled the tablecloths high with food. Anne and Adam dropped their earlier sourness and laughed with the rest of the group.

After the meal Jacqui and I made flower chains like we used to do when we were little. Then we all lounged under the trees until it was time to go back.

The shadows were getting long when the boats went swiftly downstream, the current in our favor and the oarsmen pulling strong. We came up to the dock as dusk fell. I was disappointed when the edge of my sleeve caught on the side of the boat and ripped as we were getting out. It seemed to spoil the day when I saw a jagged tear in the finely embroidered linen.

"Never mind, Marie," said Jacqui as she watched me inspect the hole. "You have better dresses back in your wardrobe."

"Yes," I said, "but this one's so pretty. Do you think there's anything nicer than all these beautiful things the count has here?"

"Maybe not." She looked up at the chateau, then said, "Let's get in the carriage."

I folded the edges of the tear into the fabric to hide it and gave my hand to the coachman. I was glad for the carriage now. Maman was right, I was tired after a day on the river.

My throat tightened when I saw Martel waiting at the top of the steps at the chateau. He laced his long fingers together as we reached him and said, "I hope you and your guests had a pleasant outing on the river today."

"We did," Anne said as she walked by him. I didn't answer. The others thanked him as they came to the top of the stairs. It annoyed me, he wasn't the host. But he smiled and nodded as if he was, and I wanted to spit on his feet.

"The count will meet you in the dining room for dinner," he said as he came in behind us, "but first he wishes to give you time to rest."

It was a relief to leave him behind as we went up the steps.

Maman was waiting in our sitting room upstairs. We told her about our day on the river and before we'd realized it, an hour had passed and several maids came in to help us get ready for dinner.

I splashed cold water on my face from the washbasin and the maid handed me a towel and pulled over a stool. "Would you like to sit while I help you choose your gown for the evening?"

I sat down. I didn't have to do anything, not even open the wardrobe door.

"Would you like this one?" she asked, pulling out a blue silk dress.

"Yes, that would be fine." I would have agreed to any of them, all the gowns were lovely.

Anne's maid took one out for her and they helped us dress. Then we went to Maman who was waiting for us in the sitting room.

"I'm tired," said Anne, covering a yawn.

73

"You'd think after farm work, a day like today wouldn't bother us," I said, yawning like Anne as the three of us went down the hallway.

When the butler opened the dining room doors the count was at the far end, standing at the head of the table. "And how was the river?" he asked as we filed in.

"We had races," I said as he took my hand and lightly kissed it, "and a picnic, and sat in the fields, and —"

He laughed. "I'm so pleased, Marie."

I felt a thrill go up my spine as he looked at me. I dropped my gaze but couldn't help smiling. Then I realized he'd called me by my given name.

"I see you are more comfortable with me," he said softly, and moved a step nearer. "I was hoping for that."

"Let's sit," said Anne, and pulled me away.

"Fresh air does sharpen the appetite, doesn't it, Lady Anne?" he said to her.

"Yes," she said curtly. I was amazed she dared to speak to him like that.

We took our seats and they brought dinner out. I no longer had trouble eating a large quantity of food and tried everything they put in front of me.

"Slow down, Marie," said Maman, tapping my hand with her fork. "You're acting as if you haven't eaten for a week."

"She's welcome to have anything she wants," said the count, leaning back in his seat and watching me with obvious amusement.

I put my fork down, feeling warmth creeping up my face. "It's so delicious, Maman, it's hard to stop."

More meat, this time venison, appeared. I didn't want to look greedy, but we never got venison at home. I took some.

People started talking around the table and I realized how quiet it had been. Finally full, I put down my fork. There were several conversations going on at once, and everyone seemed happy. Maman, Adam and Anne were discussing something about the mill, and I stole a look at the count. He was so handsome tonight, with his dark, wavy hair, dark eyes and lovely clothes. The

74

candelabras on the table threw part of his face into shadow and made him look alluring and mysterious.

He saw me looking at him and smiled. Feeling almost brazen, I smiled back. His face was mesmerizing, and the conversations around me rose and fell in waves of noise. It seemed there was no one in the room but the count and me, and I couldn't take my gaze from his face. He leaned forward, never taking his eyes from me, and said my name. I felt as if I was falling.

"Marie, are you all right?" said Anne.

I didn't want to stop looking at the count, he was so lovely. But he broke his gaze with me and spoke to her. "I think perhaps she's gotten a bit more sun than she's used to, out on the river. It's different on a boat than on land. The sun reflects up into one's eyes and tires one more quickly."

"Is that it, Marie?" She sounded concerned.

"I think so," I said. "I'm very tired."

"You'll sleep well tonight," said the count, and reached into his pocket. "But before I lose all of you for the evening, I wish to give a surprise to my two special guests and their mother. I thought these little gifts would amuse you," he said, nodding to Maman, Anne, and me as he drew out three small boxes tied with satin ribbons.

"First is yours, Lady Catherine." He put one of the boxes in front of her. Maman untied the ribbon and opened the box.

She gasped. "Oh, Count, how beautiful. Topaz." She pulled out a necklace of gold and brown stones.

The count nodded when she thanked him. He slid the next box over to Anne.

After staring at Maman's necklace for a few moments, she looked down at the box, then at Adam.

"Open it," Adam said with a shrug.

She pulled out a pair of emerald earrings and a matching necklace. "To match your eyes, Lady Anne," said the count.

"Thank you," she said, but I knew she didn't like them.

He smiled at me. I tugged on the black satin ribbon and it fell away. I lifted the lid on the box and drew in a long breath as I looked at diamonds sparkling against the black velvet lining. "Oh, Count, they're beautiful. I've never seen anything so beautiful."

75

"I have," he said, and I looked up at him. He was staring intently at me, his eyes boring into my soul. I felt I couldn't breathe.

I looked back down at the box and then held up the diamond earrings and pendant. "Look, Maman."

I heard the others whispering as they saw what he'd given to me. Maman said something, but I wasn't really listening. My head was spinning. I was afraid to look back up at the count, afraid that he was still watching me.

"Thank you, Count de Roesch," I said, still looking at the diamonds.

"You're quite welcome, Lady Marie. I hope all three of you enjoy your gifts." He rose from his chair. "And now you must excuse me for the evening. Good night."

He bowed deeply and everyone said goodnight to him. He quickly kissed the hands of Maman and Anne, and bent over my hand. "The lovely Lady Marie deserves much more than a token such as this," he said, and his kiss, harder than usual, burned on my hand.

Anne ruined it all later when we were in our sitting room. "We can sell these jewels. Marie, Maman, give me your boxes. I'll keep them all together."

She held out her hand. I leaned away from her. "I don't want to sell them."

"Marie, this is how we'll pay our taxes. Don't you see? He's given us a way." Her hand was still extended, waiting for the box. But I didn't want to give up my beautiful diamonds.

"Let's wait," I said. "Maybe he'll do something else to help with the farm and we can keep these."

"What's the matter with you? We can't have jewels like these. Maman, tell her. We have nowhere to wear them."

"Let's do what Marie wants," said Maman, looking at her box. "We'll wait. Perhaps the count does want us to keep these."

Anne looked angry as she rose to go into our bedroom. "All right, you can wait," she said over her shoulder. "But I'm selling mine."

76

I looked over at Maman. "We'll see," she whispered, and smiled.

Chapter Twelve

The next day passed quietly. We played card games and strolled in the gardens near the house. It didn't matter that we weren't doing very much. Everyone was thinking about the ball that night.

During the evening meal we were all told our clothing had been delivered upstairs. But when Anne and I went to our room, nothing was there.

Then a maid appeared at our door. "The Count de Roesch has sent special gowns for you." She stepped aside and two more maids came in and hung our dresses on our wardrobe doors.

"This one is yours," one of them said to me. It was a gown of cream-colored silk which seemed to shimmer in the light.

Anne's dress was emerald green velvet. I felt a stab of envy when I looked at it knowing how green her dress would have made my eyes. But mine, I decided, was prettier.

Anne went over to the dresses and held out the skirt of her gown. "These are beautiful," she said. For once, there was no undercurrent of resentment in her voice. "The emeralds will match it perfectly."

I bit my tongue so I wouldn't remind her she wanted to sell them.

The maids helped us dress, then did our hair. They pulled it back and shaped it until we had long curls, wound through with pearls and ribbons. Then they brought powder and rouge for our faces. Our new jewels were the perfect finishing touch. I felt waves of excitement thinking of the count's approval.

78

Maman looked regal in a silver dress with white lace. She smiled her approval at Anne and me.

When the dining room doors opened and we entered, the count was standing at the head of the table waiting for us. He watched only me as we approached him. After Maman greeted him, I extended my hand to him. He bowed over it, and then held it to his lips. When he straightened up, he didn't let go of my hand for several seconds. I was sure everyone noticed. I didn't mind at all.

At dinner, I hardly even tasted what was served. I felt triumphant. I was the one he was watching, I was the one he spoke to the most. Anne had a worried look which I found annoying. I was fully capable of taking care of myself, and there was nothing wrong with the count being interested in me.

But underneath my pleasure, I still felt a thread of unease. And it wouldn't go away.

After dinner the count took Maman's hand and tucked it under his arm. He kept his hand on hers as we followed them through the hallway to the ballroom. Two servants opened the double doors and we swept into the room.

It was lavishly decorated. Ribbons twisted through the standing lamps and hung from the ceiling. Bouquets of flowers overflowed their vases. Sofas and chairs lined the walls. The musicians were at one end of the long room and played softly as we entered. There were other couples, too. I wondered if they were the parents of those who were staying with us for the week.

The count danced first with Maman, holding her hand up high between them. Anne and Adam followed, and slowly the rest of the group paired off. All except me.

I went over to the sofas and sat down, spreading my gown around me. Somehow it didn't seem quite as beautiful now that I was the only one not out on the floor. I folded my hands and stared at a small mark in the highly polished wooden floor. Why hadn't he asked another boy here to be my partner? Didn't he know this would happen? I felt like crying.

79

Someone walked over to me. I didn't look up, I didn't need to. I knew who it was. "My dear Lady Marie," the count said softly.

I kept my eyes on the floor and squeezed my hands together.

He knelt in front of me and covered my hands with his. "The princess of the ball shouldn't be sitting on the side," he said.

"The princess doesn't seem to have a prince." I could feel my face crumple and began to cry.

"You don't need a prince," the count said, pulling me up. "You have already won the heart of the king. So don't cry, my queen for the evening." He wiped my tears away with his fingers, and I was surprised at how gentle his touch was. "Tonight this ball is for you."

We glided out onto the floor. Why had I ever been uneasy around him? When our eyes met, his were warm and alive. And his smile was soft and inviting.

The rest of the night passed in a blur. We danced minuets, contredances, and variations of the village's country dances. Anne gave me sharp looks across the floor. Maman had a satisfied smile as she watched me with the count. And I saw envy in the eyes of the other girls. It made me feel giddy. The music slid through the air, into my fingertips, and out my toes. The candles on the chandeliers high above us seemed like stars, and I wanted to dance with him forever.

But others danced with me, too, and I found myself watching the count when he wasn't with me. When he and another girl laughed, I felt a twinge of jealousy. I wanted him to be with me.

"Our generous count certainly seems to be making you happy tonight," said Adam when he was my partner.

"Perhaps," I said, irritated at his condescending tone.

"Don't forget this is the man who told you he would take your father's farm unless you or Anne married him." His eyes searched mine. "You *have* forgotten, haven't you?"

I stopped dancing as the magical air crashed down around me. "Why are you trying to spoil my evening? I haven't forgotten." But I had.

"Marie, look through him. Why is he doing this? He wants a wife, and he wants it to be you or Anne. And it's not going to be Anne, he can see that now. So he's trying to charm you instead.

80

And it's working. This isn't what you are, Marie. You're a village girl, not a countess. Don't you see what he's doing? He's —"

"Stop! I don't want to hear what you think!"

"Come sit with Anne and me," he said, trying to guide me to the chairs. I planted my feet and he bumped into me.

"I don't want to go over there," I said.

"Marie." Anne called to me and patted the seat next to her. Adam gave me a little push in the small of my back. I walked stiffly over to her.

"Do you want to ruin my evening, too?"

"No, I want to sit with you a while." She patted the chair again, and I sat down.

"The count is paying quite a bit of attention to you," Anne said. I didn't answer. "I saw him kneeling by your chair. What was he saying?"

"It doesn't matter," I snapped.

Anne sighed. "Marie, he makes me uncomfortable. I know Maman loves this, but I still wish we weren't here. And it frightens me, how he's behaving with you."

"I haven't done anything wrong," I said.

"Anne didn't say *you're* doing something wrong," said Adam. "It's the count who worries her. He worries me, too."

"Maybe he's trying to find someone to be his friend because no one trusts him," I replied.

Anne took my hands in hers. "I know this is hard. He's paying a lot of attention to you, and that can be a wonderful thing, a man's interest. But not this man."

"I think you're all being unfair," I said, tightness squeezing my chest.

"Marie," said Adam, so softly I could barely hear him. "Four wives now. And the last one went through a window. No one knows for sure what happened. And he wants you to be next. It's not safe up there. There's something wrong with that place. We don't want to see you living at the chateau."

"You don't want me happy, you mean," I said, angry with both of them. "You don't want me to have nice things and not worry about how to get food or —"

"Shh," Anne said. "Don't shout."

81

"I'm not shouting." I pulled my hands away from her.

"What about Thomas?" she said.

"What about him? He didn't want to be here with me. He doesn't care at all." I started tearing up again.

"He *does* care for you, Marie," Anne said gently. "He always has."

"No he doesn't." I wiped my tears away. "He only wants to work."

"Who's talking about work tonight?" The count's voice boomed out near us and we all jumped. "Come back and join the party, my friends. Lady Anne, would you be my partner? It's the end of the evening, our last dance." He held out his hand to her.

She hesitated, but then took it and rose from the chair. Adam and I came onto the floor behind them, and we danced for the last time that evening.

I wished I was dancing with the count.

Chapter Thirteen

The next morning was cloudy and gray. Anne and I dressed quietly with the help of a maid, both of us tired from the ball. We had spoken very little to each other since arguing the night before.

"The count had to leave early this morning. He said to bring breakfast to your room," the maid told us. "We'll do the same for the other guests. Since it's Sunday, there will be a short service in the chapel when everyone has awakened."

Two servants entered carrying trays with breads, pastries, and coffee. We sat at the low table with Maman while one girl poured our coffee.

"This is much more than we could ever eat," Anne said.

"The count wanted to make sure you had an adequate selection," said the maid. "If there is something you would like that isn't here, we'll get it for you."

"This is fine, thank you," Maman said. "That will be all."

They left, and the three of us were alone. "One tray would have been plenty," said Anne.

"It's the graciousness of the count," said Maman rather sharply. Anne looked up at the ceiling. I was glad Maman didn't see it.

We finished eating in silence. Maman retreated to her room and Anne and I wandered downstairs. It was drizzling outside and all the rooms had fires in the grates. We settled into chairs in one of the rooms and a servant immediately appeared to ask if we wanted anything.

"Does the count always have fires in the rooms, even when they're not occupied?" I asked.

"No, he ordered it today so your guests will be comfortable in any room they choose."

"I can't imagine wasting all that wood," Anne said. The maid didn't answer, and there was a stretch of silence.

"Thank you," I said. "That will be all."

When she had left, I turned to Anne. "Why are you criticizing him so much? First it's breakfast, now the firewood."

"It's overwhelming, don't you think?" she said. "It makes me uncomfortable to be around excess like this."

"You're insulting him."

"And you're fascinated with him," she said. "Don't forget what this man's trying to do to us." She got up from the chair and faced me, her chin set. "Has he dazzled you so much you've forgotten who you are and what he wants? Don't do this. Don't be deceived by his riches."

"I'm not deceived! You're jealous because you're going to marry Adam and you wish you weren't, because you can't have this and I can."

The words were out before I had time to think. Her mouth dropped open. We stared at each other, Anne with a look of shock still on her face and me smoldering inside. I didn't dare say any more. She turned and left the room without another word.

I stared at the fire, its warmth on my face. Fine, she could leave. I was right. She wished she was in my place and the count was paying more attention to her. I was the lucky one.

I watched the flames, trying to ignore that uneasy feeling which never seemed to leave. Anne wasn't going to ruin my delight in the count's attention.

But now she was angry with me, and I felt all alone.

We went to the service in the small chapel behind the chateau with the other guests. I sat apart from Anne. She didn't even look at me.

After it ended we went back to our rooms. When I walked in, Anne and Maman were already reading by the fire. Maman smiled

84

at me, but Anne didn't look up. I went downstairs and played games with the others. It rained steadily and the day passed slowly.

At the mid-day meal Anne acted as if nothing had happened, so I relaxed and asked her if she wanted to play chess after we ate. It was while we were playing that I asked one of the servants about the count's previous wives.

"His wives? I don't know about them, Lady Marie. I'm new here," she said.

"Someone else must have been here long enough to know, Marie," Anne said, moving one of her men. "You can ask them."

"No, Lady Anne, the staff is all new," the maid said.

"Everyone?" Anne said.

"The butler, he's been here, but he doesn't talk to us," the girl said.

"I don't like it," Anne said, watching the girl walk away.

"Check," I said, moving my queen.

"Checkmate," she answered absently, pointing to her rook and its path to my king.

I sighed. She always won games. "Want to play again?"

"No, I'm going to help Adam at cards."

I felt out-of-sorts again and was delighted when Peter, one of the other guests, saw the empty seat and sat down across from me.

The dinner bell rang while I was winning the second game. At the meal, the count charmed everyone. Our end of the table was constantly in laughter from something he had told us.

There was a concert in the music room after dinner again, and then the count retired. All of us went upstairs shortly after he left; the evening seemed flat with him gone.

Maman, Anne and I all found flowers on our pillows. Maman's were yellow and Anne's were white.

Mine was a single red rose.

The first thing I saw in the morning was my rose in a small vase by the side of my bed. I smiled and snuggled down under the covers. The count was wooing me and it was wonderful.

85

But I was disappointed when he wasn't at breakfast. "The count is in his office," the butler told me when I asked. "He will greet you later this morning."

I hardly answered Maman and Anne when they asked if something was wrong. I wanted him there, to look at me with tenderness in his eyes, telling me I had won the heart of the king.

He appeared briefly in the parlor at the end of the morning, kissed the hands of Maman, Anne and me, and talked with everyone. We were having a picnic later in the day, and at first he said he couldn't come. My face must have shown disappointment because he said, "Perhaps I spoke too soon. Let me rearrange a few things, and I will join you. Does that please you, Lady Marie?"

Aware that everyone was watching me, I nodded, looking down at the floor, and felt myself blushing. When I raised my head, he was gone.

He came to the picnic, just as he said. He strode across the lawn as the servants were putting out the meal on large cloths under the trees. "I didn't forget my promise, Lady Marie," he said as he bowed over my hand. I could hear one of the girls giggling.

When a servant tried to put a plate in front of him, he brushed it away. "No, no, I'm only here for the company." He chatted pleasantly with everyone as we ate, and then moved closer to me. "I'm so pleased to see you enjoying yourself," he said. "Your maman and sister are enjoying their time, too."

"Yes," I answered, "Maman hasn't been this happy for a long time." She was laughing with Peter as I spoke, and when she saw us looking at her, she waved.

Anne, seeing the count sitting so close to me, watched us suspiciously. I hoped he didn't notice.

Then he bent nearer to me. "You can have all this, Marie. Think of how wonderful it will be to become mistress of a chateau and how happy it would make your maman. And Anne would be able to marry Adam, who I can see is a perfect match for her, don't you think?"

I nodded, glancing over at Anne again. She was still frowning at us.

86

The count seemed too close to me. I moved the edge of my gown away from him. Immediately he rose and bowed, first to me and then to the rest of the party. "It has been a pleasure to join you, but I must return to the chateau. I will see you again this evening."

As he walked away I had a sick feeling in my stomach. He had left because I pulled away from him. First I wanted him close, then I didn't. What was wrong with me?

I was restless. Everyone was sleeping in anticipation of another late evening of music and games, and the halls were quiet. I went down the broad staircase, sweeping my fingers along the smooth, polished banister. There wasn't a speck of dirt anywhere, even in the corners of the steps. The count's army of servants made sure everything here sparkled.

At the bottom of the steps I looked up at the ornate gold chandelier with dozens of unlit candles. The ceiling above it was high and vaulted, divided into four quarters, with paintings of angels and clouds in each section.

I looked around at the polished floor, the rooms off the hall, and the heavy wooden front doors. How would it feel to be the mistress of this chateau? The thought made my head spin. To have all this as my own, to live in such grandeur, wear these beautiful clothes every day, and have servants to do whatever I wished, was more than I had ever imagined. And that's what was being offered to me. All I had to do was marry the count. So much would be solved. The farm would be safe, Anne could marry Adam, Maman would be provided for. And I would have this.

I had a sudden image of him the day we buried Papa, with his eyes glinting at me. My chest grew tight and I reached for the railing. His eyes had gleamed at me like that at his other chateau, when Maman and Anne and I first went there for dinner. And Martel – he crept around here, too, just like in the village, watching us, gathering information. He seemed so like a devil. He would be with the count, near me all the time. I grew so frightened I couldn't breathe. The walls seemed to move. Darkness edged my vision.

87

"Marie!" It was the count's voice and I saw his face as I felt myself sway. His arm went around me and pulled me down to sit on the staircase. I buried my head in my arms.

"Get water for her," he said, and I heard someone running. Everything seemed to be spinning around and I felt sick to my stomach.

Then I heard whispers and a woman said, "I'll take her there, Count." Then she said, "Lady Marie, can you stand?"

She waited until I finally nodded. When I stood up, slowly and carefully, the count was gone. "Let's go to the smaller salon," she said, "and have you lie down."

She helped me to the room and I sat on the sofa. The count came in and took my hand, looking worried. "Marie, you're not well. Your constitution isn't used to these late nights. I'm sorry, my dear, I've been selfish."

"I thought I wasn't tired," I said, "but I must have been wrong. I should be resting like everyone else."

The worry on his face eased. "The maid will help you upstairs and we'll make sure everyone has an early night tonight." He patted my hand and rose. "No more fainting spells. I want to take care of my favorite guest, not make her ill."

He motioned for the maid and she came over. "Take her back upstairs and help her into bed," he told her.

"Thank you, Count," I said as he kissed my hand a little longer than necessary.

Just before the count straightened up I sensed movement at the door. I glanced over and saw Martel backing up into the hallway. To my surprise, he looked furious.

88

Chapter Fourteen

"Wake up, Marie. Remember what today is?"

I groaned and pulled the soft down pillow over my head. "It's too early."

"No it isn't, the breakfast bell already rang," said Anne as she pulled at the pillow. "You shouldn't have stayed up last night. Was the count with you?"

"He was with all of us."

"There were only two others with you when Adam and I came upstairs."

I didn't answer her. I had only stayed a minute or two after everyone left. Just long enough for the count to tell me how marvelous it was to spend the evening with me, and how he was looking forward to seeing me today. And for him to ask me how I was enjoying my time here, kiss my hand, and tell me to rest well. I really wasn't alone with him very long at all.

"You're birthday's today."

"I know, Anne." I blinked as the maid opened the drapes.

"The count sent this up to you, Lady Marie," the maid said, and handed an envelope to me.

Excitement rippled through me as I saw my name written with his flourish. I thought of how he had walked me to the staircase the night before, pressing his hand on mine as I held his arm.

Anne watched with a frown while I opened it. "Did you tell him?"

"No, of course not." I unfolded the letter. "'My dearest Marie,'" I read out loud. "'May I be the first to offer you congratulations on your birthday. I hope the year ahead is graced with all your dreams fulfilled and untold happiness for you. Perhaps I will have the honor of bringing some of those wishes true. Your most humble admirer, Count de Roesch.'"

My heart seemed to soar as I looked at his name. "My admirer, he said. The count called himself my admirer."

"Yes, I heard."

"Oh Anne, please let's not argue. Not today."

"Marie, be careful. He's –"

"Yes, I know," I said, folding the letter and putting it back in the envelope. "And today's my birthday and tomorrow we have a masquerade ball and it's been a lovely time. And then we'll go back to the farm."

She sighed but held her tongue. We dressed in silence and went downstairs with Maman.

"The count will join you later this morning in the garden," a servant told me when I asked where he was. I tried not to be disappointed.

Maman and Anne gave me ribbons for my hair after breakfast. Jacqui cut some flowers and had them put in a vase and sent up to my room. Everyone wished me a wonderful day.

And all the while I longed to see the count.

He finally came out to the garden, looking terribly handsome in his gray coat and silk shirt, his dark hair flowing down to his shoulders and his beard black and shining. He walked straight to me.

"Lady Marie, it's a glorious day just for you," he said as he bent over my hand. "And there is a surprise waiting for you and your guests in the front of the chateau."

"In the front? What is it?"

He seemed to enjoy my curiosity. "That is for you to discover, Lady Marie," he said, offering his arm. "Come and find out."

Everyone crowded close behind us as we went through the chateau to the front doors.

"I thought a special form of transportation would fit you today," he said with a sweep of his arm.

90

At the foot of the stairs was a beautiful white carriage trimmed with gold. Behind it there were two more carriages, not as grand, which I knew were for the others.

"It's beautiful," I said. "It looks like a royal carriage."

"It was." He patted my hand. "And now you will be royalty for the day. I'll escort you through my park and show you some of its special places. There's also a picnic basket for you and your guests to enjoy after that."

"I've never seen anything like it," I said, still looking at the carriage.

"Any time you are here, it is yours."

I didn't know what to answer since I wasn't ever coming here again, but I thought it was a grand gesture on his part.

The count helped first me, then Maman into the carriage. The others came behind us as we were driven through the chateau's park. The count was pleasant and amusing and had Maman and me laughing several times. The ride was far too short.

"Our morning together has taken up much of the day," he said when I told him it ended too soon. "I cannot compete with the rest of the guests for your time. The carriage will take you to the stream where we saw the large meadow, and you may have your picnic there."

He kissed Maman's hand and then mine. Then he held my hand to his cheek. "It is always sad to leave your side, my beautiful Lady Marie. Perhaps someday it will not be necessary." He kissed my hand again and my heart jumped.

"But I don't want you to leave, Count," I said before I could stop myself, and I felt Maman's hand on my arm.

He chuckled softly. "That is what I wish to hear," he said, and stepped out of the carriage.

The picnic was long and boring without him there. I couldn't wait to get back to the chateau. Anne could tell. Every time I caught her looking at me, she was frowning.

When we got back I immediately went up to my room. "To rest," I told everyone, but it was really to get away from Anne's disapproval.

Maman came into my room a short while later to check on me.

91

"I'm fine, just tired," I told her when she asked if I was ill, and then pulled the covers up higher.

"The maid told me the count will have something else for you this evening."

I opened my eyes and sat up. "Really? What?"

"I don't know. That's his secret. You'll have to wait."

"I hate waiting. He tortures me with hints of secrets." I threw back the covers and got up.

Maman gave a soft laugh. "He enjoys playing with you like that. Be glad. It shows his interest."

I followed her out to the sitting room. "I wish he didn't show it that way," I said. "It makes me think of a cat playing with a mouse." As soon as I said that, I had the uncomfortable feeling Anne had once told me exactly the same thing.

Then Anne came in from the hall. "Why are you looking so unhappy, Marie?"

"The count has another little surprise for her tonight and she wants to know what it is," said Maman.

"Isn't a gilded carriage enough?"

"Don't be cross, dear. How did you like the outing?"

"It was boring." She sat down in a chair. "I'm getting tired of the other guests. They never have anything worthwhile to say. I'm going to change and go back out with Adam. We're walking down to the canal. Do you want to come?"

I didn't, but Maman changed her shoes and went out with her. I went to Jacqui's room and we spent the rest of the afternoon talking about the carriage and the picnic.

The count was at dinner that evening, but he said nothing about another surprise. And afterward, in the large salon, he played cards with the boys and hardly spoke to me. I wondered if he was angry with me about something.

I knew I looked disappointed, and near the end of the night, even Jacqui tried to reassure me. "He's their host too," she said. "I'm sure he's not ignoring you on purpose."

I didn't want to stay any longer. "I'm going upstairs."

"It's been a tiring day for you," said Maman, looking worried. "You need rest." It seemed that had become her cure for everything.

92

"I'll thank the count for the day and go up, Maman."

"I'll go with you," said Jacqui. I took her hand, appreciating her loyalty.

The count stood when we came to his table and bent over Jacqui's hand first. Then he took mine.

"The lovely Lady Marie. And how was your special day?"

"Very nice, Count de Roesch. Thank you for the carriage ride."

"I'm pleased that you enjoyed your day," he said. "And when you retire, you will find another small gift to remind you of your afternoon of royalty. I hope it brings you pleasure.

"And I hope, too, that you will forgive my inattention to you during the evening. I have found you so enchanting, I'm afraid I have neglected my other guests."

Warmth rushed up my neck and face as I looked into his eyes. He wasn't angry with me. He was enchanted. "Of course, Count. All is forgiven."

I knew I was smiling like a fool as he bent over my hand and gave a lingering kiss. Once again my heart raced and I felt a fluttering in my stomach. It confused me but it was exciting, too, and I didn't want him to stop. But he let go of my hand and we said goodnight.

Maman came upstairs with us and we entered the sitting room. There was no box on the table or anywhere else.

"He said there was another gift for me. Do you see it, Maman?"

A maid had followed us into the room. "In your bedroom, Lady Marie."

I saw it as soon as I stepped into the room. A white winter cloak, made of fine wool with heavy gold embroidery and lined with white satin, hung on my wardrobe door. It even had white fur trim around the hood and down the edges.

"I've never seen a cloak so perfect." I touched the satin and traced the gold design with my fingers.

Jacqui stroked the fur. "It will keep you warm, but where does he think you'll wear it?"

"To church," said Maman. "Why don't you put it on?"

The maid took it down and helped me. It draped beautifully, sweeping across the floor and framing my face when I put up the hood.

93

"He certainly knows what will make you look lovely," said Maman.

I looked at myself in the mirror wearing my beautiful new cloak. It would be so hard to go back to the cottage and leave all this behind. The village seemed drab and gray, the count blazed in color next to it.

I wished our time here would never end.

Chapter Fifteen

It was our last full day at the chateau. It had been a week of living as I had never imagined. There were servants to do everything for me, lavish dinners each night, and parties or concerts every evening. The other guests the count had invited had been friendly after the first day. The young men were amusing and although the young women were more aloof, they also had been enjoyable.

I knew, though, they had never worked hard in their lives and most of what interested them was frivolous. So even though I liked them I grew tired of them by the end of the week, just as Anne had. It was hard to believe my parents had grown up with people like them.

But it was still fun, more fun than I had ever had, and I was sorry to see it end.

We didn't know yet what we were going to be for the masquerade ball that night. The count said our costumes would be a surprise.

"We won't be able to recognize each other!" said Jacqui.

Anne snorted. "Yes we will."

Jacqui looked disappointed.

"I'm sure we won't know right away," I said, and she smiled again.

I knew a little about mine. "My queen will wear a costume befitting her," the count had whispered to me two nights ago after

95

dinner. "But don't ask me what it is, fair Marie." I didn't that night. I was content to know I would be his queen again.

But when I saw him the next day I badgered him until he laughed and told me, "If you don't stop asking, I'll not give you a costume. You'll have to come in rags." I stopped, but I couldn't help wondering.

The day stretched on endlessly. If I could have hurried time, I would have done it. The count left mid-morning and I wandered through the gardens and the house, restless and bored.

When I saw an empty carriage in the courtyard, I went back to the gardens for Anne and Adam. "We can go to the village down below us," I said to them. "We haven't been there at all, and I want to see if it's like home."

But when we asked the butler, he said the count had told him the carriage wasn't to be used.

"I thought we could do whatever we wanted while we were here," said Anne to Adam as we walked back to the gardens.

"Maybe he doesn't want us in the town," Adam said.

"Why not?" I asked.

Adam shrugged.

"The town isn't too far from here. We can walk," I said. "Let's see who else wants to come."

Only Jacqui wanted to go, so the four of us set off. The walk down the road, first through the woods and then past farmers' fields, was refreshing after being in the chateau so much.

"I'm glad we came," I said as we reached the outskirts of the village. Two mangy dogs barked at us, then ran off. We passed several cottages and then the village square came into view.

It was market day and a few of the stalls were still open. We wandered over to them and when the vendors looked at us eagerly, I was ashamed to realize we had brought no money with us.

Anne must have thought of it at the same time, because she said to one of them, "I'm sorry, we've just walked down from the chateau and have no money."

"The count's credit is good with us," he told her.

96

Of course it was. His credit was good in our village, too. The chateau workers took what he needed and the villagers kept a record of it. I looked over his stand.

"Could we have some apples?" I asked.

He reached behind a bench and pulled up a basket. "These are the best. I was saving them in case the chateau needed them." He pulled four beautiful, firm, red apples from the basket. "Here."

I took a bite. "This is delicious," I said. "Can the rest of that basket be sent to the chateau?"

"It will be there within an hour," he said with a small bow.

I realized I could have whatever I wanted sent up to the chateau. The power was heady. The farmer stood by his stall, watching us quietly as we moved on. What did he think of us, three women and a man in fancy clothes, walking down from the chateau and poking around his village?

I wondered if any of the count's wives had visited here before. Perhaps the second one had come from near here. I hadn't asked his other guests at the chateau anything about him or his previous wives. Talking about the count seemed an uncomfortable subject with them.

Anne pulled on my arm. "There's a woman who looks like Widow DuBois."

I peered down the row of stalls at a small, older woman, watching us with obvious interest.

"I wonder if she's the village gossip," Anne said.

If she was, she'd be the one to ask about his wives. I wandered over to her. "Good afternoon," I said. She dipped her head. "We've just come down from the chateau to see your village. It's very much like ours."

"You're from a village?" Her surprise made me want to laugh.

"Yes, the count invited us to visit for a week."

She eyed my dress and I felt uncomfortable. "It's not mine," I told her, "it's just to use while we're here."

She nodded but didn't reply.

I felt the urge to explain more. "He invited my sister Anne, my mother, and me. Our mother was... is nobility. Our father, he was too, but he died. The count is being very kind to us."

97

She covered a smile with her hand, then said, "I'm glad to hear our good Count de Roesch has found someone who interests him."

"You make it sound as if he's never been married."

She chortled. When she replied, the sudden loud sound of wheels clattering on the cobblestones made it hard to hear her. What I thought she said was, "We've been waiting years for a good wife." She eyed my figure.

Unsure if I had heard right, I said, "Didn't any of his other wives visit here?"

"Other wives?" She looked confused.

"Count de Roesch had —"

A hand gripped my shoulder. "Lady Marie," Martel's syrupy voice cut in. "We've been looking everywhere for you. You have to come back to the chateau immediately."

He turned me and moved me toward the carriage that had pulled into the square. That's what the clattering wheels had been. I shrugged off his hands but he put them right back on my arms. "Stop pushing me," I said. "You interrupted us, and I don't want to go back to the chateau yet."

"Your mother isn't feeling well," he said, "and it would be best if you and your sister were with her."

"Maman is sick? What's wrong with her?" I asked him. He didn't answer, just kept walking me back to the carriage.

Jacqui, Anne and Adam saw him and came over. "Your mother isn't well," he repeated to Anne.

"Oh, Adam, we shouldn't have left the chateau," said Anne.

"We haven't sent for the doctor," said M. Martel. "We were waiting to see if that's what you wished."

We all got into the carriage and Martel climbed in after us.

"What's wrong with her?" I asked him again.

"She said she has pain in her head," he said, and looked out the window as we passed the woman who looked like Widow DuBois. He didn't seem to want to tell us anything more. We covered the distance back to the chateau with the horses at a trot.

Anne and I flew up to our rooms and found Maman in the sitting room, sipping a cup of tea.

98

"Maman, what's wrong?" Anne knelt by the chair and I stood in front of her, taking her hand.

"What do you mean? Goodness, girls, why are you running in here like that?"

"Martel came down to the village to find us," I said. "He told us there was something wrong with you."

She looked puzzled. "He must have overheard me talking to the maid. I told her you had gone to the village and I had a headache and would like some tea, but that's all. It was certainly nothing to make a fuss over. What a shame he ruined your trip. I can't imagine why he thought you needed to be here."

"He told us to see if you needed a doctor," said Anne, still looking worried.

"He could have asked me." She took a sip of her tea. "But since you're here, why don't you have some tea with me?"

Anne sat back on her heels. "Adam was right. He didn't want us in the village."

"Who didn't want you in the village?" asked Maman.

"The count," said Anne, "or Martel."

"Don't be silly," said Maman.

"I think Anne's right, Maman," I said. "The butler wouldn't let us use a carriage today when we asked to go down to the village. We had to walk."

"Well," Maman frowned. "I'm sure there's a reason."

A maid appeared with two more cups and set them both on the low table. Then she left.

"Maman, there was someone who was just like Widow DuBois," I said as Maman poured tea. "She didn't seem to know the count had ever been married."

"Village gossips don't know everything." Maman dismissed it with a wave of her hand.

Maybe not, I thought as I drank my tea. But they'd know if their count had been widowed four times or they wouldn't be a very good gossip.

99

Chapter Sixteen

The count wasn't at dinner that night and we ate quickly. Everyone knew our costumes were going to be brought up while we were in the dining room.

"I can't wait to see what I'm going to wear," said Jacqui. "It won't be anything like what we do at the village for masquerades. That's just masks."

"It will be much more than masks," Maman said with a smile. "You'll all look lovely."

"How can you not wonder what it'll be, Adam?" said Jacqui, watching him eat. "I'm so excited I can't even think of eating."

"I don't care what it is," he said, "as long as it's comfortable."

Jacqui wrinkled her nose at him. "Maybe one of us will be the Fairy Queen."

"I'm sure if someone's a queen, it'll be Marie," said Maman.

"I tried to find out what mine is," I said, "but he said everyone's is secret, even mine."

Jacqui went back to picking at her food. I couldn't eat and moved what I had around on the plate to satisfy Maman. I looked at the count's empty chair several times, wishing he was there.

Finally they cleared our plates and dinner was over. I ran to our room. The maid opened the door, smiling, and beckoned to me. "Your costume has arrived, Lady Marie," she said. I went in.

The dress was hanging on the wardrobe door. It shimmered in the fire light, made of material that looked like spun gold. When I reached out and touched it, the fabric was smoother than satin. I

100

pulled out the skirt and it swung up, yards and yards of golden fabric. I stretched it above me and still there were more folds, hanging in waves from the high waistline. And when I let it go there was a long, wide, golden train pooling on the floor.

Then I saw the hat. It was a high cone, with yards of beautiful lace spilling out from the top in a long sweep. The hat had the same golden glow as the dress. And there was a golden mask nestled next to the hat to cover the top part of my face.

I heard Anne's footsteps behind me and her intake of breath. "Oh, Marie."

Then I noticed her dress. It was hunter green velvet, the same style as mine, with a hat to match. Her high conical hat had lace streaming out from it, too. "Anne, you'll be so elegant in that dress. He seems to like you in green. And Adam will love you even more when he sees you tonight."

"Yes. And yours, I've never seen anything like that. He really is dressing you like a queen."

Then Maman came up behind us. "Oh, girls, how lovely. Marie, what a dress! The count has outdone himself, my dear." I couldn't see her face, but I could hear the satisfaction in her voice. It would have annoyed me a short time ago. Now it gave me a warm glow.

"What's yours look like, Maman?" I asked.

"You'll see when I'm dressed."

She went back to her room to get ready. We dressed quickly with the help of our maids, then went to our sitting room to wait for Maman. Someone knocked on the door.

"Come in," Anne said.

"Guess who?" Another costumed guest came in, holding her mask up to her face. The rose-colored gown and mask didn't hide her giggle.

"I know it's you, Jacqui," I said.

"Didn't you wonder, just a little?"

"I would have if you hadn't been laughing."

"Oh." She put her mask down and looked at my dress. "Yours is beautiful. Mine is, too, but that's so much nicer."

I swept the skirt around and smiled at her intake of breath. She was right. I would be radiant tonight.

101

"Everyone has this style dress and hat," Jacqui said. "I wonder what the boys are wearing."

"Whatever they used to wear when women wore these dresses," said Anne. "Are we ready?"

Maman had just come from her room. Her dress was an echo of ours. Not quite as extravagant, but quietly beautiful. It had the same tall hat and her costume was a sparkling bright blue. "This will be a splendid evening, don't you think, girls?"

"Yes, Maman," I answered, wondering what the count would wear. Would it match mine?

We filed out of the room, stepping carefully around each other's trains. None were as long or as full as mine.

Several others were waiting in the upstairs hallway by the staircase. Each girl had a dress similar to Jacqui's and the boys had formal pants and jackets or military uniforms.

The talking stopped when we walked up. All eyes were on me. I held my mask up on its stick although everyone knew who was wearing the golden dress.

Finally someone spoke. "It looks like we're ready to go down," Adam said, acting as if everything was normal.

"Oh, Marie, it's stunning," whispered one of the girls. "It's the prettiest one, isn't it, Lady Catherine?"

"It is," Maman answered. "And now it's time for the ball."

We went down the stairs. The butler, dressed in a cavalry uniform, led us into the ballroom.

My gaze swept the room for the count but he wasn't there. Several dozen other guests were there, all in costumes. I wondered who they were.

The butler gave a little bow to Maman as she let go of his arm, then he leaned in to me and said, "The count will arrive shortly and would like to have the first dance with you." With a quick bow to me, he disappeared through the door.

The musicians played softly as we waited for the count to arrive and I wondered what had kept him from greeting us. We didn't have long to wait. The butler reappeared, announced "The King of the Evening," and the count walked into the room.

I couldn't help smiling as soon as I saw him. His dark hair fell in waves to his shoulders, shining in the candlelight. A matching

102

golden coat, shirt, and breeches, made from the same material as my dress, swathed his strong frame. His black beard glimmered as it spilled out under the mask. His mask wasn't on a stick, it had a holding band going around his head like a crown.

We were perfectly matched.

He looked across the room and when he saw me, he strode across the floor and took my hand. "Lady Marie, my Queen for the night," he said, and kissed my hand.

He held up my hand as he looked over my costume. "Exquisite, my dear, as I expected. Please excuse my lateness, I had some business to attend to with M. Martel." I didn't ask what it was, I wanted him to forget everything but me. He smiled at me and my heart raced.

He led me out to the floor and we began the dance. I felt chills race down my back every time he told me how captivating I was. I felt as if my feet had grown magical. Never had I danced as well or as long as I did that night with Count de Roesch. The dancers swayed and moved gracefully through the steps, the other guests spoke to the count as they passed us, and they all looked approvingly at me.

Near the end of the evening he took off his mask and brought me through the doors that led out to the gardens. "Are you warm enough?" he asked as we stepped into the night's chill.

"It feels good out here after dancing so much," I said. "The ballroom was getting stuffy."

"Then I'm glad we came out." He drew my hand through his arm. I held it lightly as we strolled along the paths.

"The stars look clear and pure," he said, and I looked up. A canopy of sparkling lights hung above us. "They remind me of your eyes and the way your face glows when you're happy." He paused. "You have been happy this week, Marie. Am I right?"

"Yes, Count, I have."

"I thought so." I knew he was smiling. "I cannot express how pleased it makes me to know that I've brought you pleasure. You, too, bring joy to me, my dear Marie. Your purity and simple desire to please others — it has been wonderful to be near that this week."

103

He stopped and pulled me closer. "You have the power to make me very happy, Marie. More than anyone else on the earth. But I'm afraid."

"Of what, Count?"

"Of me. That I can't give you what you need, what you desire. That I cannot make you happy enough. That something might –" He shook his head. "I couldn't bear it if harm came to you, Marie. What should I do if marrying the woman I love brings her harm?"

"The woman you love?" My heart soared. No one had ever spoken those words to me.

He drew me to him and kissed me. When he let me go, I took a deep breath. It took a few moments for me to be able to think clearly again.

"But how would you harm me?"

"Perhaps I should not have put it that way. My other wives – they met with such unfortunate ends. What if they hadn't married me? They would still be alive."

"It's not up to us to question things like that."

"Yes, you're right, my dear." He kissed my hand, then held it tightly. "You have the key to my heart, Marie." He leaned closer. "But I must warn you, I fear that it is a dark place, with forbidden rooms that frighten even me."

"I will unlock them, my count, and flood them with light."

"Then there is hope even for me?"

"Father Samuel said there is hope for everyone, as long as they still breathe."

He drew back when I mentioned Father Samuel. "An unfortunate end for him, too," he said. There was coldness in his voice, jolting to hear after such warmth with me. "A selfless man, to be sure."

"As a priest should be," I said, wondering why I felt I had to defend Father Samuel.

"Of course, all priests are selfless," he said, and the warmth was back in his voice. "As you are, Marie."

Anne would argue with that, but I basked in his praise.

"Don't listen to the things others say about me," he said. "Help me."

104

He kissed me again. I didn't care about the stories of a curse on the hill. I didn't believe he had anything to do with the death of his wives. He was lonely. He needed someone. And he had turned to me.

He took my hands in his. "Marie, will you marry me?"

Suddenly it felt as if an abyss opened wide in front of me. I had felt this way before, but I couldn't remember when, not with the count standing so close. I closed my eyes and pushed it away.

"Yes," I whispered.

As he kissed me once again, I felt as if I had fallen into it.

When we re-entered the room, he wrapped my hand around his arm and covered it with his hand as he had done with Maman. He pulled me close to him and I saw Anne's eyes widen in alarm.

He leaned toward my ear. "May I make the announcement?" He was so close, his breath moved my hair. Anne rose from her seat and came toward us.

"Yes," I said, just before she reached us.

"May I borrow my sister, Count?" Anne said.

"Not yet, my dear. We have something to announce."

Anne's hand stopped part-way up to my arm. She looked stunned as the count moved us past her. She knew.

He stopped by the harpsichord. "Ladies and gentlemen, I have a joyous announcement to make," he said. At the sound of his raised voice, the room quieted. All eyes turned to him and then me, standing so close to his side.

"The Lady Marie has consented to become my wife."

After a moment of surprised silence, all the guests crowded around us, giving best wishes and congratulations. The feeling that I had fallen was replaced with excitement when I saw their reactions.

Maman kissed me. She twittered something I didn't hear because I saw Anne, standing with Adam, watching us with a look of horror as the count put his arm around my shoulders.

And then I remembered when I had felt that abyss in my life before. It was when Papa had died.

105

The room seemed to recede as I had a sudden stab of fear and clutched the edge of the harpsichord. Is this what Papa would want? Would he give me his blessing? Or would he be grieved?

The count took his arm from around me to shake the hands of the men who had come to him. Anne came to my side. "Are you insane?" she whispered into my ear. "Tell him no!"

"Don't tell me what to do, Anne," I said to her, my fear turning to anger. "I'm going to marry the count and you can't stop me."

She pulled me away from him. "Marie, think of what's happening. He has you under his spell here – it will be different when we get home. You can't do this."

"Yes, I can." I shook her arm off as the count came over to us.

"One last dance, Marie," he said. "Come, dance it as my betrothed." He reached for my hand. He seemed so helpless one moment and yet so commanding the next. It confused me.

As we glided across the floor, I glanced up at his eyes through his mask. For a second I thought they glinted, hard and cold and calculating. But then they were warm, dark eyes, eyes I could get lost in.

"You will come home in my carriage tomorrow," he said as we danced.

I started to protest, but he shushed me and said, "Your Maman has said she will come with us as chaperone. The rest of the party will leave early in the morning, we'll follow later."

When the music ended, we went over to Maman and the count escorted us to the foot of the stairs. Anne and Adam came up and he pulled Maman to the side and spoke with her. She nodded and he kissed her hand. Then he walked back to me.

"Lady Marie, thank you for your beautiful presence this evening. You have made my joy soar to new heights. And good night, Lady Anne," he said with a nod at Anne. He gave a little bow to both of us, then left.

We climbed the stairs with our friends, complimented each other on our costumes one last time, and said goodnight.

I had lingered in the hallway a few minutes, not wanting to face Anne. When I got to our rooms she and Maman were sitting by the fire, already out of their costumes.

106

"When you've changed," Maman said, "come back out and we'll talk." I didn't look at Anne as I went into the bedroom.

The maid helped me out of my costume and into my sleeping gown. I pulled on a robe, went back out to Maman and Anne, and sat in a chair by the fire, ready to face Anne's disapproval.

"I don't think you should marry him," said Maman.

"What?" Anne and I said in unison.

"Well, I'm not sure now it's best." She looked at her fingers.

"Maman," I said faintly. I felt dizzy. The only one who'd thought this would be good had changed her mind.

Maman pulled a handkerchief out of her pocket and started twisting its edge. "I'm just not sure, Marie," she said. Her voice sounded strained.

"But the farm! It would save Papa's farm," I said.

"This is not a good time to decide you don't want this, Maman," muttered Anne, "even though I agree."

"It isn't only the farm, Maman," I said. "He's lonely and hurt. I can help him."

"You can't fix things for him, Marie, and that's what you think you'll do. You can't change his past hurts." Maman's voice sounded stronger. "I know. Papa and I thought our past wouldn't matter. But it did, and it was hard to break away from it."

"But you're glad you did, you always said so," I said, still bewildered by her change of mind.

"Yes, but it was hard in the beginning, and it's different from what you're doing with the count. We didn't marry to get wealth. We were leaving it."

She pulled on the edge of the handkerchief. "I'm not sure this is right, Marie. I don't think you should sell yourself for the farm."

And then my support – what there was of it – came, of all places, from Anne. "She's not selling herself, Maman. That sounds awful. She's doing what she thinks is right."

I gave her a grateful look. She sat down next to me and took my hand. "Don't misunderstand me, Marie. I don't think you should marry him either. But I believe you're trying to help us. And I appreciate that."

107

She kissed my cheek and I started to cry. "This is the best thing for all of us," I said. Then I brushed away my tears and hiccupped. "It solves everything. And he's not a monster, Maman."

"I never said he was," she answered.

"I'm going to marry him, even if you think I shouldn't."

We were silent, and then Maman got up and kissed my cheek. "Then you have my blessing, child. I pray all goes well."

Anne kissed me, too, but she didn't say anything.

"I'm going to bed," said Maman. "And the count told me just before we came up that you and I are going home with him tomorrow."

"Oh?" Anne sounded alarmed. "Why?"

"To extend his time with Marie, I would think," answered Maman. "They are betrothed now, remember.

"We'll have an early morning, girls. Anne, don't forget to thank M. Bellamy as soon as you get home for taking care of the animals while we were gone."

"Yes Maman," Anne said as Maman left the room. Then she frowned. "Marie, there's so much about him that doesn't seem right. He says things that don't seem true. He's had four wives. And there's the curse up there..."

"Village gossip," I snapped as I followed her into the bedroom.

"It's more than gossip. It shows –"

"It shows there are stories, Anne. But nothing else."

"There's always been talk of a curse on the chateau and that family," Anne said. "I've never really believed it either, but what if it means *something*?"

"It doesn't."

"Oh, Marie," she said. I could hear her exasperation, but I didn't care. I hung up my robe in the wardrobe.

"We were wrong about him, Anne," I said. That's what I wanted to believe, what I had to believe. "He's kind, and he's lonely."

"You'll be his fifth wife," she said.

"I can count. What do you think, he killed all his wives? Be reasonable. They died from sickness, and the last one was an accident. He couldn't kill them. No one could get away with that."

She looked uncertain. "Well, up there, away from everyone –"

108

"He has servants. They'd talk."

"I don't know, Marie. I don't like this. I don't think you'll be safe."

We climbed into bed. "You're right down in the village. I'll still see you all the time. And we won't lose Papa's farm, Maman will be cared for, and you'll have a dowry."

She gave a deep sigh. "Maybe it should be me."

"What do you mean?"

"I'm the oldest. Maybe I should marry him."

"But you love Adam!"

"You're my younger sister, Marie. I can't let you do something if I don't think it's safe."

"You're going to marry Adam and you'll have a wonderful family and be happy."

"Marie, I don't care about any of that if you're not safe."

"I've already given my word to him, Anne. You'll marry Adam and I'll marry the count. Everything will be fine."

"I pray you're right, Marie," she said, and pulled the covers up to her chin.

I prayed the same thing as I drifted off to sleep.

Chapter Seventeen

The morning dawned hard and clear as a fall chill crept into the bedroom. I didn't want to get out from the warm covers, but Anne was already up and I could hear Maman talking with a maid.

Everyone seemed to be dressed and down for breakfast faster than any other morning. Too soon Maman, Count de Roesch, and I stood on the steps outside and said goodbye to everyone. Adam, Anne, and Jacqui pulled away first. I could see the envy in the other girls' eyes as they said goodbye to us, and I felt excitement fluttering in my stomach again as their carriages left. I knew they wanted to be me.

But it didn't last long. As they went down the hill, another carriage came up and pulled around to the steps. I watched curiously as the footman opened the door. To my surprise Father Gregory stepped out.

"Good morning, Count," he said as he puffed up the steps.

"Good morning, Father Gregory," said the count. "How was your trip?"

"It went well. I stayed in the abbey we spoke of. How are you, dear ladies?"

"We're fine, Father Gregory," Maman replied. "How nice to see you here. What brings you so far from the village?"

He smiled at her. "Business of Count de Roesch's in another town." He bowed slightly to us and then he and the count walked in front as we went back to the door.

110

The count turned to us in the hallway. "I need to go over a few things with Father Gregory. I'm sure you can amuse yourselves for an hour or two until I'm ready to leave."

"Of course," Maman answered, but he had already turned away. Father Gregory followed him and they disappeared into another room. Maman and I were left in the hall.

"Come, Marie, let's go to the garden," Maman said. I followed her outside and we sat on a bench by a low stone wall.

"Why did Father Gregory come?" I asked Maman.

"I suppose he helps the count in some way from time to time. He's a man who can converse with him in ways the villagers can't. A priest has to have education and I'm sure the count appreciates someone who's had schooling."

"Father Gregory doesn't seem very smart to me."

"Hush, Marie, don't be insulting." I saw her glance at the nearby windows. I sat silently after that, wishing we'd left with the others. Finally Maman grew bored and we went inside to the library. We waited there over an hour until a servant came to tell us our baggage had been put in the carriage and the count was ready to leave.

We went out to the drive where the count was waiting in a large dark blue carriage. Maman stepped into it as if she rode in a carriage every day. The footman helped her in with a flourish of his hands, and then turned to me with a bow.

I felt like royalty. I stepped up and settled into the deep velvet seat next to Maman. The count sat on the seat across from us.

Father Gregory stepped up and leaned into the carriage. "I'll follow later," he said.

The count nodded. "Does he know?"

"No." He passed an envelope to the count and withdrew, shutting the carriage door with a jarring bang. I wondered what they meant but he didn't explain. Instead, he put the envelope in his pocket and smiled at my mother.

"I hope you don't mind a detour on the way home," he said. "Father Gregory brought something which necessitates a stop for us."

"Of course not," said Maman, smoothing down her skirt. "It was lovely of you to bring us home. Anything you wish is fine."

111

"Now that Marie has pledged herself to me, I don't want to let her out of my sight." He took my hand and leaned forward. "And we have something to accomplish before we reach the village."

"We do?" I said, surprised.

He gave a little chuckle, let go of my hand, and settled back in the seat. "You'll see, my dear."

We rode without talking for some time, then he and Maman chatted about the week and how much everyone seemed to enjoy it. I watched the fields and woods pass by without joining in their conversation. I tried to think of what the count could have meant. Anxiety settled over me again. My shifting emotions were exhausting, and I wanted to be home. I still wasn't sure I was doing the right thing. I needed the familiarity of the cottage around me again to think everything through.

After several hours the carriage clattered into a stone courtyard. We had arrived at a small monastery. We walked across the barren courtyard to a large door and it opened immediately.

"You are expecting me," the count said to a robed monk in the doorway. The monk nodded and ushered us in.

"I will return shortly," the count said to us, and he followed the monk down a hallway.

Maman and I looked around. We were in the middle of a long stone corridor stretching to our right and left. It had a bare wall along the outside wall; the inside had arches running its length, all opening onto a lovely garden courtyard in front of us. We could see a stone chapel at the far end of the courtyard. It was silent and no one was around.

We went through an arch and over to a small stone bench outside the chapel, out of the sun, but the count reappeared before we could sit down. He was trailed by a priest.

"This is Father Marcus. He has agreed to help us." The count reached for my hand.

"Help us what?" I said as his fingers closed over mine.

Count de Roesch pulled me past Maman to stand next to him. "Father Marcus will perform our marriage ceremony."

Shock raced through me. "You thought I would marry you *today*?"

112

"This is quite sudden," said Maman, sounding shaken. "Why didn't you say something before?"

"I thought Marie would know," he said, concern in his voice. "But she, too, is surprised? After our walk in the garden last night, Marie, didn't you know then?"

"I... no, I didn't realize it would be so soon..."

"Marie, you said this is what you want. Why should we wait?"

His smile seemed warm but his eyes were hard. That strange combination. I pulled my hand from his and covered my face. "I don't know what I want. This is too fast."

The priest cleared his throat. "Perhaps I should come back after you discuss this?"

"No," the count said. "We'll go inside out of the sun."

He moved me forward into the chapel. I was aware of the damp-smelling stone walls around me, shafts of sunlight coming from the high windows, and the odor of burning candles. We walked past empty rows of wooden benches, our footsteps on the stone floor echoing in the shadowy chapel, and reached the altar. I felt oddly abandoned even in this holy place.

I was aware of the count telling the priest to proceed. Then he put his arm around me. The priest began to speak. I couldn't concentrate on what he was saying. I should be home with Anne, not standing in front of an altar with a man I barely knew.

Then the count pulled a ring from his pocket. I felt as if I couldn't breathe. The vise that crushed my chest when Papa died was back. My hand hung limply at my side. Surely this was a mistake.

I looked at Maman. Her face showed deep lines that hadn't been there before Papa was sick. Her fingers picked nervously at her neckline; she knew I was upset.

"Marie," she whispered softly, shaking her head.

My mouth was dry. I swallowed. I couldn't go through with this.

Then I thought of the farm, our house, Papa working the land. That's where Maman belonged, on Papa's farm. And if I didn't marry the count, we would lose it and strangers would live in Papa's house and till his fields. He would be completely gone.

"Do you take this man for your husband?" said the priest.

113

"Yes," I said, and my voice echoed in the stone chapel. The priest spoke again and the count answered him.

The count slipped the ring onto my hand. I looked down and saw diamonds and rubies circling my finger. It was done.

Then he passed an envelope to the priest, the same one Father Gregory had handed to him when we'd gotten into the carriage. "Here is my wife's genealogy for the registry," he said.

I looked at Maman again. She seemed dazed. What she had wanted so badly had happened. One of her daughters had just become the Countess de Roesch.

The rest of the ride back to the village was quiet. I seemed to have lost my voice after speaking in the chapel. Maman, for once, didn't want to chat. The count read papers he had brought with him. I felt numb.

It was late afternoon when we rode into the village and stopped at our house. Anne came to the door and, when she saw the carriage, turned and spoke to someone in the cottage. I thought it was Adam.

But it wasn't. It was Thomas.

The footman opened the door and Maman stepped down. I rose to follow her, but the count's arm held me back.

"No, my dear, you can visit some other time. We're going home now."

My stomach twisted. The cottage wasn't my home any more.

"What are you doing with Marie?" said Thomas. He looked angry.

"I think, young man, what I say to my wife is none of your business. You repair wheels, do you not? May I suggest you continue with your trade and keep your comments about the Countess de Roesch to yourself."

Thomas's shocked look tore through me. I sat back down.

How could I have been so stupid? I had married the wrong man.

114

The Countess

Chapter Eighteen

I cried all the way up to the chateau.

"Take this," the count said, handing me his handkerchief. It seemed improper, using an item so personal to him. But I took it and wiped my face. Then I dropped it, crumpled and wet, into my lap.

I turned away from him and looked out the carriage window. The trees seemed to choke the road as we drove up the hill, pressing against the edges of the drive and leaning over the carriage. The sun's rays were too slanted to reach any ground in front of us, and the woods were dark and still as we passed through.

I wanted to be home with Maman and Anne in the brightness of the cottage, not riding away from them. We were going uphill but I felt as if I was traveling down into a dark pit.

The carriage, which before had seemed large and luxurious, now made me feel trapped. It was taking me away from my family – and from Thomas. My Thomas. What had I done? I cried harder.

"Marie, this is not how a new bride should be acting."

The carriage circled around to the front steps of the chateau. The windows were empty eyes, the stone walls cold and forbidding. "I should be home with Maman and Anne in my cottage," I said. "I don't belong in a chateau."

"Of course you do," he replied. "You were born to be the mistress of a grand house."

117

I was silent as the footman opened the door and helped me down. The count took my elbow as we went up the steps. Martel was waiting at the top, looking annoyed.

"Why have you brought her here?"

"You are speaking of my wife. Please do so courteously."

His mouth dropped open. "What? I don't think —"

"What you think doesn't matter, Martel. It is done," said my new husband with a dismissive wave. "Lady Marie is now the Countess de Roesch."

We swept by him and went through the front door. The butler stood inside, waiting for us.

"I have brought back the Countess de Roesch, Henri. Please inform the staff of their new mistress."

The butler showed no surprise or curiosity as he bowed first to the count, then to me.

"Welcome, Countess," he said. "Your trunks will be brought up to your rooms and unpacked immediately."

"That will be all," said the count. Then he motioned to a maid as we walked down the hall. "The countess would like some tea." She scuttled through a door. He led me into the salon where Maman, Anne, and I had been so very long ago. Was it really less than a fortnight?

We sat on a sofa and he took my hand. "I think it's always an adjustment for a young woman when she first comes to her new husband's home. You'll learn to appreciate it here and everyone will work to make you comfortable."

His voice was warm and kind as it had been the night of the masquerade ball. I realized with a jolt that was only last night.

"I'm sure you will find being the Countess de Roesch a fulfilling life. Think of all the good you can do for the village."

"But that's where I want to be, not hidden away up here," I said, and my eyes filled with tears again.

He shifted away from me on the sofa. "You'll see your family and the villagers, Marie. They're not far."

I sniffed and rubbed my nose.

"What is your name?" he said to a maid who had just entered the room.

"Jeannine, sir," she said with a curtsy.

118

"Jeannine, get a handkerchief for the countess," he said. I had already lost the one he had given to me in the carriage. I sniffed again and wiped my eyes with my hand. Then I got the hiccups. The count sighed.

When Jeannine reappeared, he rose from the sofa. "Who is to be her personal maid?"

"I am, Count de Roesch."

"Sit with the countess until she collects herself and then take her up to her rooms."

He left. Jeannine sat next to me and held out a handkerchief. I took it from her and hiccupped again.

"I get those when I cry, too," she said. "Take a deep breath, that's what my maman always tells me."

She had a friendly face and I was glad she was sitting with me instead of the count. I wiped my eyes and blew my nose and she took the handkerchief from me.

"There now. Let's go upstairs. We'll have your tea brought up. Are you ready?"

I nodded. She helped me stand and held my arm as we went up the staircase.

I shuddered as we passed the colored glass window on the landing. "I want to go home," I whispered to her.

"I cried for days when I first came to work here," she said softly as we climbed the next staircase. "I wanted to be home, too." She squeezed my arm and I felt better. At least I had found a friend.

We came to the top and walked down a hall. "These are all guest rooms," Jeannine said as we passed several doors on each side. "Your rooms are near the end, and Count de Roesch's are next to yours, at the very end of the hallway. Beyond that is the servants' staircase."

We came to what looked like a sitting room. Jeannine let me enter first. A large, gray cat with round, yellow eyes rose from a sofa and slid past us. "He belongs to Madame Vacher," said Jeannine.

"Who's that?" I asked as his tail disappeared through the door.

"She's the head of the household staff. You'll meet her later."

The sitting room was almost as large as our entire cottage. A door to the right opened onto a bedroom and we went in. Four tall windows lined one wall. There was a big canopied bed between the two middle windows with sky blue bed curtains pulled back to show a matching bed cover.

I felt Jeannine's hand on my arm again. "Look over here." She turned me around to see what was behind us.

By the door was a huge white wardrobe. Next to that was the largest mirror I had ever seen. I walked up to it and spread my arms out. It went from the fingertips of one hand to the fingertips of the other.

"Why would anyone need such a large glass?"

"That's what we said," Jeannine answered.

"This was put here for me?"

"No," she said, looking at me cautiously. "It was for a previous countess. She was very beautiful and – not that you're not beautiful, Countess," she said, stumbling over her words. "It's that his third wife was, well, very interested in how she looked, and wanted large mirrors in her rooms – this isn't the only one, you'll see more in the dressing room." She fell silent and looked at me, twisting her hands.

"It's all right, Jeannine, I understand. I saw her once. They went by in the carriage when she first came. Even seeing her through the window, she was lovely. I remember she had dark black hair and eyes. You're right, she was very beautiful. It was so tragic that she died."

"Yes, it was a shock to everyone. She wasn't particularly kind to any of us, but still."

"And then so soon after that, his fourth wife fell," I said. "Finding her dead in the courtyard must have been awful."

"Oh, she was still alive when they carried her in, moaning and crying. It was terrible. The count was most attentive and had her taken to a room. He sat with her all through the night. But by morning she had died. Father Gregory had already come and she was in the coffin."

"Did you see her?" I asked, thinking I shouldn't show such a morbid interest.

120

"The coffin was already nailed shut when the staff paid their respects," she said. "But the one before, she was always wanting new dresses and such, even though they didn't go anywhere. That's why there are all these mirrors. There's another one over there," Jeannine said, pointing. "And there used to be more."

I saw a small table with a seat and another mirror sitting on it.

"Two mirrors in one room! I'll get tired of looking at myself. Must I keep them all?"

"Not if you don't want them."

"Then that one will go," I said, pointing to the large one. "I'll keep the small one by the table to fix my hair."

"You may want a bigger mirror, too. One you can see all of your dress in. There's one in the dressing room over here."

I went through the doorway. It was another room, smaller than the bedroom, with two large windows and several mirrors. Three wardrobes lined the walls.

"This mirror will be enough, the others can go," I said, looking at one. "I can see my dress in it."

"These are your gowns," said Jeannine as she opened the doors of one of the wardrobes. Eight dresses hung inside, all made of rich fabrics and sheer laces. "The seamstress will come tomorrow to measure you for more. And you also have what you brought home with you today."

"Why are there already dresses here? Were these hers?"

Jeannine looked confused. "Hers? You mean the other countess? No. The count told us –"

She was interrupted by a knock at the door. "Come in," I said as we went back out to the sitting room.

The door opened and an older woman stepped inside, glancing over Jeannine before she curtsied to me. Her dark hair was pulled back into a tight bun and her mouth made a thin line across her face.

"Welcome, Countess. I am Madame Vacher, the head of the household staff. I hope your trip was pleasant. Please let Jeannine or me know if you need something. Have you found everything to your expectations?"

"Yes, Mme Vacher, thank you." I wasn't sure what else to say, and after a few moments she curtsied slightly again and left.

121

"She's a little frightening," I said.

"She's not as fierce as she seems. She's demanding with us, but I've seen her be kind to the stable boys. And the last countess liked her."

"Does she ever smile?"

"Not much with the servants. But you mustn't be afraid of her. She'll do whatever you want, Countess."

"I don't feel like a countess. I feel out of place, like I should be downstairs in the kitchen or out in the garden."

"You can't let the servants hear you talk like that, they won't respect you."

"But I don't know anything about being a countess, Jeannine. I'm a village girl."

"That's not what we were told. We heard your parents were highborn."

"They were, but they left that behind when they fell in love. They haven't spoken to their families since they married."

Someone knocked on the door again. "Come in," I said.

"It's your trunks, Countess," said a male voice.

Jeannine opened the door. "Put them there," she said, pointing to the dressing room.

I watched while they brought three large trunks into the dressing room and left. Then I followed Jeannine back into the dressing room and sat on a big velvet chair while she unpacked the dresses.

"I wore that to one of the picnics," I said as she pulled out a lavender gown. "And I wore that one on the first night we were there, and that one when we were boating. I ripped the sleeve."

Jeannine examined the dress. "They must have fixed it, there's no rip now. Your gowns are lovely," she said as she carefully hung each one.

"Yes," I said. "When I first touched them, my skin was so rough it caught on them. Then the maid gave me cream." I held my hands out to her and she took them, turning them over and feeling my fingers.

"We have cream here, too. And I can make your nails look better. I'll get all that dirt out and shape them."

122

I examined my hands. I'd stopped chewing my nails when Thomas made fun of how they looked. Several of them still had farm dirt at the edges as Maman's had. I felt a pang of loneliness when I thought of Papa's fields. I put my hands down and tried not to think of the farm.

"Were his other wives anything like me?"

"Not his last two. I didn't know the first two."

"The third one, who wanted all the mirrors, what was she like?"

"Haughty. Oh, I'm sorry, Countess, I shouldn't speak like that." She looked frightened.

I smiled at her. "You can speak your mind with me. I'm just a village girl, remember?"

"Yes, Countess."

"Do you have to call me that?"

"What would you prefer?"

"Marie."

"I couldn't call you by your given name. It isn't proper."

I sighed. "Tell me more about his wives, then. What do you know?"

"Well, I know his fourth one came from Germany and the third from far away. I'm not sure where she came from, though, nor the second. The first one came from a chateau south of here."

"A chateau? The count said she was from the city."

Jeannine frowned. "That's not what I've heard."

"The one second one, she died of plague?"

"Yes, after a ship's captain came to visit the count."

"And the first one, was that from fever or consumption?"

"Consumption. Fever took his third wife."

"That's what we'd always heard, too, except when he spoke of his wives, he said the first one died of fever and the third of consumption."

"That's odd," Jeannine said. "I was here for the third and it was fever. We weren't allowed to see her the last two days when she was sick, and then she was gone."

"Maybe I'm remembering it wrong. Oh, Jeannine, I feel so much better since I've met you."

"Thank you, Countess. It will be a pleasure to serve you."

123

I smiled and watched her hang up my beautiful dresses. Perhaps being married to the count wouldn't be as difficult as I had thought.

Chapter Nineteen

The count came to my room that night. Early the next morning, he kissed me tenderly and told me I had already made him forget his other wives. I believed him.

And later when I sat down next to him at the breakfast table, he smiled and said, "I think this will make you happy, Countess. As a wedding gift, in addition to forgiving the taxes your family owes, I will also cut in half the taxes for the rest of the villagers."

"Oh, thank you! What a wonderful gift. It will make so many people happy."

"I want them to share in our joy, Marie," he said, and kissed my hand.

My new husband was charming and attentive. My daily questions seemed to endear me to him and I saw him smiling to himself when he didn't know I was looking. I worked hard at learning what was expected of the mistress of the chateau. Within a few weeks, the village and the people I had known all my life grew farther away. Everything I had ever wanted, I found in the chateau at the top of the hill.

Or so I told myself.

Each morning I went down to breakfast in a new gown, my hair styled by Jeannine in front of the small mirror. And each morning at the table my husband greeted me with affection, even if he had already seen me upstairs.

The morning routine didn't change very much. The count often had a ride on his favorite horse before breakfast. Sometimes

125

he would come in right from the stables, still smelling of the outdoors. He seemed happier on those mornings. Each day after breakfast he went to his office where Martel or Father Gregory often joined him. Martel seemed to avoid talking to me, but I ignored the insult. His presence always made me uncomfortable and his falseness was even more apparent now when he feigned acceptance of me as Countess. And Father Gregory often faded quietly into the shadows when I was near.

Mme Vacher would send the next day's menu to me shortly after breakfast. I always approved it since she knew better than I did what the count would like. When the weather permitted, I sat or strolled in the vast gardens behind the chateau. If I stayed inside, I went to the library or back to my sitting room, where I'd spend the day with Jeannine. There she and I would read aloud or embroider. I found myself spending more and more time with her.

Sometimes I would see the count again at mid-day dinner. Other times he would take the meal in his office or I would be told he had left for the day to conduct his business elsewhere. I never knew where he went, but he was always home at night.

But the days were long and I had very little to do to keep me busy. Not having chores wasn't as delightful as I thought it would be. I sometimes watched the maids with envy as they hurried past me to their next duties.

The first Sunday we went to the church in the village, Thomas came up to us before Father Gregory had even ended his prayer.

"You'd better not hurt Marie," he said to the count, his fists clenched. "No accidents or illnesses as your other wives have had."

"My wife's title is The Countess de Roesch and you will refer to her in that manner."

"She's Marie to me."

"No, village boy, she is Countess to you. And it is not wise to threaten me."

"Don't harm her, Count," he spat out.

The count smiled at him and gripped my arm so tightly I almost gasped. But I didn't want more arguing, so I let him steer me away.

"I'm watching you," I heard Thomas say to him as we left.

126

The count laughed. When we got into the carriage, he let go of me and shook his head. "Quite a troubled boy, such a shame. I think we will have services in the chapel at the chateau instead of coming down to the village."

I tried to ignore the throbbing where he had squeezed my arm. "Oh, but I want to go to the village church. I want to see everyone."

He smiled. "Whatever you wish, my dear. But for a while, I think, we'll have Father Gregory conduct a private service for us after he does one for the village. It will give someone's temper time to cool."

I didn't want to go to the chateau's chapel. I'd heard all of his previous wives were buried there. I started to protest again, but he took my hand and gave it a lingering kiss.

My resolve melted with his touch. "I'm sure you know what's best," I said, my heart beating faster. He smiled, tracing a pattern on my cheek with his finger.

But that night an unsettled feeling came over me when I thought of the stones which must be there, each with the name of a countess who had come before me. And when I looked at my arm I saw purple marks where his fingers had gripped me. Thomas must have upset him more than I'd realized.

I had been right. The chapel had been used as the chateau's burial place for generations. Although the stones of the crypts were beautifully chiseled, to me it was a room full of dead people. And there were four newer stones on one side. I avoided them.

Then early one Monday morning the count took my hand. "You have been my bride a little more than a month, my dear," he said, "and already I have to go away on business. The carriage is waiting." He held up his hand when I started to protest. "No, Marie, I must. But when I return, we'll go to the village again on Sunday. And I'll bring home a surprise for you."

"I'd rather have you than a surprise."

He seemed pleased. "What a lovely wife you are. I'll be back in several days. Why don't you have your sister up for company? I'm sure your lady's maid gets tiresome at times."

"Oh, no, she's never tiresome."

"I'm glad Mme Vacher chose wisely for you." He smiled, and his eyes sent a spark through me. I wondered how I'd ever thought those eyes frightening. I felt myself blush as I always did when he looked at me that way. It made him laugh.

"Where are you going?" I asked.

"To a chateau of mine south of here, to look over some stock. Stop frowning, Marie, I'll be back soon. I promise. And I'll remember to bring your gift."

"What is it?"

"Patience, my charming Countess, you'll see." He leaned forward and kissed my forehead, then left the table.

I went upstairs to my room. Jeannine was there as I'd expected, brushing dirt off one of my gowns.

"Jeannine, the count is going away, and he told me to have Anne come stay for a visit. How do I get word to her?"

She lay down the brush. "I could ask Mme Vacher to send someone, or perhaps I could go myself."

"You go, Jeannine. She'll listen to you."

"Of course, Countess. I'll leave right away."

I waited almost an hour for Jeannine to return with Anne, and it seemed like forever. I paced by the front windows in the salon, constantly peering down the drive. Finally, the small carriage came into view. I was already at the bottom of the steps when it pulled up.

"I'm so glad to see you," I said to Anne, throwing my arms around her as soon as her feet touched the ground. "I've missed you."

"We've missed you, too," she said as she gave me a kiss. "The cottage isn't the same without you. Even Adam says so." I was surprised to see tears in her eyes.

"Is everything all right? Is Maman not well?"

"We're fine." She searched my eyes. "And you?"

"I'm wonderful."

She seemed to relax. "I'm glad, Marie. Maman sends her love. I think she was a little insulted you didn't invite her, too."

128

"I didn't think of it, but don't tell her. Actually, it was the count who suggested I have you here while he's gone. He knew I'd be lonely, even though Jeannine's here and she's wonderful."

"She helped me with the chores so I could leave faster," Anne said.

"It was nothing, Lady Anne. Those were my chores, and more, when I was still home." Jeannine followed us up the stairs to the front door.

"Welcome, Lady Anne," Mme Vacher said at the door as she curtsied. "There is tea in the smaller salon."

"Thank you, Mme Vacher," I said as we passed her. "But we're going upstairs to my rooms." We started up the stairway. "It's more private in my rooms," I said softly to Anne. "I'm still uncomfortable acting as if the servants are invisible. And M. Martel seems to hear everything. Jeannine, can you get the tea? We'll have it in my sitting room."

When Anne and I reached my rooms, she stood in the middle of the sitting room with her hands on her hips. "This is yours?"

"Yes, and the bedroom in here," I said. "And there's a dressing room through that door."

"What do you do with all these rooms?"

"I live in them."

"These are larger than our whole cottage."

"I know. At first I felt there was too much space around me. I've gotten used to it, though."

Jeannine came into the sitting room with tea and another maid followed her in with a tray of food. Sitting across from Anne I could almost imagine myself back in the cottage.

"I remember how marvelous everything tasted when I first came," I said as Anne looked over the tray.

She reached for a piece of iced bread. "It is good," she said, her mouth full. "What's the rest of the chateau like?"

"I don't know."

"You haven't looked at it yet?"

"No. Most of the time I stay in my rooms or the gardens."

"Let's look after we're finished eating."

I put down my teacup. "I'm done."

129

"I'm not. This may not be much of a meal to you, but it's a feast for me." Finally she wiped her mouth and said, "I'm ready now. Where do we start?"

I looked at Jeannine, at a loss to know what to suggest.

"I can show you the guest rooms," she said, "or you can go to the ancient part of the chateau, if you want."

"What's there?" Anne asked.

"Almost all that's left is a tower. It's part of the original building, and it's hundreds of years older than the rest of the chateau," said Jeannine. "The servants swear it's haunted."

"How do we get there?" I said.

"It's past the kitchen and through the far hallway. I'll show you," Jeannine said.

We followed her down the hall. "Why don't we use those stairs?" Ann asked, looking back at the small staircase by the count's room.

"I can't go down any of the back stairways," I replied. "Those are for the servants."

She didn't say anything, but I could feel her disapproval.

We went past the main staircase and through the halls until we came to another large, open staircase. At the bottom we paused.

"On the left is a door to the main ballroom," Jeannine said, "and on the right is the back door to the music room."

I hadn't seen the ballroom here yet. I pushed open one of the doors. A slightly smaller version of the ballroom in the other chateau stretched before me. It had a long, wooden parquet floor, large windows that opened out onto the garden, and tall mirrors on the walls across from the windows. At the far end was a raised floor where the musicians would be. I could almost see the ghosts of dancers crossing the floor in front of me.

"When was the last time this room was used?" I asked Jeannine.

She shook her head. "I'm not sure. I think it may have been with the Count's first wife."

"Yes, I remember seeing the carriages on their way to his balls," said Anne. "They would go through the village and I always wondered who was in them."

130

"You did?" I was amazed. "I thought you never cared what went on in the chateau."

"The carriages were all so fancy and I'd never seen anything like them. Don't you remember?"

"No."

"It must have been when you were off somewhere with Thomas."

A wave of sadness swept over me. "How is he?"

"Not happy. He eats with us sometimes now. Maman is trying to get him interested in Jacqui."

I bristled. "Why would he be interested in her?"

"You sound jealous."

"Well, she's not right for him."

"He needs someone," Anne said.

"He should —"

"What? He should what, Marie? Never marry anyone because you thought you were too good for him and married someone else?"

"No, that's not it! Is that what he thinks?"

"What's he supposed to think? Everyone thought you'd marry him. You've been his shadow since you were little."

Tears stung my eyes as I tried to think of a reply.

Anne sighed. "I'm sorry, Marie. I don't want to quarrel."

"Do you want to look around more?" said Jeannine. I nodded and brushed at my eyes. We left the ballroom and followed her farther down the hall, through a doorway and into a smaller, drafty hallway, lined on one side with old windows set far back in the thick stone walls.

"Where are we now?" I said.

Jeannine reached up and tapped the stones on the wall across from the windows. "This is the kitchen's back wall. We're in the oldest part of the chateau."

The floor was stone, too, and the ceiling low with dark, massive beams. It felt cold and oppressive and I shivered.

The passageway took a turn and got narrower. At one of the doors along the hallway I paused and turned the handle. It was locked. "What's in these rooms?"

131

"The ones we passed before are storage," said Jeannine. "I think the ones along here are empty."

After another turn we came to a heavy oak door with large black hinges. An open lock hung on the black latch. Jeannine stopped. "This is the tower. I've never been this far. None of the servants come back here."

I looked behind us. The narrow hallway was empty. I felt as if someone was near, watching us, but that was silly. It was only because Jeannine had told us it was haunted.

"Let's go in," I said. The feeling grew stronger, pressing down on me.

Jeannine didn't move. "They say there are ghosts, Countess," she said, almost as if she could read my mind. "Sometimes there's lights."

I lost my courage and looked over my shoulder again. "Maybe we should go back."

Anne went around us, opened the door, and stepped through. After a moment, we followed her in.

Chapter Twenty

It wasn't how I thought a haunted tower would look. We stood in a small, musty entry room. The sun gave light through high windows. A circular stone staircase went up in front of us. The air felt chilly and I touched the curved stone wall in front of me. The stones were cold. I rubbed my hand along the surface and some of the ancient rock crumbled under my fingers.

"I thought it would be dark and full of cobwebs," I said, "like the loft in the church."

Jeannine studied the flagstone floor. "This has been cleaned recently. There's even dampness in the cracks, see?" She pointed with her toe to the packed dirt in between the stones. It was, indeed, damp.

"Maybe it leaks when it rains," Anne said.

Jeannine shook her head. "The stones are clean. There's not a mark of dirt on them."

"I thought you said no one ever came here," I said.

"They don't. I've never heard of anyone even wanting to go near this tower. If a girl is sent to get something in a storage room back down that hall, she never goes alone."

"Then who cleaned the floor?"

Jeannine didn't answer. I felt a chill pass over me. The feeling that we weren't alone grew stronger.

"I'm cold," said Anne, hugging herself.

"So am I," Jeannine said. "Do you feel it?"

"Yes, I'm cold too," I said.

133

"It's a ghost passing by," said Jeannine, shivering.

"Don't say that! It's because the stones are damp and it's chilly in here." I tried not to sound frightened.

We looked around. There was a small passageway to the right between the curved outside wall and the curved stairway wall. I wondered if it led to a room underneath the stairs and took a step in that direction.

But Jeannine moved at the same time. She reached out and touched the wooden railing that disappeared up the stairway. "This has been polished."

I turned back from the passageway and went over to her. "Someone from the chateau has been coming here."

Jeannine's eyes were huge. "Maybe the stories are true and it really is haunted," she insisted.

"A ghost doesn't clean floors," Anne said.

"If it was the ghost of a servant girl, it might," she replied.

"The whole floor is clean – except for right here," I said, nudging some dirt with my shoe. "It looks like someone sprinkled dirt here."

Anne looked at the wall. "What's this?" She felt one of the stones. "This stone is loose, see? The mortar around it is cracked." She grasped its jagged edge and pulled.

Before I could stop her, the stone moved and a few grains of dust settled down on the floor with the other dirt. "There's a hole behind it," she said as the stone came clear of the wall.

I reached into the hole. "It drops down in the back and something's in there. I've got it." I pulled my hand back out and held up a box.

"What's in it?" said Anne.

I opened the box and lifted out a pouch which had an embroidered scene of a mountain village, covered with snow that sparkled with tiny diamonds and pearls. I gave it to Anne. "Open it," I said.

She loosened the string and tipped out a pair of diamond earrings. "I wonder who these belong to," she said.

"Let's see what else is here." I pulled out an emerald pendant from the box, handed that to Jeannine, and took out the next

134

treasure. It was a gold and diamond ring. "It looks like a wedding band," I said, turning it over in my hand before giving it to Anne.

"There's one more thing," I said, and lifted out a small box. It was covered in ornate carving. On the lid was a long, thin dragon, painted red, that stretched the length of the top. I lifted the top. Inside, nestled in a velvet compartment, was a string of small, perfectly round pearls. "Oh, it's beautiful," I said. "Look how they glow." I held them up, lustrous even in the shadows of the tower.

"That box belonged to his wife," said Jeannine. "At least, I think it did. The one who had all the mirrors. I wasn't her maid, but the girl who was talked about the box."

"Then why is it here?" I said.

"I don't know," said Jeannine. "Maybe it's not the same one, I never saw it. But I know she had a box with a red dragon on it."

With a sigh of regret, I put the pearls back in and shut the lid. "We have to put everything back."

"Why?" said Jeannine.

"Well, it's not ours." I paused. "And I think it's best if no one knows we found these."

"I agree," said Anne thoughtfully. "Jeannine, not a word."

She nodded. I laid everything back in the box and put it into the hole. Anne pushed the stone in place and Jeannine brushed away the dirt on the floor with her foot.

"I wish I knew who put that there, and why," said Anne. "Four things, Marie."

"So?"

"Four wives."

"Stop it, Anne," I said. "You're just trying to frighten me."

"I'm not trying to be mean, Marie. It's just –"

"I don't want to hear it. Not now. We've come this far," I said. "Let's see what's upstairs."

We climbed the narrow, steep stairs that curved along the tower wall, passing two windows that faced nothing but a stone wall. It seemed far away from the rest of the chateau. The hair prickled on the back of my neck and I tried to ignore the quiet eeriness around us.

"We should go back," Jeannine said in a whisper.

135

I turned around and saw Anne hold her finger up to her lips. Jeannine nodded.

We reached a small landing. The only light came from a little window above it. There was a plain wooden door, closed, on the other side of the landing.

I hesitated for a moment, then walked across and tried the knob. It was locked.

"We can't come all this way and not go in," Anne said softly.

"But we don't have the key," I said.

Jeannine took a deep breath. "If you're sure you want to go in, Countess, maybe the key's up here." She reached up along the door frame.

I felt along the rest of the top of the frame. "Nothing," I said.

"Look on the sides. Maybe it's hanging from a nail or a hook."

I felt down the side. "You're right, Jeannine. Here's a key." I pulled a large, ancient-looking key off a hook and held it up.

"The lock might be too old to work," said Anne.

I found myself hoping she was right and it would be too rusty to turn, or the key wouldn't fit, or it would jam. I put it into the lock. The key fit easily. I turned it, heard a clink, and tried the knob. With a glance back at Jeannine and Anne, I pushed open the door. It swung open without a sound.

We filed in and stared at a small sofa with cushions, two upholstered velvet chairs, and a low table, all grouped near a deep, tall window. There was a carpet on the floor and an empty vase on another small table. Several candlesticks with partially used candles were on the tables, and a ruffled cloth covered a third small table. The round walls of the tower circled us, and an empty fireplace was set into the curve.

"It's a woman's sitting room," said Jeannine in a hushed voice.

"What's a locked sitting room doing at the top of a tower that no one uses?" said Anne.

"Could it be the count's?" Jeannine said.

"No, I don't think so," I answered. "He has rooms of his own, and he wouldn't have a ruffled cloth or soft colors in a room for himself. This is definitely a woman's room."

"But whose?" Anne said.

Jeannine moved around, scanning the furniture and the floor with a practiced eye. "It's been cleaned recently. The candles look old – except for this one, it's newly burned. But the room doesn't really look like it's used."

I ran my hand along the back of the sofa and then looked out the window. "You can see the village right over the trees," I said as I put my hands on the broad window sill and looked out. "Everything's so small. There's the village green, and the marketplace, and the shops. It's too far away to see who anyone is."

Anne came over to my shoulder. "Let me in," she said.

"I never saw this tower from the outside," I said as I made room for her.

"It's set far back, Countess, and covered with ivy, so it blends in," said Jeannine.

Anne looked down. "There was an old moat. I can see an impression in the grass. See, it disappears into the newer wall."

She was right. It circled the tower's edge and stopped at the chateau wall. "The entry hall at the bottom of the steps must have been part of the original chateau," I said. "I wonder how much else of the building is left."

"I think just this old tower, Countess," said Jeannine. "Even the hallway behind the kitchen is newer than this."

I pulled back inside the room and looked around. "I'd like to know who's been up here."

"I'm sure it's none of the servants," said Jeannine. "Everyone is afraid of this tower."

"That leaves the count and M. Martel," said Anne. "And I don't think either one of them would want a room like this."

"What about Father Gregory?" I said.

"Well, he *is* strange," she said, "but I can't imagine why he'd want a room like this when he doesn't even live here."

I walked around the room, searching for something that would show whose room it was. There was nothing.

"I feel as if we shouldn't be here," said Anne.

"I feel the same way," Jeannine said, still looking nervous.

"We can go wherever we wish," I said, my hands on my hips. "Why shouldn't we be here?"

137

"I don't know, it's just an uneasy feeling," said Anne.

"I think it's a lovely room, and we should come back to it," I said.

"Come back?" Jeannine said.

"Why not? There's a beautiful view. Look, we can see the road from the village, and the drive up the hill where it comes out onto the courtyard. Anyone who comes here can be seen approaching. We could see when the count comes back from his trips –"

"Yes," said Anne dryly, "and you can run back to your rooms because you can be anywhere in the chateau."

I felt a rush of coldness. "Let's go back," I said.

No one argued as we left the room and locked it behind us.

Anne stayed with me for two days. She and I explored the rest of the chateau, although we didn't go back to the old tower. We both thought we'd find something mysterious tucked away in at least one of the rooms, but the only interesting thing we found was Martel's rooms. They were unlocked and although we didn't enter, we peered in from the doorway. The rooms were crowded with expensive furniture. Silk-covered pillows were everywhere, and a large mirror which looked like the one I'd had removed from my room was leaning against one wall. We left quickly. Neither one of us wanted to explain to him why we were there if he appeared.

"Martel always unsettles me," I said to Anne when we went back to my rooms that day. "He's hiding something, I know it. He's evil."

"What he's hiding is that he's learned the right things to say and do so he can hang onto the count and live in rooms with gilded mirrors and satin pillows," replied Anne. I hoped that was all it was.

"Let's go out to the dovecote," she said the morning she was leaving. "I've never been inside a large one."

We walked out to the big, circular building at the edge of the lawn. "Do you think the doves at home would rather be here?" I said as I looked up at the birds. There were several of them

138

roosting together above us, crowded onto flat stones that jutted out from the building.

"They're just birds. They don't care," said Anne as we neared the door. "And I'd miss them if they were here."

I lifted the latch, opened the door, and we peered in. Feathers and bird droppings were scattered on the floor, and hundreds of square nesting holes started a few feet off the floor and went up over our heads. Several birds swooped across the open space, disturbed by the opening door.

We stood in the doorway until they calmed down. Soft cooing surrounded us. "I don't think it's been cleaned out yet this week," I said.

"It isn't too dirty," said Anne, and she went farther in. Shafts of light came down from the holes near the eaves. She turned slowly, looking at the birds. "Who takes care of these?"

I shrugged. "I've never asked. Does it matter?"

"No, I just wondered." She smiled. "They sound so content."

"Yes, I miss that sound from home," I said.

"You do?" She stared at me in the softened light. "I would, too." Then she turned toward the door. "Let's go, I've seen enough."

We went back to the house. Before the mid-day meal she went home.

The count returned that evening. I flew down the stairs when I heard his carriage, wondering what he had brought for me. At the bottom of steps I waited impatiently for him to come through the door.

"Countess," he said when he came in, and kissed my hand. "Have you been running?"

I slowed my breathing. "Only from my room."

He laughed, handed his cloak and hat to Henri and tucked my hand under his arm. "Come, we'll go to the small salon. I have something for you."

He sat next to me on the couch in front of the fireplace. "What is it?" I asked, looking at a bulge in his pocket.

He laughed again, and I knew my eagerness delighted him. He pulled out the box and pushed my hand away. "No, no, Marie. Let me open it for you." He took off the lid and lifted out a small

139

crystal bottle. "This is perfume from the flower fields near my southern chateau," he said, pulling out the stopper. "Smell."

I sniffed the bottle. "It's heavenly."

"This is how to wear it," he said, taking my finger and putting it over the open bottle, then tipping it. "You put it here, and here, and here," he said, guiding my wet finger behind my ears and on my opposite wrist. "Now do the same with your other wrist."

I wet my finger and put perfume there, too. Then he guided my finger to the base of my throat. My heart started beating faster, the perfume lifted up and surrounded me, and the count leaned forward to kiss me.

"Your papers." Martel's silky voice cut into the room. I pulled back, angry that we had been interrupted.

"Put them on the table here," the count said, still looking at me. But the moment was shattered for me, and I rose to leave.

Martel approached us and inhaled, leaning slightly toward me and flaring his nostrils. "You are intoxicating tonight, Countess," he said.

I was repulsed by him, angry that the count wasn't addressing his forwardness, and disappointed that my welcome to my husband had been ruined. "I will be upstairs," I said coldly, and left the room.

Our first argument was later that night. He brushed off my anger at Martel's intrusion, cut our time together short, and left me feeling devastated and alone.

140

Chapter Twenty-One

The count never brought up our argument. I felt distanced from him until several mornings later.

"Countess!" Henri's voice was usually calm and soft-spoken, but this time it was loud and piercing. I knew something was wrong. I ran down the stairs to where he stood by the front door. "The count needs you, his horse went down."

"Where is he?" I said.

"He is being helped to the chateau. We'll bring him to the salon."

Just then the count came in the front door, supported by one of the gardeners. "Can he not be saved?" he said to someone behind him.

"I'm sorry, Count, the leg is broken through."

He leaned on the edge of the doorway, looking sick. "Shoot him, then. He's in pain and there's nothing to be done."

I heard someone run down the steps behind him and the count walked heavily to the salon, leaning on the gardener. When he reached the door, he took my shoulder. "To the couch," he said, his face full of grief.

"I'm so sorry," I said as we walked. "What happened?"

"He snapped his leg in a hole. Broke clean through. I knew when I heard it he was gone."

"Are you hurt?"

"No, just sore. He didn't roll on me, I think he was careful when he went down." We sat together on the couch, and the

141

count waved away Henri and several servants who were hovering nearby.

A gunshot sounded through the window and he rubbed his hands across his face. "He was a good horse."

"I'm so sorry," I said again. "I know you were fond of him."

He stared at the window. "I've had some good horses. He was one of the best."

I took his hand and he gave a thin smile. Trying to distract him, I said, "What were your others?"

His face slowly relaxed as he told me of his horses. He even smiled as he talked about a stallion which broke through a stall door in a temper. "Thank you Marie," he finally said. "You knew just what I needed." He pulled me to him and held me gently. "You are my perfect wife."

I gave a sigh of contentment and sank into him. I was the most fortunate woman in the world. I had a man who loved me and a beautiful chateau to live in. What more could I want?

"Your sister has asked you to visit her." The farm worker stood in front of me, looking dirty and uncomfortable in the salon.

"When did she want me to come?"

"She said come when you can."

"Tell her I will be there tomorrow afternoon," I told him.

He gave a stiff bow and left, and I went upstairs.

The count's reaction surprised me when he came into my sitting room a short while later. He frowned as he stood by the fireplace. "So soon?" he said, sounding annoyed. "Can't she go for a few weeks without seeing you?"

"I haven't left the chateau except to go to church since we've been married. I miss the village."

That seemed to placate him. "Very well, my dear, if that is what you wish." He picked up my embroidery hoop, commented on how much better my work was, gave me a quick kiss, and left.

The next day I went home. "Where's Maman?" I asked Anne.

"Visiting Widow DuBois, but she'll be back. I have something for you," she said, and lifted up a small wooden cage. "This and the one on the table."

142

I peered into the cages. A bird was in each one. "Anne! You can't give me your doves."

She stuck out her chin. "Yes, I can. I want you to have them for two reasons. First, because you miss the cooing. I would, too, if I couldn't hear them every day. It made me sad, to think of you missing that. And second, we can use them for messages."

"Messages?"

"Yes. If you let them out, they'll come back here. We'll have a code. If you send the white one, it means you're coming down that day to see us. And if anything ever goes wrong, and you need help, send the black one back."

"But they're yours. You love your birds."

"I have others, and we won't eat all the squabs this year. That'll build the flock back up. You'll have to make sure they stay inside somewhere. Do you have a place for them?"

"Not the dovecote?"

"No, they'll just fly back here if you let them out. You need to keep them inside the house in their cages."

"Oh. Well, I can keep them in my room, I suppose, as long as the count doesn't mind."

"Why would he mind?"

"He won't. This is fun, Anne! It's like a secret language. No one will know if I send one, but you'll know I'm coming down."

"And the black one, Marie, he's important. If you ever need me there, send him home. I'll know there's danger and come right away."

"Danger?" I said. "What kind of danger?"

She looked uneasy. "Let's say trouble. I'm still not sleeping well at night thinking of you up there, Marie."

"I'm fine, really I am. And I have Jeannine."

"I know. But if anything happens, any reason at all that you want me up there, send this one home. As soon as I see him, I'll come up and find out what you want."

"All right," I said.

Maman and Widow DuBois came through the doorway. Anne told them our game and they thought it was a clever idea. Widow DuBois watched me carefully as I talked of living at the chateau

143

and of the count, and when I left with the cages, said, "Keep them safe, Marie."

"I will," I replied, and Anne kissed me good-bye.

"Don't forget," Anne said, "if you send the black one, I'll come up."

I waved goodbye and sat back in the carriage, surprised that I was torn inside. I had wanted to go home so badly, and it had been wonderful being in the cottage again. While I was there, though, I wanted to go back to my rooms at the chateau. I wanted to be in both places but felt like I didn't fully belong in either one.

Then one of the pigeons fluffed his feathers. "With you, I'll have part of the cottage with me, even though I'm at the chateau," I told him, and felt better.

But when I got back, the count wasn't pleased. "What do you have?" he said when he saw me going up the staircase with their cages.

I came back down. "A pair of doves. They were a gift to me from Anne."

"Why are they inside the house? They should be out in the dovecote."

"Oh, no, that's not what they're for. She knew I missed their cooing, so she gave me these to keep inside."

"Inside where?" he said.

"In my sitting room – if you don't mind, of course," I added.

"In your room?"

I nodded. After a pause, he said, "If you wish, Marie. Why are they not matching?"

"Anne said I can send messages to her with them. They'll fly back home if I let them out. If I send the white one, it means I'm coming to visit."

"And the black one?"

"It means I need her here."

"Why would you need her here?" he said sharply.

His reaction surprised me. "If I'm lonely for her, or need her help with something."

Martel stepped out from behind the count. I hadn't even realized he was there. "Filthy creatures," he said. "They should go out to the dovecote."

144

"It is not up to you," I said coldly, "and the count has already said I may have them here."

Martel turned to the count. "It would make me uncomfortable, Count, if my wife were sending secret messages to anyone."

"I have no intention of keeping secrets from my husband," I said, angry now. "I just told him exactly what they mean. And perhaps feelings such as those explain why *you* don't have a wife, M. Martel."

The count chuckled. "Claws in, my love. You may have your pets. Come, Martel." The count bowed to me and they left.

I went up to my room, still fuming. When I saw Jeannine I said, "He's far too bold."

"Who?" she asked.

"Martel," I said, and told her what had happened.

"Never mind, your birds are here now," she said soothingly.

"Where should I keep them?"

"How about on the table by the window, so they can see the sky."

"Perfect," I said as she spread a cloth over the small table. I put the cages side by side and gave them food and water. We settled down in chairs across the room from the doves.

"They're not cooing," said Jeannine.

"They will, once they feel safe. Give them time." As we sat quietly and heard them fluff their feathers, I felt more contented than I had since coming to the chateau.

Fall was over. With the chill of winter Jeannine and I stayed indoors in front of a warm fire, drinking hot tea. My rooms were like a welcome hideaway now and I loved being in them, especially when the pigeons softly cooed.

The count was preoccupied and the affection he had so freely given to me in the first months of our marriage seemed to cool. I found myself ashamed to speak of it to Jeannine. Finally, though, I felt I had to get advice from someone.

"He's changed," I said to Jeannine one morning as we sat in the sitting room, embroidery spread across our laps. "He doesn't

145

look at me the same way he used to. And last night at dinner we argued again."

Jeannine came over and sat next to me. "Perhaps it's because he's busy. Men get like that sometimes, my maman says so."

"I don't know what I've done," I said. "He doesn't seem to think of me the same way anymore."

"Maybe there's a present you can give to him," Jeannine said. "He's given you gifts and it always makes you happy. You could leave it in his room for him to find tonight. Then he'll know you were thinking of him today."

"That's a good idea. But what could I leave?"

"You've been working on that piece of embroidery, haven't you? And it's almost done."

I nodded.

She sat back. "There, then. That's what you'll do. You can finish it and leave it where he'll see it."

I thought for a moment. "I'll leave it on his pillow, under the spread."

She smiled and went back to her chair. I picked up my embroidery and within an hour said, "I'm done." I held it up. It was a tree much like the ones in the chateau's gardens with a man standing under its branches. "Should I add words?"

"No, it's perfect like that," she said. "It even looks like the count. I'm sure he'll like it. Go put it in his room."

But the thought of entering the count's room without his permission was unnerving. "You have to come with me, Jeannine."

"I'll come with you to the door," she said, "but I don't think I should go any farther."

That was better than nothing, so we went through my bedroom to his private door.

I tried the knob. The door opened. I went through his dressing room and into the bedroom, then beckoned to Jeannine.

"Oh, no, Countess, I mustn't."

"No one's here, Jeannine. Besides, how can you get in trouble? I'm the one telling you to come in."

She took a timid step in, looked around, and then scampered over to me.

146

I went to the side of the bed. "I'll leave it here." I left it on the pillow and turned to go. "What's this?" I leaned down and picked up a folded piece of paper that was on the floor by the side of the bed. There was writing on the outside.

Jeannine came over. "It's M. Martel's writing, Countess. It looks like a page from a ledger."

I unfolded it and saw more of his fancy looped writing. Then I saw something in the crease of the paper. I opened it wider. "Look at this, a blue thread. Several of them."

Jeannine leaned closer and said, "They're not threads. It's hair from a beard." She paused and then said, "And they're black, not blue, Countess. You gave me a start, saying they were blue."

I felt a chill run down my spine. "But they *were* blue, Jeannine. When I opened the paper they were blue."

"Look at them," she said. "They're black."

She was right, they were black.

"The count must have had his beard trimmed and some fell into the paper," she said. "Or maybe they're M. Martel's."

The thought of holding Martel's beard trimmings made my stomach lurch. I glanced around the room, suddenly afraid of being caught. "I put the count's present on his pillow. Let's go. And you're right, those are black, Jeannine," I said as I dropped the folded paper back down onto the floor.

Except I could have sworn they'd been blue.

When we sat back down in our chairs, my heart was thumping so hard I thought Jeannine would hear it.

"I didn't like being in there," she said. "I felt something."

Another chill passed through me. But I said, "It's just a room you didn't think you should be in."

"Maybe there *is* a curse up here," whispered Jeannine, leaning forward. "I've heard of it, the servants have talked. It's a curse put on the ancient part of the chateau. Someone will carry it, someone in the family, and you'll know because their beard turns blue. Or maybe it's their hair and it's a woman. I'm not sure."

"Jeannine, there's no curse. There can't be."

Jeannine spoke slowly. "The count's other wives. Maybe that's why they've all died. Maybe they weren't natural deaths."

147

I felt a chill go up my spine again. "It's just a tale. Why are we even talking about this? Hair can't change color and chateaus aren't cursed. And if you're suggesting they were killed, neither my husband nor Martel, as much as I dislike him, has killed anyone."

She didn't answer.

I pressed on my temples with my fingers. "Jeannine, a man's beard or a woman's hair can't change color. And that curse story is an old village tale."

"Maybe it happens when the moon is full or when it rains or something."

"Jeannine, there's no curse."

She pressed her lips together and didn't reply.

I couldn't believe the chateau or anyone in it was cursed. But that uneasy feeling wouldn't go away.

At least not until the count found my gift and came to me that night. He was warm and caring, and once again I was happy.

Christmas came and went with little celebration. On Christmas Eve the count gave me a beautiful emerald and diamond necklace with matching earrings and I gave him a new gold-tipped walking cane. He also surprised me with the white carriage from my birthday which he brought over from his other chateau. "Now you will ride to church like a queen," he told me when I saw it.

It didn't excite me as it had before, but I thanked him and told him I would wear the matching cloak, too.

We attended church in it on Christmas morning, came back up to the chateau with Father Gregory and Martel, and had a large meal.

The next Sunday, Thomas came up to me after church. "Marie, I want to talk to you."

I glanced over at the count. He was with Father Gregory and hadn't noticed us together. "What do you want?"

"Look at yourself, Marie. You never would have been like this before. Now you come to church wrapped in a fancy cloak and riding in a fancy carriage —"

"I am the Countess de Roesch," I said to him coldly, furious that he chose to criticize me after months of silence. "I can wear

148

what I please and ride in as elegant a carriage as I wish. You would not understand these things."

I swept past him, my head held high, and the coachman helped me step up into the carriage. The count followed right after me. "Words with your friend?" he said.

"It isn't important at all," I replied, and he smiled.

I knew Thomas was watching as we pulled away and I refused to look at him.

After that Sunday, Jeannine went home for several days and Anne came up. I enjoyed being with her again and she said she had to leave far too soon.

"Maman needs my help."

"Maman should let me do more for her," I grumbled as I watched her pack.

Anne folded a blouse. "What has she told you?"

"She said she still has to live in the village and she can't put on airs. She thinks the neighbors resent the help she has already, so she has to be careful. I don't know why. I thought she wanted more in life. Isn't that why she was so pleased I married the count?"

"I think Maman is finding it more difficult than she expected," said Anne as she placed a pair of gloves on the bed. "Are you sure I should take all this?"

"I have more than I can wear in a year, Anne. Take it. And what's difficult?"

Anne stopped packing. "I think Maman expected everything to go back to what it was like when she was young. But it didn't, it can't. And she doesn't really want all the things she thought she did." Anne sat on the edge of her bed. "She still cries some nights, I hear her. All she's ever wanted was Papa. She misses him so."

The room seemed emptier as I thought of Papa. "I still miss him, too."

"So do I," said Anne.

"I wish Maman would let me make things easier for her."

"Well, she has Adam to help her. And Thomas, until he leaves."

"Leaves?"

"Yes, he's leaving the village."

149

"Why?"

"I don't think he wants to be here anymore."

"Why not?"

"Because of you."

"What have I done to him?"

She snorted. "You've only married someone else. It's hard on him, seeing you from afar on Sundays before the count whisks you back up here. Christmas Day, after seeing you at church, he hardly spoke to anyone. He refused to come over for dinner. Maman and I had to bring it to him later."

I sat next to her on the edge of the bed, an empty weariness pulling me down.

"You fought with him at church on Sunday, didn't you?" she asked. I didn't answer her. "Whatever you said, it must have been pretty bad."

"He just wants to criticize me."

"Oh, Marie, you are so exasperating. He cares about you and he wants you to be safe."

"That's not his business any more. It never really was."

"A friend is always his business."

A pang went through me, and I hardened myself. "I don't care if he leaves."

"Well, I suppose that makes it easier for you. I care, and so do Maman and Adam."

"I didn't mean that, Anne." I started to cry. "I don't want him to leave. I've missed him, but I always knew he was near, in the village." I covered my face with my hands, ashamed of my tears and of what I'd said.

"Oh, Marie," she said again, but gently this time. She wrapped her arms around me, pulling my head to her shoulder. She held me while my weeping turned to sobs. Then, finally, I grew quiet.

"My poor sister," she said when I stopped crying. "What are we going to do?"

"There's nothing that can be done," I said, using my sleeve to wipe my face. "I'm married and I can't undo it, and Thomas doesn't want me now anyway."

150

"I don't think that's true, Marie. That's why he's leaving. He doesn't want to do anything improper by you, and it's agony for him to see you. My poor sister," she said again.

I gave a bitter laugh. "Yes, I'm the poor sister. The one who is the countess and who has all the wealth of the land at her fingertips." I wiped my face again. "You, Anne, are the rich one. You have Adam."

She sighed deeply. "Some lessons seem too hard to bear."

"I used to think it was a curse to be poor," I said. "It isn't. It's a curse to be rich."

"Maybe," Anne said softly, stroking my back.

"Is he really, truly leaving?"

"Yes, I think so."

I could feel the tears start again.

"Marie, you have to stop thinking of him."

"I know, but it's hard. Thomas and I were friends from when we were little. And the village won't be the same without him."

"I think it's better for him," Anne said gently, "and for you."

The next day Thomas closed his shop and left the village.

Chapter Twenty-Two

Jeannine and I visited the room in the tower several times before we discovered the drawer.

The first time we went back we didn't stay. It was too cold and we were still frightened. But the next time we were braver. We smuggled up some firewood and with a small fire burning in the grate, the room warmed up quickly.

We came in one afternoon and lit the fire again. I was sitting on the sofa with Jeannine when we heard a squeak. Hearing a mouse wasn't unusual in the chateau, there were mice everywhere. But this one ran out from under my dress. I jerked up my skirts and it scurried across the floor and disappeared under the table covered with a ruffled cloth.

"I hope he doesn't have friends in here." I fluffed my skirts to make sure. "He must have been under the sofa. Does he have a hole under that table?"

"Let's look," said Jeannine. We flipped the cloth over the top of the table. "That's where he went," she said, pointing to a large crack between the floorboards.

But I had already forgotten the mouse. "Look how thick the table is. I wonder if there's a drawer." I pulled up the cloth around the table edges. "There's nothing here. Help me move the table away from the wall so we can see that side."

We pulled it out and pushed back the cloth. "Look, there is a drawer!" I pulled it open. "And there's a book in it, someone's journal." I opened it. "Oh, it's in German. I can't read it."

152

"Maybe it belonged to the count's last wife," said Jeannine. "She was German, remember?"

I carried it back to the couch, flipping page after page of small, neat writing. "Why would it be hidden up here? Shouldn't the count have a journal his wife kept?"

I was more than half-way through the pages when I came upon some writing in French. "I can read this."

"What does it say?"

I sat down, the journal open on my lap. "It says, 'I shall practice French in my journal. Mme V. tells me I must do so to be a good wife to a French count. It is hard to do French always, I do easier in German. But I will try.

"'As I say before, Mme V. gives me the journal so I am not so lonely. I write what I think about. It is always Germany; it is hard to write of my home in French when I want to write in German. But I will do this.

"'I miss my mother and father and brother and sisters. My count keeps telling me I can visit, but then he does not send me. I try to not complain.' Then it goes back to German, and I can't tell what it says."

"Is there more?"

I turned the page. "Yes, it starts up in French again. It's dated, let me see, 7 February. 'It is cold and wet, not like my winters in Germany. There it is beautiful white snow. It stays white all winter in my mountains. But here it rains and ices and when it snows, it doesn't stay pretty and white. In a few days, it is mud.' Then it goes back to German again." I flipped through several more pages.

"She sounds lonely."

"Yes, she does. I would be too if I didn't have you, Jeannine."

"At least she had Mme Vacher."

"I can't imagine her being friendly. She always seems so formidable." I turned another page. "Oh, there's more French. 'He has given me a small dog, a white one, he says, to remind me of the snow in Germany. He can be very kind, my count. I must have spoken to him of the snow. The dog follows me everywhere. She is next to me now, sleeping on the couch. She barks at M. Martel and doesn't like him. I do not like him either, but I never

153

say so. He is a close friend to my husband. They spend much time together.

"'My new dog I call Schnee, snow in German. She brings more comfort to me, saying a German name. Mme V. says I should call her something in French, but I prefer German for her.' Then it goes back to German again, but she says the dog's name twice, so she must be writing about her."

Jeannine frowned. "Yes, I remember that dog. She disappeared when the countess died."

"Here's more," I said. "'Schnee follows me everywhere. She sits by my chair when I eat. I think the count does not mind. He saw her this morning and said he was glad I liked his gift. She is afraid of my count, I do not know why.' Then it's German. I wish she kept writing in French."

"It must have been easier for her to think in German," said Jeannine.

"There's more after another page. 'Mme Vacher is my friend here. She knows of my village in Germany and we speak in German sometimes. That is always good. I think I would go mad without her comfort. She is the one who shows me this room and tells me no one will disturb me in the tower. She is the only one who knows what I write. I keep my journal here a secret from others, but not her.'"

Jeannine looked up at the window. "We should get back. It's almost time for the dinner bell."

"Let's hide this again. We can read the rest when we come up next time. I don't want it to be in my room."

"Why not?" Jeannine looked surprised.

I couldn't explain it to her but I felt it should stay hidden. "She left it here, so I think we should, too," I said. Thankfully, Jeannine just nodded.

We put it back in the drawer, pushed the table to the wall, and covered it again. Then we went back. I wondered about the journal constantly that night and wished I'd brought it down to my room in spite of what I'd felt.

It was late the next afternoon when we ventured up to the tower room again. We pulled the table out and opened the drawer. But the journal was gone.

"It's the ghost," Jeannine said, her voice tight.

I glanced around the room. "The candle's been moved."

"It's the ghost," she said again. "We have to leave, Countess, before it comes for us."

"Jeannine," I said, "I think someone's been up here. The candle's by the chair, and wasn't it on the table? I remember we had to put it back after we moved the tablecloth. A ghost wouldn't need a candle."

Then Jeannine pointed at the velvet chair. "Cat hair. Gray."

"Mme Vacher's cat," I said with relief. "It was her. She knew about the journal, remember? And they were friends. She's been here with her cat."

Jeannine gave a relieved sigh. Then she looked more closely at the chair. "She sat there, too."

There was an impression on the cushion where someone had been sitting. "She must have come up to the room last night," I said. "That's why she needed the candle."

"It's her that's been doing the haunting," said Jeannine slowly, "coming here at night and scaring everyone."

"Maybe," I said. "We're going to find out. I want to ask her why she took the journal."

"But she'll know we've been here."

"I'm the countess, I can go where I please in the chateau." I marched out of the room, pulling the door shut after Jeannine and locking it.

We found Mme Vacher at her desk in a small room near the servant's quarters.

"Countess," she said, laying down some papers. "What brings you to the servant's wing? Is there something wrong?" She didn't look guilty, just surprised.

"If you don't mind, Mme Vacher, I would like to ask you about something," I said, pulling a small wooden chair over to the side of her desk.

"Of course, Countess." She pushed her chair back from the desk and folded her hands in her lap. "Have I done something to displease you?" She looked at me expectantly, and it made me uncomfortable. How is one supposed to question the staff about a haunted tower?

155

"No, Mme Vacher, you haven't displeased me." I heard Jeannine make a small noise behind me and Mme Vacher's gaze darted to her and back to me. Still, she only looked confused.

"Please, what is it, Countess?"

"Last night, Mme Vacher, were you in the old tower?"

Her face turned white and her hands flew to her throat. She made a garbled noise. "Yes, Countess," she finally whispered. "Why?"

I ignored her question. "Did you know I had been there?"

"I knew someone had, but I didn't know who." She was still whispering.

"Is that why you took her journal?"

"Oh, Countess." She put her hands to her face and began to weep.

That was not what I had been expecting. I put my hand on her arm. "Mme Vacher?"

She raised her head, tears streaming down her cheeks. "Forgive me, Countess. I..." Her voice trailed off and she looked at me helplessly.

Jeannine, bless her, knew what was wrong. She came from behind me and said gently, "Was it because you miss her, Madame?"

She nodded.

"I'm sorry," I said. "I didn't realize how close you were."

"She was like a daughter," she said, still weeping. "I knew her town, you see. My mother was German and came from the same area the countess did. She was a delightful girl, and so lonely. We grew close after only a few days." Mme Vacher dabbed at her eyes with a handkerchief. "It was terrible, when she fell. I never saw her again. The count moved her to a room. We were kept away until her funeral."

"He was the only one who helped her?" I asked.

"No, M. Martel did, also, and the priest went in – Father Gregory. Her death was very quick."

"What happened to Schnee, her puppy?"

Mme Vacher brightened when I mentioned the dog. "Oh, little Schnee, she kept digging at the tower door, trying to get in. She

156

must have thought her mistress was there. Then she tried to bite the count and he said I had to dispose of her."

"Kill her dog?" I said, aghast.

Mme Vacher smiled. "I took it to mean have Schnee removed from the chateau. I sent her home to my nieces. I've never mentioned it to anyone here. They love her, and she's happy there."

"She tried to bite the count?" said Jeannine.

"Yes, she was quite aggressive toward him at the end. She used to follow the countess around all day, always underfoot." Mme Vacher sighed. "She missed the countess terribly at first, but now she follows my younger niece everywhere.

"Did I do wrong to take the journal, Countess? I didn't know who was in the room, and I didn't want them reading it."

"No, I understand. Most of it I couldn't read, it was in German. But the French parts I could. There were still a few pages we hadn't seen, the dinner bell rang yesterday and we had to leave."

"I have it, Countess." She reached forward, opened a drawer in her desk, and pulled out the leather-bound journal. "Would you like it? I don't think she would have minded you reading it."

I took it from her and opened it to where we had stopped. It was German again, and I turned the last few pages that had writing on them, looking for more French. "There really isn't any more I can read except this part. 'The count is going away tomorrow for business and I will be here alone again. He has grown colder with me and I do not know what I have done to have him dislike me. I will do what Mme Vacher tells me and try to be a good wife to him.' Then it goes back to German again."

Mme Vacher twisted her hands together. "I can tell you what the rest of it says. No," she said as I tried to hand it to her, "I've looked at it so many times I don't need to read it. She says she wants so badly to go back to Germany and see her family, but she will stay here until the count arranges a trip for her. She says little Schnee helps her get through the days, and that I do too." She began to cry again. "She says M. Martel seems to dislike her too, and then speaks of the count again. She wonders what she did to displease him. Then she says he was very affectionate with her

157

right before he left. She seemed happy. And then, nothing." She dried her eyes. "I am sorry, Countess. I should not cry with you."

"It's grief for your friend, Mme Vacher, and I understand," I said.

She nodded and wiped her eyes again.

"I think this is yours now," I said, handing her the journal. "I'm sure she would have wanted you to have it."

"Thank you, Countess," she said, holding it tightly.

"And the identity of the ghost in the tower is over, too," I said, looking at Jeannine.

"Ghost?" said Mme Vacher.

Jeannine colored as I explained. "We didn't know who was cleaning the room, and the servants always said there was a ghost."

"It was her favorite place. I keep it clean and swept in her memory. Is that acceptable, Countess?"

"Yes, please continue. I, too, enjoy that room, and it's much nicer because you've taken care of it. You may want to be careful of burning candles at night; occasionally someone sees them." I turned to Jeannine. "Let's go to my rooms." We left Mme Vacher clutching the journal.

"The tower room will seem emptier," I said to Jeannine. "I had looked forward to reading her journal and even trying to figure out some of the German."

"You did the right thing, Countess," she replied. "She would have wanted Mme Vacher to have it."

I felt a bond to the countess after reading what she had written. We shared a husband and a home, and now we shared her journal. I wished I had known her before she died.

158

Chapter Twenty-Three

Winter passed slowly. It was too chilly to go outside, and although my rooms were warm and bright, the days dragged. The count noticed and said he had a wonderful idea for me. "You will be instructed in how to play the harpsichord, my dear," he said. "The chateau needs music in it again." I protested, but the lessons began the next day.

I hated them. Every other morning I sat at the harpsichord with an old man sitting next to me who criticized the curve of my fingers, the placement of my hands, and the awkwardness of my elbows. How could I concentrate on the notes? It made me long to be back at the cottage with chores to do instead of here with music lessons.

The count asked me constantly how I was progressing, and I finally told him the truth. "I'm not progressing at all. M. DuPont criticizes me so much, I can't play the right keys. Then he tells me I'm not paying attention. I can't even begin to learn my lessons."

He chuckled. "M. DuPont sounds like a hard master. Would you rather have a different teacher?"

"I'd rather not have music lessons at all."

He ignored that and drummed his fingers on the table. "I'll make a change. His wife can teach you both instrument and voice. I'll have Mme Vacher tell them. You'll have a few days off, and then start fresh with her next week."

The maid came in with coffee and the discussion ended.

159

Later, I went up to my rooms and found Jeannine. "What am I going to do? Now I have to take voice lessons, too."

She stopped cleaning a pair of my shoes. "I've heard you singing. You have a beautiful voice. And having Mme DuPont teaching you will be much better than her husband."

"It won't be fun," I said, feeling cross. "It will take something that *was* fun and make it work."

She pressed her lips together and went back to the shoes. I knew that look by now and dropped down in a chair without saying more.

She put the shoes back into the wardrobe and stood up. "I know what you need, Countess. Fresh air. It's finally spring and it's lovely outside. We can go for a cart ride in the park."

I felt better at the thought of getting away from the chateau. "That's a wonderful idea. We'll take a picnic, too."

"I'll have a cart brought to the front and tell the cook to get a basket ready," she said, then disappeared out the door. I found a parasol while I waited.

"Are you going to use that?" she asked in surprise when she returned and saw what I was holding.

I made a face. "I don't like it, but the count told me he didn't want my face getting too much sun. He gave two of these to me when he came back from his last trip." I opened it and then twirled it around. "I think it's bothersome, but I tried to look happy when he showed them to me and promised I'd use them."

"We can go down, the cart should be waiting," she said.

"Thank you, Jeannine. You knew exactly what I needed today."

The stable boy was surprised to see the cart was for us. He walked the horse up to where we were standing and said "I'm sorry, Countess. I must have heard wrong. I thought a cart was wanted, I'll bring a carriage around right away."

"No," I said, "this is what I wanted."

He looked unsure, but Jeannine stepped up onto the seat. "I'll take care of her, Raoul, don't worry."

He still looked concerned, but he helped me into the cart. "You'll not go out of the chateau's park in this, will you?" he said to Jeannine.

160

"No, I promise," said Jeannine. "And we'll go on the back path, not down the drive. No one will see the countess in a farm cart." She smiled at him and picked up the reins.

He looked relieved to hear that and stepped back. "There's mud from the spring rains in spots," he said.

"I'll be careful," Jeannine answered.

A kitchen maid appeared with a large basket. "Raoul, can you put that in the cart?" Jeannine said over her shoulder, and I saw the boy leap to do her bidding.

As we pulled away from the stairs I looked back and saw him watching her. "Do you know him?"

"He's from my village. We grew up together," she said, and smiled as she turned the horse off the main drive onto a smaller path. I thought of Thomas and wondered if they were friends as he and I had been.

She pointed ahead. "See how the path splits? We'll go into the woods there. One way goes through those posts – that's the way to the gamekeeper's cottage. We'll go the other way, through these trees."

We went under the branches and entered the cool forest. Trees rose up on both sides but the woods didn't seem dark and forbidding, not on a path in a farm cart with Jeannine next to me. It was a friendly forest today, like the woods at the edges of Papa's fields.

The ride was surprisingly smooth and there were beautiful field flowers along the grassy cart path. Once, through the tree branches, I could see an abandoned cottage with no roof. Sunlight filtered down through the leaves, and from time to time a bird would flit across the path ahead of us. I breathed in the forest smell around us. The scents reminded me of when I was younger and following Thomas through the woods as we explored.

We went over a small wooden bridge with no sides and although the cart didn't go near the edge, I was relieved when we pulled back up on hard ground. "There's another bridge a little farther up," said Jeannine. "It's not quite as wide as that one was."

"Then let's find a place to turn aside," I told her.

She shook the reins and the horse moved forward. "There's a clearing up ahead, around that bend."

161

"When did you come here before?"

"I've been here with Raoul. He was taking something to the gamekeeper's cottage and turned the wrong way. He hadn't been here very long."

I wondered, as I saw a blush creeping up her neck, if he really hadn't known the way to the cottage. But she didn't tell me any more.

"This is perfect," I said as we rounded the corner and a small glade opened up on the side of the path. We pulled over to the edge of the trees and stopped. I heard a bird sing, far away. Another, closer, answered it, then more joined in.

"You're right, it is perfect," she said, and jumped down from the cart. I followed a bit more slowly while she unhitched and tethered the horse.

"He'll enjoy that for a bit," she said, slapping his rump as his nose disappeared into the meadow grass. "Do you want your parasol?"

I moved farther out from the shade and sat down. "No, the sun feels good."

"You'll get color."

"I've always had color. I look sick most of the time now."

"Oh, no, Countess. Your complexion is much nicer. You've lost the ruddiness from the farm."

"I know, Jeannine, that's what I mean. I don't look like me. I look like a high-born lady, not just Marie. Oh, all right," I said when I saw how concerned she was. "You can give me the parasol."

But when she handed it to me, I laid it down on the grass unopened and turned my face to the sun. Its warmth felt like a familiar friend. Now that the cart noise had stopped, I could hear more noises in the woods; rustlings, chattering, a twig snapping. I felt all the tension I had been carrying ebbing away, and finally relaxed.

Then I realized I was hungry. "I wonder what they packed for us."

Jeannine got the basket down from the cart and opened the top. "There's chicken, bread, cheese, and a jug of water. They

162

didn't know it was for you, Countess, or there would have been better food, and far more."

"This is fine. It would have been a feast for me not too long ago." I pulled off a piece of bread. "I never thought I'd say this, but all the food we have at every meal is getting tiresome. I'm a farm girl, Jeannine. The fanciness of being a countess was fun in the beginning, but it didn't last." I bit into a piece of chicken. "And this tastes better than anything I've had for a long time."

"It's the fresh air," she said.

We ate, watching the horse slowly moving and grazing in the meadow grass. "I'd forgotten what it's like to spend a day outside." I breathed in deeply, smelling the rich forest aroma. "I miss the farm. When I go home to visit, I sit inside the cottage. I'm never out in the fields anymore." Jeannine didn't answer, but I knew she understood.

We finished eating and stretched out on the grass. I had just closed my eyes when Jeannine spoke. "I saw your friend," she said softly, "the one your sister said left the village."

I sat up. "Thomas? Where?"

"Here in the woods."

"Did you talk to him?"

"Yes, he wanted – oh, Countess, I don't know that I should be telling you this."

"You *have* to tell me. What did he say?"

She bit her lip. "He asked how you were. He said he couldn't leave unless he knew someone was watching over you. He asked me to, and I said of course I would, I didn't need to be told."

"Did he say anything else?"

"He said he needed to find out something. I asked what, but he wouldn't say. He seemed very worried about you." Jeannine looked concerned. "I shouldn't have told you, he asked me not to."

"Yes you should have, Jeannine. It's all right. He's always looked out for me, ever since we were little. Where was he staying? His house in the village has been empty since he closed his shop."

"When he left, he walked toward where the gypsies were camped. Raoul said they're gone, though. If he was with them, he's left, too."

163

"You told Raoul?"

"He was with me. We'd gone for a walk and your friend was by the cart when we got back."

So he wasn't here now. Still, he had wanted to make sure I was safe. At least we were still friends.

"And what were you and Raoul doing?" I teased.

"Just walking," she said, but she blushed.

"He's a nice young man," I said. "I'm glad you both could work here."

"So are we," she said eagerly. "He's the one who told Mme Vacher about me. She hired me before she even met me. I never dreamed I'd get a position in the count's chateau, it was all because of Raoul."

I smiled at her. She looked so happy when she spoke of Raoul. Then I said, "Jeannine, I think you shouldn't tell anyone else that you saw Thomas, or what he said to you."

"Yes, Countess."

I got up. "Let's go for a walk."

"There's a path on the side of that rock." Jeannine pointed to a trail which disappeared into the shadowy woods.

We put the remaining food back into the basket and closed it tightly. Jeannine put it into the cart and we started off, the trees closing around us as we followed the narrow trail. I was glad to be busy. I didn't want to think about Thomas.

"This path isn't used often," Jeannine said as she led the way. "It's mostly a game trail for deer."

I hadn't known how much I missed the smell of damp earth and leaves. Every few steps I took a deep breath, trying to sort out each different scent. How I missed working the farm.

We came to a stream which ran across the path. "Someone put down stepping stones," Jeannine said as she leaped across the stream, balancing on large, flat stones.

I followed her. "Is this the same creek we crossed with the cart?"

"Yes," she replied, shaking out her skirt and turning back to the path. "It twists around a bit. I see a fallen tree up ahead. We can sit there."

164

I was glad to hear it, I was getting tired. And my feet hurt in their shoes. I wished I still had my old boots. At least I'd changed out of the fancier shoes before we left.

We reached the fallen tree and clambered up onto the broad trunk. Jeannine stretched out along it and I sat with my back against a branch that was reaching toward the sky, my feet dangling over the edge. We talked for a bit, and after a while lapsed into companionable silence.

"Jeannine, do you hear that?" I whispered after a few minutes. She sat up. "What?"

"It sounded like an animal." I heard it again. "Something's whining."

"Is it a wolf?" Her eyes grew large as she looked around at the forest.

"A wolf would growl. Listen. It sounds like it's coming from under the tree trunk." I pulled up my feet.

"Oh, Countess, what if it attacks us?" she asked. The chateau seemed much too far away.

The whimper came again, and then a little yelp. "It's a dog," I said.

We scrambled down off the tree trunk and peered into the shadows under it. "Look, there's a hollow," Jeannine said. "And you're right, it's a dog."

A large, filthy dog looked beseechingly at us as his tail thumped the ground.

"He's caught in a snare, Countess. See the cord around his neck? The gamekeeper must have set it along the path. The animals come along here to get water."

I looked more closely at the dog and could see a thin cord around his neck, pulled tight.

"When he moves back to get away from it, it chokes him," she said. "He must have gotten caught by mistake. He crawled under here and sprang it."

"How do we get him out of it?" I asked.

"We have to get him to come forward. That way the snare will loosen and we can slip it off his head." We both looked uncertainly at the dog, and then Jeannine said, "Do you think he'll bite?"

165

"I don't know," I answered, and his tail thumped again. I got down on my knees and slowly put my head and shoulders under the log, then extended my hand to him. He crept forward and licked it. "Good boy," I said, and raised my hand to pat his head.

"Hey! What goes on there?" A man's loud voice startled both the dog and me, and I snatched my hand back. "Get away from that tree, you two," he said.

I pulled back out from the log and looked into the angry face of a thin, wiry man.

He glared at me. "Get up from there!"

"This is the Countess de Roesch," said Jeannine.

His eyes widened. "Oh, so it is. I'm sorry, Countess, I didn't recognize you down there on the ground." He pulled off his cap and twisted it in his hands.

"I'm sure you didn't. I'm not usually covered in dirt," I said as I brushed some of the smeared soil off my dress.

"There's a snare in there, you see, Countess, and I –"

"Yes, we know. And it's caught a dog. Is that what you were trying to get?"

"A dog? No, Countess, that's not what I'd be expecting from my snares. I was looking for a fox." He knelt down, flicked something, and snapped his fingers. "Come on out."

"Is he yours?" I asked him.

"I've not seen him before," he said as the dog crawled out from under the tree. "He looks like he's been on his own for a while."

He did, indeed. Now that he was out, I could see how thin and scraggly he was. His fur was dirty and matted, there were cuts on his face, and a dark patch of fur showed where there was old dried blood over an ugly gash. But his face was whiskery and his expression sweet, and I already loved him.

Once again, I extended my hand to him. He sniffed it and sat down, his nose right by my hand, and looked at me expectantly.

The gamekeeper chuckled. "He's a nice one. Too bad he's got no place to go."

"He's got a place now," I said, patting his head. "I'm taking him home."

"Are you sure, Countess?" said Jeannine, eyeing the filthy dog.

"Yes, I'm sure."

166

"Would you like me to clean him up for you?" said the gamekeeper. "I can wash all that dirt off and bring him up to the chateau for you later."

"Could you? That would be wonderful."

"He may work up real nice, once I've got all the dirt and burrs off him," he said, studying the dog. "He's got a good build."

I knelt down on the ground again and held the dog's head in my hands, looking into his eyes. "You go with him, boy, and get cleaned up. Then you can come to the chateau and – oh, Jeannine, do you think he can come up to my rooms?"

"If you want him there, Countess."

"Good, then that's where you'll be." I patted his head again and got up, smiling at the gamekeeper. "And thank you – I'm sorry; I don't know your name."

"Philippe, Countess. I've been the gamekeeper here for years."

"Thank you, Philippe."

"I'll wash him up real good for you, Countess. You won't even know it was the same dog. When do you want him up there?"

"Whenever he's ready is fine."

He bowed slightly and waited for us to leave, one hand on the dog's head. The dog watched us turn away and I heard him whine again.

"Don't you worry, boy," Philippe said. "You'll see her again. But first you'll get presentable. If you show up at the chateau the way you look now, I'll lose my job for sure."

When I turned back around to see the dog one more time he was watching Philippe, who was reaching under the tree. "Re-setting his snare," said Jeannine, following my glance, and we went back across the stream to the waiting horse and cart.

167

Chapter Twenty-Four

Later that afternoon there was a knock on the door of my sitting room.

"The gamekeeper is downstairs at the kitchen door," said the maid. "He has a dog he says is yours. I told him you don't have a dog, but he keeps saying 'he belongs to the countess.'"

"He's right. We found him today in the woods. Tell Philippe to bring the dog around to the front hall, we'll meet him there."

She curtsied and left and I looked around the room. "Where should he sleep?"

"You really want him in here with you?" Jeannine said.

"Yes, at least in the sitting room. I've never kept a dog indoors before. What does one do with them?"

"I'm not sure. But the last countess had hers in here, too. Ours were outside farm dogs. Except for my brother's hunting dog, that one came inside with him. He let him sleep by the bed."

"Maybe this one can sleep by the window near the doves," I said, "on that small rug. Let's go down and get him."

Philippe was waiting in the hall, but there was no dog. He bowed, hat in hand, and looked uncomfortable.

"Where's the dog?" I asked him.

"He's just outside the door, Countess. I didn't know if it would be proper to bring him into this part of the house. He may be used to the outdoors, you see." He looked even more uneasy. "He may not know how to behave inside a house. I didn't want him to do anything wrong, Countess."

168

"Bring him in, Philippe," I said. "If he doesn't know, he'll soon learn."

Philippe gave another small bow and went out the front door, reappearing a moment later with a dog on a leash.

"Is he the same dog?" I said in surprise.

"Yes, Countess, cleaned and brushed for you."

"I hardly recognize him!"

Standing in front of us was a large, dark brown dog with beautiful long, wavy fur, a tail that curved upwards, and a whiskery muzzle with a pink tongue lolling out the side of his mouth. It was still the same friendly, bearded face I had seen under the tree, though that was the only part of him which showed it was the dog from the woods. He blinked at me, but his tail didn't wag.

"I think he's a bit undone, being inside here," said Philippe. "If you don't mind my saying this to you, Countess, if you get down on his level, more eye-to-eye."

I laughed out loud when I saw the same beseeching look on the gamekeeper's face I had seen earlier on the dog's. "I understand, Philippe."

I knelt in front of them and the dog stepped forward, his tail moving slowly at first, then, when his nose touched my hand, faster.

"He thinks well of you, Countess. And you, too," he said to Jeannine, who stroked the dog's side while I patted his head. "Dogs know people, they can tell the good ones from the bad ones."

Philippe handed the leash to me and I rose. The dog was so large my hand could still rest on his head.

"What will you call him?" Jeannine asked.

"I don't know."

"It will come to you," she said, still stroking his fur. "He's so soft now that he's clean. I can't believe he's the same dog we found under the log."

"He'll need extra food for a while until he fills out some," said Philippe. "He's had a spell of bad times, from the looks of him. He's mostly skin and bones."

"He'll have plenty to eat here," I replied.

169

Philippe gave another little bow. I could tell he thought his job here was done, so I thanked him and he left.

We looked at the dog. "What should we do with him?" I asked.

Mme Vacher spoke from behind us on the stairs. "He doesn't need a walk, Philippe just brought him up from the cottage. I see he also gave him a collar and a leash. But he's quite thin. Perhaps you should feed him. Where did he come from?"

She came down the last few steps and the dog went right over to her and sat down by her feet. She smiled at him.

"We found him caught in one of Philippe's snares," I said as she looked over the dog. He flopped down on his side with a sigh.

"I don't recognize him from around here," Mme Vacher said. His tail thumped on the floor at the sound of her voice. "He seems to be a nice dog. Cook will have something he can eat. Philippe probably gave him a meal, but it wouldn't hurt to see if he'll eat a little more. Don't let him bolt it down, though, or it will all come back up." The dog sat up. She touched his head lightly and, still smiling, went back up the stairs.

"She's not leaving, boy," I said as he whined. "You'll see her again.

"Let's take him to the kitchen." I pulled on his leash and he came slowly.

"I don't think he's ever been inside a house before," Jeannine said as he peered around the doorway before cautiously following us into the dining room.

The cook looked disapproving when he saw us come through the door. I couldn't blame him, especially when I had to pull my new dog down from the table where a roast was waiting to go into the oven.

"He's not scared to be inside anymore," I said under my breath as his nose twitched and his ears moved with each noise. "He's having a grand time."

The cook finally put a plate with a few scraps on the floor for him. The food disappeared instantly. Then he tried to follow the cook around the kitchen.

"I'm afraid you have a new friend," I said, pulling the dog away from him.

170

He didn't answer me, but I did see him slip the dog another piece of meat. I decided we'd better leave before the dog's stomach held too much.

"Jeannine, let's show him his bed."

He wasn't sure about the steps at first and we went up slowly. "He's not going to like going down," Jeannine said as we got to the top and he looked back down the staircase.

"He'll learn."

And he did, not much later. We showed him his rug in my room and put a dish of water down for him. He drank, sat down on the rug, then got up and lifted his leg near a table.

"No!" Jeannine screeched.

He put it down and looked around. We rushed him back down the stairs and out the door to a bush where he relieved himself.

"We'll have to watch him, Countess, and hurry him outside if he needs to go."

"How often?"

"Whenever he looks ready."

He looked ready fairly often, and after two more frantic flights down the staircase we spent the rest of the afternoon and evening downstairs so he would be closer to the door. I was glad the count wouldn't be home until late that night. I wasn't sure how much he would like our new dog.

But later, in my dark room, it was comforting to know he was near when I was lying in bed. And when he padded into my room, I let him up on the bed with me and fell asleep with my arm around him.

Must you have that creature?" said the count the next morning when I came down, the dog trailing me. "If you wanted a dog, you should have let me know. I can get a dog for you, a fine one that fits your rank. That one is just a mutt."

"I don't want another dog. I want him."

"There are things you must think about when choosing a pet, Marie."

"But I love him already."

171

He looked over the dog who sat patiently under my hand. It was probably the same way he looked at stock for the chateaus.

He shook his head but said, "Very well, Marie, if that's what you want. Where is he sleeping?"

"In my sitting room, there's a rug for him by the window."

"Don't let him up on your bed. He'll bring fleas into the sheets. And I would rather not see him at meals."

"Oh please may I bring him to breakfast? He doesn't want me to leave him."

The count glanced at the dog again. "Have him sit on the far side of your chair. I don't want a dog watching me eat."

I patted the other side of my chair. He went around it and sat down.

"Have you named him?"

"Yes, Renard."

"Fox? That's a foolish name for a dog, especially one that big."

"He was caught in a snare the gamekeeper had set for a fox."

"And Philippe brought him here?" He looked puzzled. "Why did he do that?"

"Jeannine and I went out for a picnic and found him in the snare. Philippe came when we were trying to get him out and wouldn't let him come here until he was washed and brushed."

"He looked worse than he does now?"

"Yes, he was filthy and covered with burrs. But he was so sweet, I had to keep him." Renard's tail moved as my hand dropped to his head.

"Marie, are you sure you wouldn't like a different dog? I could get another one for you, a beautiful one."

"No, I want Renard."

He sighed. "Whatever you wish."

I knew he didn't understand, but Renard could stay and that was enough.

172

Chapter Twenty-Five

"Countess," Jeannine said to me one morning just after breakfast, "may I have permission to be away for a few days? When Raoul came back yesterday from our village, he brought word from Papa that my maman is sick."

"Of course, Jeannine."

"Thank you, Countess. When may I leave?"

"Right away. And take some food from the kitchen." Then I remembered something Papa had told me. "Jeannine, your village is part of the count's land. Doesn't the countess visit those who are sick?"

"I've never heard any of the countesses from here doing it."

"Then I will be the first."

"There's no need for you to do that, Countess," said Jeannine.

"I want to. Besides, the count told me he'll be busy all day. I can go and come back in one day, can't I?"

"Yes, it's close enough, but you'll spend a lot of time in the carriage."

"I don't mind. Then I'll send a cart back for you in a few days."

We went down to the kitchen and I ordered four large baskets of food and had one of the kitchen boys run to the stable. "Tell Raoul I want the open carriage and he'll be driving it," I said and he dashed out the door. "Jeannine, ask the cook to make three more baskets for Raoul's family."

"They'll be grateful, Countess."

"It won't even be missed here," I said.

173

"What won't be missed?" said Martel from behind us.

"Just a few things for Jeannine's family."

"Is she planning on leaving the chateau? Her job is here with you."

"I will be with her, M. Martel," I said stiffly.

His eyes showed a flash of interest. "Surely you won't be staying in a villager's cottage, Countess."

"I'll return tonight. I'm visiting a sick villager, something my father taught me to do."

He looked as if he was going to argue with me, but then turned and disappeared into the hallway.

"He doesn't need to know what my plans are," I said crossly, annoyed that I'd told him as much as I had.

"It doesn't matter, Countess. Don't let him spoil your day."

The kitchen girls filled the baskets with food and brought them out to the waiting carriage. Just before we were ready to leave, Henri told me Mme Vacher needed to go over some things for the chateau. "I'll be as quick as I can," I said as I went back inside.

It was almost an hour before I returned. "I don't know why Martel told her to go over that with me now," I complained to Jeannine. "It really isn't up to him, and all of it could have waited."

"The count must have told him to tell her. But we still have enough time," she said as we climbed into the carriage. We sat with four of the baskets on the seats. Three others were tied to the back.

"Thank you for the food for my family, Countess," Raoul said as he climbed into the front of the carriage.

"It's my pleasure, Raoul."

He dipped his head and then, with a quick look at Jeannine, picked up the reins. Then I heard Renard bark. "Open the door, Jeannine, and see if he'll jump in," I said.

He did, and sat by our feet as the carriage rumbled out of the front courtyard to the road. He quickly wormed his way onto the seat across from us between the two stacks of baskets.

"Just like when he squeezed under the tree and got snared," said Jeannine, and I laughed.

The sky was bright blue and the air smelled sweet. I was glad I'd chosen an open carriage. "It's a wonderful day for a ride," I

174

said as we went down the hill. But when we passed through the village and went by Thomas's old shop, I turned away. I didn't want to see how deserted it looked now.

Maman was by the door when we drew near the cottage. When she saw us she came outside.

"Come with us, Maman!"

"No, I have too much to do here, child."

"I can send someone from the chateau to do it for you."

"No, dear, I don't need more help." She waved goodbye and went back inside.

"She's always like that now," I grumbled. But Jeannine didn't respond and my annoyance quickly passed.

We spent the next several hours rolling through the countryside, past fields and villages. Shortly after we entered a forest, Raoul stopped the carriage in a clearing so we could stretch our legs. As soon as we got out Renard jumped down and sprinted into the woods. "Oh, I hope he comes back!" I said.

"He will, Countess. He doesn't like to be far from you," Jeannine replied. "Shall we have some bread and cheese?"

"That would be wonderful."

I was watching the trees where Renard had disappeared and didn't hear the thieves come out from the woods. One grabbed me from behind and Raoul spun around as I shrieked.

"Look what we have here," the man behind me said. Raoul moved toward me. "No, don't you do nothing foolish and make me hurt this lady," the man said. Raoul stopped, eyes wide, and I felt a knife against my throat. Then I heard a nasty chuckle by my ear. His stench was nauseating, and the arm around my waist was filthy.

Then another man came into my view. "What do you think these good people are carrying?" he said.

"It's food for some villagers," said Jeannine, her voice strained, as he stepped up to Raoul and put a knife against his side.

"Empty the carriage," said the one holding me. He must have been looking at Jeannine, because she gave a tight nod. "And let's see what this fine lady is wearing." He kept the knife at my throat and with his other hand felt for rings on my fingers. "I think we've got some fancy jewelry here."

175

He twisted off my wedding ring and then felt my throat. I had removed my other jewels and put on a plain gold necklace before we left. He jerked it off, cutting the chain into the side of my neck and breaking the clasp.

"Don't harm the countess or you'll be dead men," said Raoul through clenched teeth. The man pushed his knife further into Raoul's tunic. The tip of the blade disappeared and a spot of blood spread on the fabric.

"Oh, we won't hurt the ladies." The man at Raoul's side winked at Jeannine. "You'll be good for sport."

That's when Raoul moved. He grabbed the man's arm and twisted it away from his side. I watched with a sinking feeling, feeling the arm around my waist tighten and knowing Raoul would never get to me in time. But then there was a ferocious growl behind me and I was flung to the ground.

I looked up in time to see Renard biting into the arm of the man who had been holding me. Then he leaped across the grass and jumped to bite the face of the other man. The man screamed in pain. Renard didn't stop. He was like a whirlwind, attacking both of them time after time.

Then he put himself between us and the robbers, snarling fiercely. The men, bleeding, backed away from him. More blood was on Renard. I wondered if it was theirs or Renard's. Everything seemed to move slowly but it was really only moments. Then the two men bolted into the trees.

"Get in!" Raoul shouted. I snatched my necklace from the ground where it had dropped and saw my wedding ring, half-hidden in the grass. I scooped that up, too, and dashed for the carriage. Jeannine pushed me up and jumped in after me. Raoul leaped into the front, grabbed the reins, and raced the carriage down the road.

"Wait! Renard isn't with us!" I shouted. But Raoul couldn't hear me.

We charged through the forest, finally emerging on the far side with wide farm fields around us once again. Raoul kept the horses running. I looked back and saw with relief Renard running after us. It wasn't until we were on the outskirts of the next village that Raoul slowed the horses.

"Countess, you're hurt!" Jeannine's horrified voice made me realize my neck was stinging.

I touched the side of my throat and my fingers came away with blood on them. "I think that's from the necklace he pulled off."

"I put you and Jeannine in danger by stopping there –" Raoul's voice broke.

"Raoul, you couldn't have known," said Jeannine. "Those woods have always been safe. I've gone through them by myself many times and nothing's ever happened. And they could have jumped the carriage even if we hadn't stopped."

"But still –"

"Jeannine's right, Raoul. It's not your fault. We'll ask at this village if anyone knows them."

"You stay in the carriage, Countess, while I find someone who can bandage your neck," said Jeannine. She jumped down from the carriage and went into the first cottage, reappearing a minute later with an older woman. "Countess, this is Mme Martin."

"Countess de Roesch, what a terrible thing to happen to you! Come inside and rest. And we'll take care of that," she said, peering at my neck.

Jeannine helped me down from the carriage and Renard came out from underneath. Mme Martin backed up. "That dog, he has blood on him."

"That dog saved her," said Raoul. "I couldn't have gotten to her in time."

She stared at Renard as if she didn't believe it, but he came to me and I put my hand on his head. "He attacked both of them and drove them off."

Then I saw Raoul wince and hold his side. "Raoul, you're hurt," I said.

"Come now, both of you, inside," said the woman, suddenly bossy like the Widow DuBois. She motioned to a boy in the doorway. "Get your father." He ran off.

She held Raoul's arm to steady him and Jeannine walked with me. I was glad Mme Martin had taken charge. I was feeling quite shaky.

Inside her cottage, I sank down on a bench. "Look at Raoul first," I said.

177

She laid him down on the bed and lifted his shirt and tunic. "He's got a knife wound here. I'll wrap it. You'll have to stay here and rest, young man."

"I'm driving the Countess. I can't stay."

"Yes, you can, Raoul. We can go on to Jeannine's and I'll visit there for a day or two."

"Oh, Countess, you can't stay in my cottage!"

"I lived in a cottage all my life until I married the count," I said to her.

Mme Martin finished with Raoul and inspected my cut. "It's not deep, Countess. I'll wrap your neck. I think that's all it needs."

She wiped it, then took a clean cloth and tied it around my neck. "There, that will stop the bleeding."

Raoul tried to rise and she turned back to him. "No, young man, you need to rest or you'll be bleeding too much again."

"Raoul, we'll be fine," I said. "You stay here."

"I can't let you go without me with those men on the road."

"My boys Jean and Jacque will drive them," said Mme Martin. "They'll be safe. And I've already sent for my husband. The men from the village will find those robbers if they're anywhere near."

"We'll be fine," I said to Raoul. He looked ashen. "You need to rest. Lie down, you're making it bleed." I was afraid he'd fall over if he kept trying to get up.

Jeannine took his hand, kneeling by the bedside as he lay back down. "Your maman would want you to stay here," she said.

"We'll tell her you'll be home when you can travel," I said. "And you stay home until you're better. She can send you back to the chateau when she thinks you're ready."

Raoul had already closed his eyes. "I'll stay here with you," said Jeannine, holding his hand.

"You go with the countess," he said. She looked about to argue, but then she kissed his hand and came back to me.

"Go find your older brothers in the near field," Mme Martin said to another young boy. "Tell them they have to take the Countess de Roesch to another village." He ran out the door and returned shortly with two young men.

To my relief her sons were large and strong. Every time I looked at their broad shoulders and backs I felt safe. And when

178

we left, they guided the carriage carefully through several villages and fields with skill that surprised me for farm boys. They probably hadn't handled anything other than a heavy, slow farm cart.

We finally pulled up to Jeannine's cottage and several children swarmed out the door. When she stepped out of the carriage, they circled around her and pulled her toward the house. "No, no, the countess is here. I need to help her. Who is watching Maman?"

"Aunt Pauline," one of the girls said.

"Go get her."

They left Jeannine and ran back inside, reappearing a moment later with a large, smiling woman. "Jeannine, dear. And who is with you?"

"This is Countess de Roesch, Aunt Pauline. She's come to see Maman. And she's brought baskets of food here for us, and for Raoul's family, too."

"How wonderful. Thank you, Countess," Aunt Pauline said as Jeannine helped me down.

"Raoul was bringing us, but he was hurt when we were attacked by two thieves in the woods," Jeannine said. Her aunt looked concerned and she added, "He'll be all right. Jean and Jacque brought us the rest of the way." The two boys nodded a greeting. "Raoul's still at their house with their mother, Mme Martin. She said he should rest before he travels again."

Renard jumped down from the carriage and one of the smaller boys flung his arm around Renard's neck. "Look, he has blood on him. Was he hurt, too?"

"No, that's from the men," I said. "He bit them."

"Good dog," he said as he patted Renard's head.

"Where's Maman?" said Jeannine.

"She's inside," said Aunt Pauline. "Countess, please come in."

She stood by the low doorway as we ducked our heads and went inside. It took a few moments for my eyes to adjust from the bright sunlight to the dim interior of the cottage, but when they did, I felt like I'd come home. There were children around us, food cooking on the hearth, and a table set for a meal. I had to smile.

179

Then I saw a small bed in the corner. Jeannine had already gone over to it. "Maman." She knelt by the bedside.

"Child," I heard her maman whisper. "You've come."

"Yes, Maman, and the countess is here, too."

Her maman turned in the bed and looked across the room. Her eyes were dark and sunken in her pale face. "Countess, please forgive me –"

"There's nothing to forgive. Jeannine was coming to see you, and I brought some food for your family."

Jeannine took her hand. "It's food from the chateau, Maman, good food." She reached over and poured a cup of water. "Here, drink this, and then we'll get something from the baskets for you."

Her maman took the cup. "How long can you stay?" she asked Jeannine.

"As long as you need her," I answered. "Her papa sent word she could be of use here."

She smiled. Even though her eyes still looked ill, it made her face looked less sunken. "Just her presence is enough to make me better."

"When did Aunt Pauline come?" asked Jeannine. She opened one of the baskets and handed her mother a small piece of bread.

"I came yesterday," her aunt answered. "Your maman's got too many little ones to tend without help when she's laid up."

Jeannine's maman peered at my neck. Jeannine saw and said, "Raoul was hurt, and so was the countess. We were attacked and one of the men cut the countess's neck, that's why there's a bandage."

"Where is Raoul?"

"At the Martin's cottage. Mme Martin, she's Jean and Jacque's mother, said he had to stay and rest. She said he'll be fine in a few days."

"Don't look worried, then," her mother said. "Raoul is strong. What happened to the men who attacked you?"

"Renard drove them away," I told her, patting his head. He had come into the cottage as we talked, and the children looked at him with awe.

180

Jeannine's maman glanced around the room. "There's nowhere for the countess to sit," she said to Jeannine, trying to get up, and I realized how uncomfortable I was making her.

I sat down on the bench along the worn trestle table. "I grew up in a smaller cottage than this." I looked around at the sparse furnishings. "I feel as if I've come home. It's lovely here, it truly is." I smiled at her mother. "You eat some of that food Jeannine brought for you and get well. Don't worry about where I'm sitting."

Her face relaxed as she lay back down on her bed. "Such a kind one, your Countess," she said softly to Jeannine. "He picked well this time." A warm wave of acceptance washed over me. I felt more welcome here than I ever had at the chateau.

A little girl no more than four came over to me. She leaned on my knee and I smiled at her.

"You're pretty," she said.

"Thank you. So are you."

She studied my face and said, "What's your name?"

"Marie, you mustn't ask the countess her name!" scolded Jeannine.

I drew in my breath to show her my surprise. "Why, Marie's my name, too!"

Her eyes widened. "Then we're name sisters!" she said, and ran out of the cottage.

"Did I upset her?" I asked Jeannine. But before she could reply, little Marie ran back in.

"Here," she said, thrusting a flower into my hands. "Name sisters always give presents to each other."

"Oh." I reached into my pocket and brought out a small purse. "Then I'll give you something, too." I pulled out a coin. "Here, this is yours now." I handed her the coin. "But your flower was much nicer."

She turned the coin over in her palm, looking at it with curiosity. I realized it had little significance for her, aside from being a gift, and felt in my pocket again.

I pulled out a small lace handkerchief. "And you can keep it in this."

181

She took the cloth with obvious delight and ran to show it to her mother, then dashed out the door.

"Wait, Marie," said Jeannine. The little girl ran back, and Jeannine held out her hand. "Let me keep the coin. You play with the lace."

Marie ran back out the door and Jeannine put the coin on the mantel. "She would have lost that before she went through the gate."

I laughed. "I don't think the lace will stay white very long."

"You're very generous," Jeannine's maman said.

"Use it to buy good food so you get strong," I told her, and added another to the mantel when she wasn't looking.

"I'd like to tell Raoul's mother what happened," I said.

"There's no need for you to do that," Jeannine told me. "You should have a meal and start back. Even then you won't be home until after dark."

"But I can stay here, Jeannine –"

"Oh, Countess, you mustn't," she said, and her maman echoed her words. Their distress at the thought changed my mind.

"Very well. I'll have a small meal, and then Jean and Jacque can take me home."

Jeannine looked relieved. She unpacked some of the food from one of the baskets and sat by the bed. She helped her mother with a piece of meat, shredding it into small bits for the sick woman to swallow.

I left soon after we finished eating. The two boys drove the carriage back to their cottage and we checked on Raoul.

"He's sleeping," Mme Martin said. "And the men didn't find those robbers. They're gone, Countess. Don't you worry."

I didn't, not with her sons sitting solidly at the front of the carriage and Renard by my side. We pulled up to the chateau late that night. Mme Vacher met us at the door with a worried look. "We expected you back hours ago. The count has been asking if you've arrived since before nightfall. You –" She stopped and her eyes widened with alarm as she saw the two boys. "Where's Raoul?"

"With their mother. He was injured and needed to rest."

"What happened?"

182

"We were attacked on the way there by robbers. Raoul will come back when he's healed."

As I stepped into the lighted hallway, she saw the bandage on my throat. "Countess! You were hurt?"

"It's hardly anything, really."

"Come in, Countess, let me see. Henri, send for the count and let him know the countess was injured. Tell me again what happened," she said as she led me to the small salon and I sat on a chair by the fire.

"It was Renard who saved us."

"Renard?"

He had followed us into the room, his tongue lolling out of the side of his mouth. He flopped down with a sigh at my feet, not acting at all like a hero.

"He really did, Mme Vacher," I said as she unwrapped my bandage and looked at the cut. "He drove them off. Raoul tried to get to me, but he didn't have time. Renard attacked them and they ran away."

I had just finished explaining everything to her when the count came and the story had to be repeated. He was very upset that I had been in danger. "To think I could have lost you," he said. "From now on you must stay in the chateau park unless I am with you. I don't want anything else to happen to you."

I felt safe and secure as I lay on the couch, the count sitting next to me and holding my hand. It almost seemed worth the danger, to have him show such concern and affection for me. It made me realize I hadn't seen it for a long time.

The boys were taken to the kitchen where, I heard later, they ate more food than the cook had ever seen two people eat before. Then they bedded down in the stable and left early the next morning.

Jeannine and Raoul came back five days later, Raoul's side healing well and Jeannine full of stories about her family.

"I'm glad your maman's better and you had a good visit," I said, "and I'm happy that you're home. It's been dreary here without you."

183

"I missed you too, Countess. Now things will get back to how they should be." I thought they would too, but we were both wrong.

Chapter Twenty-Six

Mme Vacher came into my room one afternoon while Jeannine and I were brushing Renard. She stood before me, the previous countess's journal in her hands. "I found more writing in the back of her journal and thought you would want to hear it."

"Yes, I would, Mme Vacher."

She opened the journal from the back and flipped forward several pages. "I don't know why it's back here. Maybe she wanted to hide it. Both entries are very short; that's another reason I missed them before. They're in German."

She began to read. "'I have the key but I'm afraid. Why would he forbid me to use it? I wish Mme Vacher was here, she would tell me what to do.'

"The rest of this page is blank. Then here," and she turned a page, "it continues. 'I am more curious than afraid. What can harm me? I'm going to unlock the door.'"

Mme Vacher looked up at us. "There is nothing more after that. I don't know when she wrote these. Perhaps it's the very last thing she wrote. She may have been on her way to this door, stumbled at the top of the staircase, and fell through the glass."

"Was she clumsy?" I asked.

"Oh, no, she was quite graceful."

"Have you ever wondered..."

"Have I wondered if she was pushed? Oh, I've heard the servants talk," said Mme Vacher. "But who here would have wanted to do that to her?"

185

"Might she have been running from someone?"

"From whom?" she said.

I thought of Martel with his narrowed eyes but didn't answer.

"What key does she mean?" asked Jeannine.

"I don't know," said Mme Vacher.

"Which rooms are locked?" I asked.

"Some of the guest rooms," she said, "but they're cleaned regularly. The rooms downstairs are all open. There are rooms in the cellars which are locked, but Henri has keys for them. They're for storage, except for the wine cellar."

"Maybe it's one of those," I said.

"Perhaps. There are a few storage rooms in the old hallway, but they either have supplies or are empty. There are several outbuildings, too. They might have a room that's locked," she said.

"I wish we knew what she meant," I said. "Maybe it wasn't her last entry. It could have been an earlier one, and she didn't find anything interesting."

"That could be, Countess," said Mme Vacher, and she looked toward the door as a distant bell rang somewhere in the house. I knew she needed to check on the maids before dinner, so I dismissed her. She curtsied and left with the journal.

I fell asleep that night thinking about the mysterious key and woke several hours later. There was movement on the other side of the connecting door to the count's room. He must have left his dressing room door open. He was usually careful about closing it and I'd never heard anything from his bedroom before. I felt heavy with drowsiness and stayed in bed, too sleepy to get up and let him know I could hear him.

"I'm tired of this," the count said, his voice sounding faintly through the door.

"They were sloppy." Even half-awake, Martel's smooth voice annoyed me.

"I wanted her here. I want it to be here."

One of them put something down. There was a long pause and then the count said, "Horses can be unpredictable."

"Yes, they can," replied Martel.

"But it has to be here," said the count.

186

I found the conversation unsettling and drifted back to sleep, wondering vaguely what horse he wanted here. In the morning I thought it part of a dream.

I breathed in the aroma of the woods as the cart bumped along the rutted path. It had been too long since I'd been away from the chateau's walls and as soon as the count went to his office for the morning, I asked Jeannine to make arrangements for an outing. When we were out of sight of the chateau, she stopped the cart and I climbed up to the front seat next to her.

"Where's Renard?" she asked.

"Somewhere nearby."

The trees around us calmed me and although it had taken a couple of weeks after being attacked, I felt safe again as long as we were close to the chateau.

"Stop the cart along here," I said. "I want to walk for a while."

She pulled the cart aside into a narrow patch of grass and we got down. Renard gave a short bark up ahead. "It sounds like he found something," I said.

We walked along the cart path, turned a corner, and I stifled a scream. Renard was with a stranger who was kneeling next to him. He looked like a gypsy.

But then I realized he was stroking Renard's head. He couldn't be dangerous, not with Renard so calm.

He rose as soon as he saw us. Renard whined when he saw me, but stayed with the man.

"That's my dog," I said. Then I saw two dead birds at his feet. "And you're poaching."

He didn't answer.

"This is the Countess de Roesch," Jeannine said in a quivering voice.

He gave an exaggerated bow. "Good day, Countess de Roesch."

"You're poaching," I said again.

"And you've stolen my dog," he answered.

"I've stolen nothing," I said, but my heart raced. He couldn't take Renard.

187

"I raised this dog, he's mine." The gypsy eyed me shrewdly. "Unless you'd like to buy him for two birds."

For a moment I didn't know what to reply, and then I laughed out loud, suddenly liking him. "My dog may have come from your camp, but I don't believe you raised him. Do you have a family?"

He was obviously surprised at my response. "Yes, a wife and two children."

"Take the birds, and several more, if you can catch them. Just do it quietly. If the gamekeeper finds out, tell him you have my permission. And don't take anything from his snares. He doesn't like it. That's where I found the dog."

The man pushed Renard away from him. "He was my dog, but I've got another one now."

"He's worth far more than a few birds to me," I said as Renard came to me.

"He saved the countess's life," said Jeannine.

The gypsy studied my face, then leaned over and picked up the birds. "Thank you, Countess," he said. He took a step toward the trees but then stopped and faced us again. "You're a good woman, I think," he said to me, "and I wish you well. But you'll need more than good wishes up there. It holds a curse. Be careful, Countess." And he disappeared into the forest.

I clapped and Renard ran to me. "Gypsies are so superstitious," I said as we walked back.

It wasn't until we were almost at the cart that I realized I could have asked him about Thomas.

"How are your music lessons coming?" the count asked me one afternoon.

"I'm not playing as well as Mme DuPont would like," I answered.

"That's what I've heard," he said. I was glad I'd been honest. "She did tell me you've made some progress, especially with your voice lessons, and thinks it's worthwhile to continue."

Of course she would. She was well-paid for her efforts with me.

"Thank you. I'm sure I'll get better with practice."

188

"You may show me tonight after dinner. I'd like to hear you play."

My stomach plummeted.

He kissed my forehead and went to his office. I immediately made my way to the harpsichord to practice for the rest of the day.

My first recital that evening was every bit the disaster I thought it would be. My fingers curved like talons, hesitated on the keys, and hit wrong notes constantly.

When I finished, the count came over and laid his hand on my shoulder.

"Thank you, that was quite refreshing. But I will retire for the evening now. I'm afraid my head is aching – no, my dear, it wasn't from the music," he said as I tried to apologize for my poor playing. "I've had it all afternoon."

"I'll work on another piece," I said, hoping he wouldn't want to hear it.

"Father Gregory will be here for dinner next week. You may play for us then. I'm sure he would enjoy something simple."

"I'll have Mme DuPont choose a piece for me to practice," I said, feeling my face grow hot.

"I think we'll also add riding to your schedule," he said. "Perhaps you will enjoy that more than the harpsichord. You'll be able to join me on my early morning rides. I've found my new horse quite satisfactory and purchased a gelding that will be appropriate for you. He'll arrive here in a week or two. He's a hunting horse, past his prime."

"But I've never ridden."

"It's not difficult to ride, it only takes practice."

He left looking tired. I found Jeannine and told her of the unwelcome lessons that had been added. "You may find them fun," she said, putting a dress back in the wardrobe that had been airing on its door. "And he's right, you can join him when he goes out on his horse."

I groaned. "He does that so early. He talks about seeing the sun rise. I don't want to see the sun rise from the back of a horse." I watched Jeannine look through the dresses. "He never hunts. Did he have hunts before I came?"

189

She hung another dress on the door and examined the hem. "Not that I remember. I haven't heard talk of it, either."

"I wonder why. Nobility always hunts."

Jeannine didn't answer and I decided to ask him myself at dinner. The chateau's huge park had forests full of deer, fox, and occasionally wild boar, and other chateaus had hunting parties to amuse the owners.

"I have no stomach for killing," he told me when I asked. "All that blood." He shook his head and changed the subject.

I thought it strange, I had never known anyone who was bothered by an animal's blood. But it was obvious he didn't want to discuss it, and I wondered if he was ashamed.

We were at the mid-day meal with Father Gregory and M. Martel. No one was speaking. Martel seemed to be annoyed. Father Gregory was busy eating. I was picking at my food, feeling uncomfortable at my own table. I often felt that way. The count's recent coolness to me seemed even more pronounced lately, although I didn't know what I had done to anger him.

I glanced across at Father Gregory. He looked up and caught me watching him. "Is there something wrong, Countess?"

"No," I said, and went back to my meal.

"She is very similar in some ways to your last unfortunate wife, Count de Roesch," he said, and I could feel him still watching me.

I looked up again. "No, I'm not small and my hair's dark, not blonde."

The count seemed surprised. "How do you know what she looked like?"

"Mme Vacher told me. She was German, wasn't she?"

"Yes, that's right," said Father Gregory. "But she had a trusting nature, as you do. Don't you think, Count?" The count didn't answer. Father Gregory didn't seem to notice he'd been ignored, he just went back to eating. He belched noisily and I looked away, disgusted.

"I believe there are some errands you can do for me today," the count said to Martel. "I need something from the village and also from a farm not too far from here."

190

"I have things to do also," Martel said curtly. "Perhaps Father Gregory can go to the farm."

"I wish you to go, Martel. Father Gregory will be doing something else. We'll discuss it in my office after the meal."

I found myself thinking of a chessboard and Father Gregory a pawn on it, someone for Martel and the count to move at their whim. I sighed, thinking I'd rather be playing chess at home with Anne than watching it here with them.

The count lay down his spoon. "Marie, must you be so morose? It ruins my appetite."

Unease crept into me as I looked at him. His eyes had none of the warmth I used to see in them. "I'm sorry," I said softly. "I was thinking of my sister."

"Well," he said, "invite her here. Surely she would come if you asked her."

"Yes, I think I will," I answered.

He looked at me for a few moments, then picked up his spoon and went back to his meal.

When they had finished, he said, "I will be in my office for most of the day. Enjoy your afternoon with your sister." He gave a slight bow and they left.

I found Jeannine upstairs. "I'd like Anne to come up for the afternoon. Do you know where Mme Vacher is? I want her to send for Anne."

"I'll find her, Countess."

"I'll go with you," I said. "I don't feel like sitting here."

She wasn't upstairs and we couldn't find her in the front rooms downstairs. "Maybe near the kitchen," said Jeannine, and we headed down one of the hallways.

It led past the count's downstairs office. The door was ajar, and we heard his voice as we neared.

"I don't think it's too soon. I've grown tired of her. It's time."

"No, Count." Martel was just inside the door. "I told you, not yet. This one is delicate. She's —"

They must have heard our skirts rustle as we drew closer and the conversation ceased. Martel pushed open the door.

"Ah, Countess. What brings you here?"

"We're looking for Mme Vacher."

191

"She's not here."

"No, I'm not — I didn't think she was." He waited as I stumbled over my words. "We were going to the kitchens — the downstairs rooms were empty —"

The count appeared at the door. "Countess, I do not wish to be disturbed. I am sorting though some business about the chateau's horses and interruptions are not welcome."

"I'm sorry —" I stood helplessly. I couldn't seem to get any more words out.

Jeannine stepped up to my side. "I'm sorry we disturbed you, Count."

He nodded, closed the door, and we hurried away. When we turned a corner in the hallway, I stopped.

"You're shaking, Countess."

"Did you hear what he said, Jeannine? He said he's tired of me. What does that mean? What will he do?"

"Countess, he was talking about horses. Didn't you hear him say that?"

"Horses?"

"They were talking about the chateau's horses. Why would he talk like that about you?"

"I don't know. Sometimes he frightens me. I feel like something's going to happen, something terrible. I tell myself I'm being foolish, but then he looks at me and his eyes are hard. And the gypsy, he tried to warn me."

"I'm not going to let anything terrible happen to you, Countess. And you know not to listen to a gypsy. The count is right, you do need a visit from your sister," Jeannine said. "We'll find Mme Vacher. And if I have to, I'll walk down to the village myself."

But we did find her. She was coming out of the kitchen. I must have looked wild-eyed because when she saw me, she said, "Countess! Is something wrong?"

"She heard something and took it wrong, that's all, Mme Vacher," said Jeannine. "The countess would like her sister to come this afternoon for a visit."

192

Mme Vacher, still looking alarmed, said, "Of course. Jeannine, take the carriage to the village. Countess, would you like to wait for her in the small salon?"

I nodded and she took me there, sat me in a chair, and said, "You rest, Countess. I'll get some tea for you. Jeannine's already on her way. Your sister will be here soon."

I dismissed her after she brought the tea and leaned back in the chair, my eyes closed. What was going on? I heard people talking about me, but they weren't. I saw blue hair, but it was black. I felt the count no longer loved me, yet he could be warm and affectionate. Everything was so confusing.

Maybe it was me.

I stood up and went to the window. I didn't know what to think anymore. Being in the chateau seemed to be poisoning my mind. I was growing more and more afraid and I longed to be living back in the village again, with chores to do and people to visit. I had been happy then and I hadn't even known it.

Maybe that's what all this was. I was homesick. I wanted to be with Maman and Anne again, with Adam and Thomas visiting, and not be the mistress of a huge old chateau.

I started crying but I brushed away the tears. I had to compose myself before Anne arrived or she'd be so worried she'd put me in the carriage and take me home. How nice that would be.

My mind kept going in circles until finally the carriage came up the drive. I ran out to greet Anne. "You can just send a cart for me, you know," she said as we kissed. "I don't need a fancy carriage."

"Oh, stop complaining. I haven't seen you for weeks."

Jeannine stepped down from the carriage with flowers in her hand. "These are for your sitting room," said Anne. "They're from Maman."

"I'll put them in a vase," Jeannine said.

"How is she?" I asked as we went through the door and up the stairs.

"She's well. Now that the weather's better she's back out in the fields, telling the chateau workers what to do."

We reached the sitting room and I pulled the door shut.

"How have you been?" Anne said, looking around the room. "I see you on Sunday mornings, but even after all this time he takes you away before the service has ended. And your maid said you weren't feeling well today."

"I feel fine now that you're here," I said, my voice a little too high. Anne frowned so I smiled and said, "I was confused about something I heard, that's all." I gave a little laugh and added, "Sometimes my mind plays tricks on me."

"Marie, something's not right. What is it?"

There was a knock and the door opened. Jeannine entered with the flowers in a vase and put them on the table.

I shrugged. "It's different than before. But I have Jeannine, and she makes it better."

Jeannine smiled. "Thank you, Countess."

Anne glanced at Jeannine and took my arm. "Shall we go for a walk?"

"We can talk with Jeannine here," I said. "I'll tell her everything later anyway."

"Well, that makes it easier," said Anne. She sat on the sofa and pulled me down. "So tell me, what's wrong?"

I looked down at my hands, giving up the false gaiety. "I don't know. It isn't fun to be here anymore. I'd rather be home at the cottage. I spend most of my time with Jeannine. Sometimes I go out in the garden, but if Jeannine isn't with me there's no one to walk with, so I don't go out often."

"Don't you spend time with the count?"

"No."

"Not at all?"

"Well, I see him at mealtimes and we used to spend most evenings together. But now he's usually busy."

"Even after dinner?"

"Yes." I sighed. "Maybe it will get better, now that summer's here. Jeannine and I can go out in the cart more. And I can let Renard run along behind us." I heard his tail thump across the room. "But we ran into a gypsy in the park, and he said something ominous about the curse, that I needed more than good wishes here –"

"They're superstitious, you know that."

194

"I know, but it scared me."

Anne took my hand. "This isn't like you. What's happened?"

"I don't know. I thought he'd be fun, like he was when he gave the party for us. He was warm and charming and paid a lot of attention to me.

"But he's not like that anymore and it's different being up here without any one from the village. There's Jeannine, thank goodness, but we have to be careful. The other servants don't like us being close. They say she thinks too much of herself."

"Why don't you have a big party? Invite everyone our age from the village."

"He'll say I can't."

"Oh, Marie, just ask him. He'll say yes. You're his wife and he wants you to be happy."

"Sometimes I think he *doesn't* want me to be happy."

"That's nonsense. He married you because he cares about you. He'll probably be delighted that you're doing something fun."

Her idea did sound fun. I smiled. "Having a party would be wonderful." I reached over and hugged her. "Anne, I'm so glad you're here. I feel better already. Jeannine, send for some tea, and I'll ask the count tonight at dinner."

We spent the rest of the day talking and laughing, and I felt as if I had come out from under a cloud.

Later, when I asked the count about a party, he did seem delighted. "Just the thing for you, my dear. I should have thought of it," he said as he touched my cheek. "How about waiting until my trip?"

"What trip?"

"I have to go to the city and I'll be staying for several weeks. A party here while I'm gone would be perfect." And he kissed my hand warmly when he left the table.

Anne was right. I had no reason to be unhappy. It must have been my fault that the count had grown so distant. And he wasn't cold at all when he paid me a visit later that night.

195

Chapter Twenty-Seven

"Your riding lessons will begin today," the count told me the next morning.

The warmth that had enveloped me from the night before fled away. "Must I learn to ride?"

"You'll find it enjoyable. And in a few weeks, you can come out with me when I ride."

"I've never ridden."

"A riding master will be there to help you. And I've chosen an older horse. You'll have no problem controlling him," he said. "Once the horse gets used to you, he'll want to obey you."

"That isn't what I've seen with the village horses," I said.

"I told Mme Vacher to order a riding habit for you. It should be upstairs. You can tell me about your lesson later."

When I went upstairs, I found a beautiful brown velvet riding dress hanging on the wardrobe door. It had a matching jacket and hat. I decided I might like riding after all.

Anne came back up later that morning to surprise me. I knew it meant she was worried about me, but I was glad to see her anyway. "I'll watch," she said when I told her what the count had planned for me. We walked out to the stable courtyard when I was ready.

"Your horse is here," one of the stable boys said. He pointed across the cobblestones to where a groom held the reins of a horse. It was an enormous black beast. This couldn't be the older horse the count had mentioned.

196

"He'll kill me," I said, sweat prickling the back of my neck, looking at how far his back was from the ground.

"Are you sure this is the right one, Marie?" said Anne as the horse snorted.

"He has a sidesaddle on. He must be meant for me."

"This is the wrong horse for the Countess," Anne said firmly to the young groom by the horse's head. "She needs a small, quiet mare."

"This is the one Count de Roesch told me to saddle," he said. The boy was having difficulty holding the reins. "He came out this morning and said he picked this one special for the countess."

Anne looked unconvinced. I wished it was Raoul standing with the horse, I was sure he'd never let me ride the creature.

"He knows his horses," the boy continued. "He must think she can handle him."

"She doesn't know how to ride," said Anne.

He looked uncomfortable. "I can't get her a different horse, not without the count's permission."

"That's all right, Anne, I'm not going far, and I'll have a riding master with me."

"The count said you should be mounted before the master comes so you're ready for him," the boy said. He led the horse to a mounting block.

"I think you should wait until he's here, Marie," said Anne. "That horse might bolt."

"He's not going anywhere with the reins being held." I sounded much braver than I felt as I stepped up onto the block. The back of my jacket was already damp with nervous sweat.

The boy helped me sit in the saddle. He showed me how to wedge my right knee between two pommels on the sidesaddle and put my left foot in a little slipper stirrup hanging from the saddle. Once I was positioned correctly, I leaned over to smooth down my skirts. "I don't think this will become one of my favorite pastimes," I said to Anne as I sat back up.

"Countess!" The count's voice cut across the morning air.

What I remember after that is a blur. Anne told me later the horse reared up at the sharp sound of his voice and broke away from the boy. She saw me grasp at the saddle and try to cling to it

197

as he shot across the courtyard. I slipped from his back before he even reached the drive.

I don't remember hitting the stones. Anne said I crumpled up and didn't move. She thought I'd been killed. She said when the count got there he told her to leave but she insisted that I be taken upstairs to my rooms, where she and Jeannine would take care of me.

When I woke up I was in my own bed with a throbbing leg, a sore ribcage, and a terrible headache. But nothing was broken.

"Raoul ran out of the stables when he heard you scream," Jeannine told me later when it was one of her turns to sit with me. "He saw Anne try to wake you but you didn't move. He shouted for help and I came running. Anne was furious with the count and told him it was his fault for choosing such a wild horse. I don't think he had ever been spoken to like that before. She raised her voice to him, Countess, she even stood up and stamped her foot at him."

"I've seen her angry, I know how she gets."

"Well, then he got angry too, and said you were going to a private room with him and he ordered Anne away from the chateau, but M. Martel came outside. He put his hand on the count's arm and whispered something to him and the count didn't say any more. I never thought I'd be grateful for that man, Countess, but it was him, M. Martel, who sent the count back to his office and carried you up here to your room. Then Anne and I and Mme Vacher, we took care of you.

"I wonder what Martel said to make the count change his mind," I said.

Jeannine bent toward me. "I'm not sure, but when he sent the count away, I think what he whispered was, 'It's not time.'"

I recovered in my room, resting in my bed while Anne, Jeannine, or Mme Vacher sat quietly nearby. When my headache finally eased Anne and Mme Vacher read to me. Jeannine brought my embroidery in and we stitched together. My leg, twisted when I fell, kept me in bed longer than I wished.

198

The count was concerned about me and checked with them several times a day. He also visited me for a short while each morning and evening and even postponed his trip to the city.

Within a week I was up and walking. Two days after that, to his surprise, I joined the count for breakfast. And after the meal, we argued.

The serving maid cleared away the dishes and he leaned forward in his chair. "You need to get back up on that horse. That's what riders do when they get thrown."

I stared at him.

"You can ride him again next week."

"But you said you hadn't wanted me to ride that one. You said it was a mistake, the groom confused the horses. And he almost killed me!"

"Yes, but now we know what he might do, and the riding master can lead him the entire time. He won't break away again. And he won't be startled this time. I apologize again, my dear, for being so thoughtless and calling to you. When I think of what could have happened."

He reached for my hand. I didn't want him to touch me and moved it away. We were silent as the maid returned with coffee. When she left I folded my hands in my lap and said, "I will ride another horse if you insist, but I won't get back on that one."

"You will do as I say," he said.

I heard Renard flop down by my chair.

"I told you not to bring that dog to breakfast."

"I didn't realize he was here. He's been with me constantly since I was hurt, and he must have come looking for me."

"I've decided I don't want him in the chateau, Marie. He's not the type of dog I wish to see in my home."

"But he makes me happy. And you told me before I could keep him." How had the argument shifted so quickly from the horse? And why did my voice have that whine in it? I sounded like a child. I reached down and patted Renard.

"I want him gone from the chateau this morning," he said.

"I don't want him to go."

"You're forgetting your place, Countess. A wife shouldn't argue with her husband."

199

"Father Samuel said the husband should put the wife's desires first. He said my Papa did that and that's why Maman was so happy."

"You are saying I don't provide for you?" he said sharply.

I lifted my chin and looked him in the eyes. "No, Count, I'm not saying that at all. You provide beautifully for me." Then I realized with a shock his beard had a blue sheen at the edges. I thought of Jeannine talking about the curse on the family. I froze, unable to argue any further.

"What is the matter?"

I shook my head and looked down at my plate. Jeannine was right, the gypsy was right. There was a curse here. I was sitting next to it. I was so frightened I couldn't breathe.

"Marie, look at me."

Slowly I lifted my gaze to his face. His beard was coal black. I was losing my mind.

I heard a soft growl come from the throat of Renard. He got up from the floor by my chair, stood between the count and me, and growled again.

"I do not want this cur in the chateau."

"Why does he growl at you?"

"Marie, I am trying to be patient with you. Get rid of that dog."

He hadn't answered my question. The silence grew. He was watching Renard, not me, and he looked wary. I searched for any blue at all in his beard or his hair. There was none. It had to have been my imagination.

But Renard's hackles were raised, and it was Renard who made me brave.

"I will not ride that horse, and I will not get rid of Renard. He is *my* dog. I will make sure he's kept away from you, but I will not have him removed from my home." I put my hand on Renard and he sat down. "Please call Jeannine," I said to the serving maid.

Jeannine appeared within moments.

"The count does not wish to see Renard," I said to her. "Take him to my rooms." She curtsied and left with the dog.

"Very well," he said, but then I heard him whisper, "You will regret this, my dear," so softly I was sure he had not meant for me to hear it. He left the table with a curt "Enjoy your morning."

200

The count no longer cared for me, I knew it then. But I rose from my seat feeling I possessed a new power. I had challenged him and won.

The Key

Chapter Twenty-Eight

Several days later, Jeannine and I passed the count in the hallway as he came out of his office.

"Out of my way!" he commanded Jeannine, who shrank back. I, too, pressed against the wall as he went past us. Martel emerged from the office with a grim look and brushed by us.

"It isn't you, Jeannine," I said. "He was short with me yesterday, too. Whatever bothered him, he was over it by evening."

Later the count was calm and pleasant. "Did you enjoy your day, my dear?" he asked at the evening meal, the incident in the hallway apparently forgotten.

"Yes. Jeannine and I spent the day reading and embroidering."

"You are very skilled with the embroidery hoop. I'm sure whatever you do will turn out well."

"Thank you," I replied.

He nodded and said, "I've arranged for a traveling troupe of musicians to play for us tomorrow night." I was surprised. We hadn't had entertainment at the chateau since the first few months of our marriage.

Then I noticed he was playing with something golden in his other hand. "Is that jewelry?" I asked him.

He slipped it into his pocket. "It's not yet time, my dear," he said pleasantly, and went back to his meal.

The count's odd mood swing happened again the next day. He was brusque and irritable in the morning, relaxed and attentive in the evening. And once again, he had something golden in his hand. This time I didn't ask about it, I just watched.

It took several minutes for me to see what it was, but he finally opened his fingers and I saw a small, golden key in the palm of his hand. I had never seen it before. "What a beautiful key," I said. "What does it open?"

He smiled, slipped it into his pocket as he had done before, and said, "It's a warm evening. Shall we go for a walk in the garden?"

I agreed, expecting him to show me what the key unlocked. But we strolled through the garden and he talked of the chateau, some horses he was buying, and the fields at another of his chateaus until I forgot all about the key.

And the next morning when I asked him about it, he looked puzzled and told me he didn't own a golden key.

It was Anne's birthday, and it was pouring outside.

"You will stay at the chateau today," the count said when I told him I wanted to go see her. "I don't wish to have a broken carriage wheel from the mud in the village now that the wheelwright has left."

"But I've always been with her on her birthday," I said with dismay.

"You are married now, and a countess. You can't do all the things you did when you lived in the village."

I looked out the window at the sheeting rain. It was too far to walk in this weather and Henri had heard the count say the carriages were not to go out today. For the first time in my life, I wouldn't see Anne on her birthday.

"I will be in my rooms today," I said as I left the salon.

Later in the afternoon a maid came to my door. "You sister is here, Countess," she said, stepping aside. A thoroughly drenched Anne came into my room.

"Anne! I thought I wasn't going to see you today! Did the count send the carriage for you?"

"No, he didn't." She dripped onto the floor, puddles spreading around her. "There was a boy from here down in the village and

206

I got a ride back up with him. I thought we'd make it before it started pouring again, but we didn't. Help me out of my clothes."

I hugged her, not caring how wet I got. When I stepped back, she twisted the water out of her hair. "Maman didn't want me to come at first, but I insisted I had to see you on my birthday."

The maid took her cloak and we peeled off her wet dress. Jeannine brought out some dry underclothes and Anne put them on by the warm fire.

"I'm surprised a cart from the chateau was in the village," I said as I watched the maid shake out one of my dresses for her.

"Why?"

"When I told the count I wanted to go see you today, he said no carriages could go down because of the rain."

"It wasn't a carriage, it was a cart," Anne said.

"They still have wheels," I answered. She gave me a quizzical look but I didn't explain.

The maid finished tying up the back of Anne's dress and fluffed out her skirt. Then she left us. Anne went over to the doves in their cages on the table and cooed at them.

"I have a birthday gift for you, but it's not here," I said. "It's too big."

"Too big?" She came back from the table.

"Well, it would never be able to come into my room."

"Why not?"

I settled back on the sitting room couch. "Because of the stairs."

"Don't be annoying. What is it?"

I laughed. "I knew you wouldn't want jewels or dresses or anything like that, so I got something you and Adam could use."

"What?" she said, finally sounding exasperated.

"There's a horse in the stable, a mare, for you."

"Oh, Marie!" She threw her arms around me. "How wonderful!"

I kissed her. "I know Adam's just died and this one is young. She'll give you years of use. You can breed her for foals, too."

"Thank you, it's perfect." She hugged me again. "You couldn't have given me a better gift. The count doesn't mind?"

"Of course not," I said. "But I need to tell you something."

207

"About the horse?"

"No, the count."

"What?"

"It's his beard." I pulled on the edge of my sleeve. "It seems silly now."

Anne sat very still and watched me.

I took a deep breath. "I think I've seen it, Anne. I've seen his beard turn blue. Just a little. At least I think I did."

"Marie, you know that's just a story."

"But what if it isn't? Jeannine says —"

"Jeannine is a superstitious village girl. She thought the tower was haunted, too, and it was Mme Vacher keeping it clean. We used to talk about a curse in the village when we were little, but we all knew it was silly."

"But the gypsy warned me, too."

"Marie." She leaned forward and took my hands. "You're spending too much time alone up in this chateau. I'm not saying I think it's safe here, I don't trust him and I still worry about you. But don't be ridiculous. If it's really blue, he's doing it himself."

"Why?"

She shrugged. "He thinks it's amusing. He probably enjoys teasing his young, impressionable wife."

That was a new thought. He probably *would* think it amusing.

"When I see him today, I'll look at it," she said.

"Maybe it's when he's angry. We were arguing," I said, feeling completely foolish. "I think it was a little blue. But not for long."

"It changed?"

"Oh, Anne, I don't know. I thought it was, then it wasn't. Maybe I'm losing my mind."

"I don't think that's it, Marie. How are you sleeping?"

"Not very well."

"That's probably what it is. You're tired and not seeing things right."

"Maybe so. Anyway, let's do something else. I'm tired of thinking about it."

"Chess?"

"Fine," I said.

208

After she won, we settled back into our chairs. "How is it going with M. Martel?" she asked.

"I hate him."

"He can't be that bad, Marie."

"I don't trust him and he's miserable to be around."

"There must be *something* about him you don't hate."

"Well," I said grudgingly, "he has impeccable manners. Even when he's insulting someone."

"That's it?" she said.

"That's the best I can do."

"That doesn't sound like you, Marie. Isn't there something you can do to make it better?"

I shook my head.

"Why don't you do something nice for him?"

"For Martel? There's no one I can think of that I'd rather *not* do something nice for."

"Then maybe that's exactly why you should do it."

All the irritation I felt toward Martel shifted to Anne. "That's easy for you to say. You don't have to live with him always sneaking around, whispering in the count's ear. I don't *want* to be nice to him. I want him to go away."

She shrugged. "Well, don't complain about him if you don't try to make it better."

She changed the subject and we spent the rest of the day talking, reading, and drawing. The count came to dinner with us. He was pleasant with Anne, who thanked him for the horse and then scrutinized his beard. He didn't seem to notice and told her she should stay for the night and go back to the village the next evening. "But it will have to be one of the farm carts because of the mud," he said.

"I'd rather have her go in a carriage," I said, trying to start an argument.

"The carts are sturdier than the carriages, my dear, although not as comfortable. I'm sure Anne understands."

"Don't we have any strong carriages?"

"Henri will make sure it's the best cart here," he said.

I looked at his beard. Black as midnight.

209

He visited with us for a short while in the salon after dinner, where I complained about the harpsichord and told him I didn't want any more lessons. He said I could have a break from them. And after I complained that the fire wasn't high enough and the room was always chilly, he retired to his office.

"Not blue," Anne said after he left.

We went to bed early. I lay under the covers hearing Anne's deep breathing next to me and chided myself for listening to Jeannine. I'd made a fool of myself in front of my sister.

But that unsettled feeling wouldn't leave.

The rain beating savagely against the windows woke us in the morning.

"We can't go anywhere today," I said. "The road will be all mud, worse than yesterday. I'm glad you came up here when you did."

Anne pulled aside the drapes and looked out the window. "I hope Maman is all right."

"Of course she is. All she has to do is feed the chickens and the goats."

"I suppose." She went back to the bed and sat down. "What shall we do today?"

"I'd like breakfast up here," I said to the maid who had entered. She curtsied and left. "I don't even feel like getting dressed yet. You can use one of my dressing robes, they're in the wardrobe."

Anne went over to the wardrobe. She gave me a green robe and pulled out a blue one for herself. "This is wonderful," she said as we went out to the sitting room. "How much longer before breakfast?"

A knock on the door answered her question, and two trays were brought in. One had coffee, silverware and fine porcelain; the other had bread and pastry.

She curled her feet up under her on the sofa. "I'd have breakfast in here every day."

"I do more and more," I said. "He doesn't like Renard downstairs." When Renard heard his name he came over from his rug and sat at my feet.

210

"He doesn't like Renard? Even after he saved you?"

"No."

She took a croissant. "Maman is wondering when you'll start a family."

"What?" I almost dropped my cup.

"It's what happens."

I shook my head. "Not with me. I want to be home in the cottage with you and Maman. I don't even want to be married anymore."

She was silent, studying my face.

"Besides," I said more quietly, "he doesn't come to me very much anymore."

"It only takes once, if it's at the right time. You know that."

"Oh, Anne, that would be awful!"

"Why? Don't you want to have a family?"

"I did – once. But not now. Not with him. I don't want to talk about it anymore." I leaned my head back against the sofa and closed my eyes.

"I've heard the first year is the hardest," she said.

"It's more than that. I feel as if I'm in a prison up here, cut off from everyone."

"We're not that far."

I opened my eyes. "But you are, Anne. Some nights I lie in bed and cry myself to sleep. I want to go home so much, and he doesn't even want me to visit you. The last time, when I got back and told him about it, he said that should do me for a while. He meant I wouldn't have to go back for a long time."

"Why would he want to keep you up here away from us?"

"He said he doesn't want me going places because of what happened when I went to Jeannine's village."

"I don't believe that," said Anne. "Going all the way to her village is nothing like coming down the road to us."

We listened to the pounding rain, and then she said, "Do you think he's hiding something?"

"I don't know. Sometimes I think he is."

She picked up her cup. "Maybe whatever's bothering him will pass."

We drank our coffee, and then she said, "It's stopped raining."

211

I went to the window and looked out. The dark clouds in the sky had finally passed over us, and even though there was still a light rain, the sunshine was streaming down. I opened the window and breathed the clean, fresh air. It smelled earthy and damp.

Anne came to my side. "Look, there's a rainbow." Stretching across the sky was a double bow. "It's a promise for your future," she said, and kissed my cheek.

I put my arm around her and we watched the bow's colors grow deeper and then slowly fade. When we couldn't see it any more we went back in the room.

But seeing the bright colors with Anne by my side didn't help my heaviness. I had a weight that didn't lift, even with her excitement when she saw her new horse. And the weight grew heavier as I waved goodbye to her that evening.

Chapter Twenty-Nine

The next day it rained again. I had just left the library to search for Jeannine when Henri emerged from a door near the kitchen I hadn't seen open before.

"Where does that go?"

"To the wine cellar, Countess." Henri stepped aside as I peered down the dim stone stairway.

"It's not very light."

"No, Countess, the wine needs darkness. There are small windows on the staircase, but the light is not strong in the cellar. We use lamps when we go down." He looked at one right by the door, hanging on a hook and still lit. "We take that with us, and light another down there, if we need it. Would you like to see it?"

"You don't mind?"

"Of course not, Countess," he said as he held the door. "Perhaps I should go first, in case you trip."

"Thank you, Henri." We went down the wide, stone steps. There was a railing along the stone wall and I kept one hand on it, following Henri. He descended slowly, probably thinking I wasn't able to go faster. I was tempted to tell him how many times Jeannine and I had raced down the upper staircase to get Renard outside before he had an accident in my rooms.

We got to the bottom and he held the lamp high. "Be careful, Countess, the stones on the floor can be uneven."

We were standing at the edge of a large room with a stone and dirt floor. The high windows up the staircase gave some

213

illumination, but the cellar had a dusky look, as though it was perpetually evening. There were several doors down a wide, cavernous hallway. On our left was a large wooden door and on our right, two smaller ones. I was glad I had a wrap around my shoulders; the air was quite chilly.

"The wine cellar is through that door," he said, indicating the large door with a wave of the lantern.

"There are other doors here. What's in those rooms?"

"Storage, Countess, as are the ones down the corridor."

"Do you have keys for all of them?"

"Yes, I have one key for the wine cellar, and one master key for the other doors. But only the wine cellar is kept locked. There are also two other cellars in the chateau," he continued, "and they each have several rooms."

"Are they locked?"

"The doors down to the cellars and also one room in each cellar are locked, Countess."

"Why are so many rooms locked in the chateau?"

"It is the count's wish. I have keys for them, and the count does too, of course. I believe M. Martel has keys for all of them also."

Of course he would. "Is there a small golden key for one of them?"

"No, Countess. None are of gold."

He stood quietly after that, waiting for my instructions.

"Can we go into the wine cellar, Henri?"

"Of course, Countess." He pulled a key ring out from his jacket and put one of the keys into the lock. The door swung inward with a creak and I peered into the dark room.

"Would you like me to go first, Countess?"

"No," I answered, and stepped into the room. Henri entered directly behind me, holding the lamp high. The light showed rows of shelving with bottles, and the room brightened as he lit another lamp on the wall.

"There are hundreds of bottles here. Are they all for the chateau?"

"Yes, Countess. The count also gives them as gifts."

214

I looked more closely at them. "They're all stored slanted down. It looks as if they're about to slip off the rack onto the floor."

"That's to keep the corks from drying out," he said, waiting patiently while I looked over the racks.

"That is a drain channel," he said when I asked about the indentation in the floor along the wall. "The room can get quite damp and occasionally it is cleaned. The drain makes cleaning easier. There's another drain on the other side, also."

"I'm sorry to pester you with so many questions, Henri."

"There is no need to apologize, Countess."

It was damp and chilly but I liked the chamber. I moved slowly down the middle row, fascinated with the forest of bottles. I pulled several out of the rack and studied them, and even slipped one under my wrap to share later with Jeannine. I shouldn't have felt guilty about taking a bottle of wine without the count's permission, but I did.

At the end of the cellar there were three large barrels on their sides against the far wall. The barrels were coated with a thick layer of dust.

"The count does not wish the barrels to be touched," he said from behind me, holding the light still higher.

I wondered if he held up the light because he had seen me take the bottle, and pulled my wrap tighter. "They don't have wine in them?"

"They do, Countess, but they are not to be touched," he repeated.

I resisted the urge to draw my finger through the dust. "Is that because something will happen to the wine?"

"No, it is the count's orders. The wine has been in them quite a long time."

"Is that good?"

"Wine should be tasted to see if it is ready, Countess. He has not wished to do so with these."

That was curious. Then I looked at the space in between two of them and saw a small object near the wall. "I think there's something caught in the drain behind these casks."

"I shall let the count know."

215

"No, Henri, don't bother him with it. You can't get to it without moving the barrels. It doesn't matter. I'd like to go back upstairs. I've gotten chilled."

"Very well, Countess."

We went back out and up the steps, pausing only while he locked the wine cellar door. As soon as we reached the hallway, I thanked him and hurried upstairs to find Jeannine. I hoped there was a fire in the sitting room, I was chilled all the way through to my bones. But it wasn't from the dampness of the cellar.

I had recognized what was wedged behind the barrels. I'd seen it many times, hanging on a heavy gold chain around his neck when he was leading a service or giving comfort and counsel to one of the villagers. It was Father Samuel's crucifix, and the chain was broken.

"Why would his crucifix be there?" I asked Jeannine in front of the fire, trying to get warm.

"Monks have wine cellars in monasteries," she said. "Maybe he knew about the wine and was checking the barrels for the count and his chain got caught and broke off."

"Why wouldn't he try to get it?"

"He didn't know it was gone."

"He'd know."

"Not if he came down with the plague right after that," she said. "Or maybe he did know and he couldn't reach it. You said the barrels would have to be moved. Why don't you ask the count?" she said.

"No, I'll not bother him with it," I replied, "and I don't really want him to know I've been there."

"What are you going to do with the wine?" she said, picking up the bottle I had taken and looking at its label.

"I don't know. I suppose we'll use it on the evenings we're eating up here." I could still see the crucifix lying in the dust and it made me feel cold again. The fire wasn't enough, I wanted people around me. "I'm freezing, Jeannine. Let's go downstairs and get some tea."

"I'll have something brought up."

216

"It'll be warmer in the kitchen. I'd rather go there."

I heard her sharp intake of breath. "Oh, no, Countess, you mustn't do that. The kitchen is for servants."

"Jeannine, I'm tired of sitting in a big room and being served my food with stillness around me. I want to be with people who are busy making bread and washing up. I'm going downstairs." I ignored her protests and went down a staircase – one of the back ones that the servants used – to the kitchen.

When I stepped out from the stairs, the cook and two servant girls who were helping him turned and stared at me. Jeannine stepped out from behind me. "The Countess would like some tea," she said, but no one moved. "Monique, tea for the Countess. Now."

Both of the girls scurried to heat water and get a teapot ready. The cook watched me as I sat down at the table by a pile of greens. "Is there something else I can get the Countess?" he asked, speaking to Jeannine. I felt as if an invisible wall had descended into the room.

"No, I'll just wait here," I said.

He swallowed and looked at Jeannine, who shrugged. They didn't want me sitting at their table.

Loneliness welled up inside me as the girls put a cup of tea and a teapot in front of me and then backed away. The cook stood nearby, not working.

"Jeannine," I said, my voice catching, "please bring this back up to my sitting room. I'll drink it there."

I left the kitchen by the correct door, feeling their relief as it closed behind me, and went up the proper staircase to my room. When Jeannine came to the room, she found me crying into the pillows and couldn't get me to stop.

Several days later I was going to the gardens when I saw a key in a key ring hanging from the cellar door. Without thinking, I unlocked the door and pocketed the keys.

The door swung open noiselessly and I quietly pulled it shut behind me. It was dark without Henri's lamp lighting the way and

217

I stood for a minute, letting my eyes adjust to the dimness. I went down the steps slowly, holding tightly to the railing.

What was drawing me down here again? I told myself it was to get another bottle of wine, but I knew it wasn't that. We hadn't finished the last one yet. It was Father Samuel's crucifix. It didn't matter that the count had given orders the barrels weren't to be touched. I couldn't leave his crucifix in the dust and dirt on a cellar floor.

When I got to the bottom, I unlocked the wine cellar and left the door wide open to let in some light. Once I was inside, I pulled another bottle off the rack in case I needed an excuse to be down there. Then I went back to the barrels, trying not to be frightened in the eerie, moldy dimness around me.

Very little light reached all the way to the back of the room. I crouched down, set the bottle on the dirt floor, and peered between the two barrels, searching for the crucifix.

It wasn't there. And it wasn't on the other side of the barrel, either. I looked again in the first spot where I was sure it had been. There was nothing.

Someone had taken it.

My heart started to race and the skin on the back of my neck prickled with sweat. Was someone in the cellar with me now? I told myself not to be silly. Henri must have told the count I had seen it and he asked Henri to get it. There was nothing to be afraid of.

I got up and went back out of the room, pulling the door shut and locking it, forcing myself not to run up the cellar stairs. It seemed to take forever to reach the safety of the hallway. I locked the cellar door and dropped the key ring into my pocket, and then waited until my heart stopped pounding in my ears.

Just as I started down the hallway Martel came around the corner. His eyes darted to the cellar door. Those must have been his keys I'd found hanging in the lock. I could give them to the count and make Martel look like a fool.

But as I passed him I remembered what Anne had said about being kind. Even though I didn't want to, I stopped, turned around, and held out the keys. "Did you lose these, M. Martel?"

He snatched them from my hand. "Where did you find them?"

"You left them in the cellar door."

Then I heard someone coming down the steps. It was the count. "Is there something wrong?"

"No, I'm just going to my rooms," I said as I turned and went up the stairs, certain that my kindness had been wasted.

And later, as I told Jeannine what had happened, I realized the bottle I had taken off the rack was still sitting on the floor, right next to the barrel.

Chapter Thirty

"I sent my dove to Anne," I said to the count the next morning as we sat together in the salon.

He stopped turning the pages of the chateau's journal. "And what does that mean?"

"I told you when I first got them, remember? It's our code. If the white dove goes home, it means I'm coming for a visit."

"And the other one?"

"The black one means I need her here."

"And why do you need her here?"

"Oh, I didn't send the black one. It was the white one, to tell her I'll be visiting later today."

"Ah," said the count, and glanced down at the pages. Rows of neat numbers went down one side of the page. I couldn't imagine a less interesting book. And Martel was with us. He always seemed to be at the count's side now.

"It's fun, sending a message to her like that," I went on. "Now she knows I'm coming, so she and Maman will both be there when I arrive."

"Is this the first time you've sent the bird to them?" the count asked.

"No, I've used him several times. I bring him back with me so I can send him again."

"You can send word with one of the stable boys or farm hands."

"This is more fun."

He nodded absently. "I hope you have an enjoyable visit. Don't forget Father Gregory will be dining with us tonight."

That was disappointing to hear. I had planned on staying at the cottage for dinner.

It was a short visit that afternoon. "Too short," said Maman as I left with the caged bird.

"It will be longer next time, Maman, I promise," I told her.

When I got home, Jeannine met me as I came up the staircase. "Oh, Countess, I'm so sorry. Something has happened to your other bird."

"What?"

"He got out. The cage was empty when I came in the room. He must have worked the latch loose and flown away."

I went into the room and saw the empty cage. "Jeannine, it's impossible for a bird to open this latch."

She wrung her hands together. "Then I must not have closed it tightly enough when I fed and watered them this morning. I thought I had, I'm so careful with them. I'm sorry, Countess."

"Don't worry, Jeannine. He'll just fly home and Anne will come up to see what I want. She'll wonder what's wrong, that's the worst of it. But she'll bring him back and we'll make sure it's closed tight this time."

"I hope I don't cause her to worry," said Jeannine.

"It will give the Widow DuBois something to talk about," I said. "Here, put this one back by the window," and I handed her the white bird's cage.

But Anne didn't rush up that night, nor did she come the next day. One the following day, curious as to why she had ignored the signal, I called on her and Maman.

"You came without sending the signal," said Anne as we got there. "Maman is over with Widow DuBois. If you'd sent the dove, she would have stayed home.

"You don't pay any attention when they come."

Anne bristled. "I certainly do! We were ready for you the last time!"

"You didn't come up when the black one came home."

"What are you talking about? The black one isn't here, I was just feeding them before you came."

221

"Are you sure?" I said in surprise. "He got out of the cage while I was here the other day."

"Well, he certainly wouldn't have been any good to use for getting help," she said in disgust. "He must have flown somewhere else. And he was the only black one I had."

That night, as I covered the white bird's cage, I whispered, "I'm sorry. We'll find another friend for you." He cocked his head and watched me until the cloth settled over the bars.

Renard found our missing bird the next day. When he and I went outside, he ran to a small patch of freshly turned earth and dug down, then tugged something out of the ground.

"Here, Renard, bring it here. Is that my dove? Someone must have found it dead and buried it for me." But when he brought it to me, holding it gently in his mouth, I saw that its neck had been twisted so violently the head was partially torn off.

I screeched and Renard dropped it. I picked it back up by its wing, put it into the hole, and kicked some dirt on top of it. Then I ran back inside. Renard followed me upstairs to my room and I hugged him while I tried to stop trembling.

When Jeannine came in later I said, "Renard found the black dove. Someone killed it, Jeannine. They buried it so I wouldn't know."

"Oh, Countess, perhaps you're mistaken."

"Come, I'll show you. His head was twisted almost off his neck."

But when we went back down to the garden, there was only a spot where a dog had been digging. No bird was buried in the dirt, and I truly wondered what was happening to my mind.

After that I began waking at night covered in sweat, my heart racing. I would lie in bed for hours trying to calm myself enough to go back to sleep. It rarely worked.

So I began to take walks at night. I wandered the gardens and lawns, staying in the shadows so no one would notice me. Some nights I saw the count through the windows in his downstairs study or the library, going over papers or reading a book.

222

Sometimes Martel and occasionally Father Gregory would be talking with him. I never let them know I'd seen them.

I became so exhausted the days seemed like a dream. Jeannine knew something was wrong. She would ask if I was tired, but I'd shrug or talk of something else. I didn't tell her of my walks.

One night the moon was high in the sky when I finally got up and sat by the window. The cool air on my face woke me up even more and I dressed, stole down the stairs, and went out through a side door. I had heard Renard's tail thump when I left the room. Usually I took him with me, but that night I didn't call him to come. I wanted to be completely alone.

The lawn was wide and exposed. Like a deer, I felt ill at ease as I crossed it. I glanced back at the chateau. It loomed up against the dark sky, cold and unforgiving. The woods seemed welcoming and friendly compared to the house, even though it was night. Full of life, branches swayed and leaves rustled, small creatures moved along their paths. I slid into the shadows of the trees and slowed my pace.

It felt exhilarating to glide through the chateau's forest, listening to the noises and breathing in the night smells. I followed a game path in the dark. Time seemed to stop as I went deeper into the forest than I had ever been before at night.

Then in the moonlight I saw someone close ahead on the trail, walking in the same direction. I stopped at the same time he crouched down. He made a quick movement with his arm, took something from the ground, and stood up.

I tried to back up quietly but a twig snapped and he turned around, an animal dangling from one hand and a knife in the other. I had stumbled upon an armed poacher and there was no one to defend me.

I couldn't get away, so I drew myself up and said in my haughtiest voice, "Who are you and what are you doing here?"

I heard a chuckle. "And what is my friend the Countess doing out so late?"

Relief washed over me. I knew this man.

"Catching you poaching again," I said.

"And you are meeting your lover."

"No, I —"

223

"You don't need to tell me," he said, holding up the hand with, I could see now, a dead rabbit. "Your night visits are not my business. And mine are not yours, yes?"

"Sir," I replied, "I am not unfaithful to my husband. When I can't sleep, I walk."

"With all respect," he said with an exaggerated bow, "that is hard to believe, a countess so far into the woods at night. Where is your carriage? Where are your servants?"

"It may interest you to know that I grew up in the village below and my father was a farmer."

"And who was your father?"

"Charles Moreau."

"You are his daughter?" he said with surprise.

"Yes."

"We were not aware of that," he said quietly. "All of us were sorry when we heard he had died. He was a good man and a friend."

"Thank you." I fought down the urge to cry. Blinking hard, I said, "If he was your friend, then you are a good man, too."

"Thank you, Countess." He bowed, this time without exaggeration. "I am known as Stefan."

"There was another good man, Stefan, who may have come to your camp. His name was Thomas."

"Yes, he was with us a short while. He left when we moved on last time, and we haven't seen him since we came back. He had questions about the count. He didn't tell us his business. I'm sorry, Countess, I know nothing more than that."

I swallowed hard, surprised at the lump in my throat. "Was that your snare or Philippe's?" I asked.

"It was mine."

"I hope you can hide from him better than you can from me."

He laughed. "Your gamekeeper is snoring in his cottage and will never know I borrowed a rabbit or two."

"Don't get shot in the process. As I recall, you need to go home to your wife and two children."

"And a third on the way."

"My congratulations to you and your wife. Consider the rabbit my gift."

224

"Thank you, Countess." Then, to my surprise he said, "I'm sure your father would not be happy knowing you are the countess."

"Why?"

"There is something evil up on the hill. We spoke of it, your father and I."

"And what did my father say?"

"He never wanted to think ill of anyone. But he knew there was something wrong there. Something, and someone." He shook his head. "It's an ancient building, parts of it, and..."

"Are you saying there's a curse?" I asked, my palms starting to sweat.

"It's a family curse, Countess, gone into the very stones. Sometimes it's better to pull down old walls that have seen too much evil. I think you've felt it, too. I can hear it in your voice. Four wives there, all gone. I'm sorry to hear it is the daughter of Charles Moreau who is his fifth. You must not trust anyone there."

"What do you mean?"

"Only what I said."

I had to remember this was a gypsy who lived in a traveling wagon. Solid walls couldn't be cursed. I wasn't going to listen to such superstition. "Thank you for the warning, Stefan," I said stiffly. "I will keep it in mind."

He slipped into the darkness and I was alone.

I found I was trembling and had to sit down on a nearby tree stump for several minutes until I stopped shaking. As I turned back to the chateau, pulling my cloak tighter, the woods no longer felt friendly. They were dark and forbidding and I felt alone, vulnerable, and too far from safety.

I made my way back to the chateau and lay on my bed, wide awake. I couldn't keep from thinking of his warning that the walls were cursed. Maybe he was right, it wasn't just a person, it was a place. All four countesses died. His mother, a countess also, didn't want to live here. Did she know? Did the walls hate anyone who was a countess? My heart beat faster. I was the countess now.

225

This was silly, I told myself. Stones can't hold a curse. But I felt my mind slipping away from me in fear, and I tossed and turned all night.

I tried to tell Jeannine what had happened in the morning and thought she'd be frightened by his warning. Instead she was horrified that I'd spoken to a gypsy at night. "You mustn't go out like that, Countess, it's not safe."

"He knew my father, Jeannine, he wouldn't harm me." But she wouldn't even listen to what he had said to me. I finally promised her I wouldn't go out at night again, feeling awful because I knew I would.

And several nights later I went out again. It was chilly, and I pulled my shawl more tightly around my shoulders. I walked along the garden path and heard an owl hooting. It was a lonely sound and made me want to go inside.

I climbed the garden steps and saw the count in his downstairs study with the window open. I heard Martel's voice, drifted closer to the window, and watched them from the shadows.

Martel picked up a glass and sipped it, placing it carefully back down on the desk opposite the count. Then he leaned back in his chair and watched the count.

The count drummed his fingers. "It isn't the same. It needs to be here, with me. And she would have been too damaged." My skin prickled. They weren't talking about horses.

"There would have been no questions," Martel said, lacing his long fingers together.

"I can stop questions. I'm the Count."

"You can't stop everything," Martel said.

"She will fail."

Martel sighed. "Don't test her and she won't disappoint you."

"I have to. You don't understand."

"No, I don't. Let's leave it at that."

The count leaned forward. "Don't cross me, Martel."

Martel shrugged and reached for his glass. "As you wish." The last thing I saw before I backed away was Martel delicately sipping his drink.

I crept into the house, shaking with fear. I needed to find Jeannine. As noiselessly as I could, I climbed up the servant's

226

stairway and slipped into Jeannine's small room. Almost all the space was taken up with her bed, a washstand, and a small chest, so I sat on the edge of her bed and shook her awake.

"Countess," she said, her eyes opening wide in alarm. "What's wrong?"

"I was walking in the garden and I heard the count talking to Martel. They were talking about me, Jeannine!"

She sat up. "They were in the garden?"

"No, they were in the study. I heard them when I was going back inside."

"You must have been dreaming."

"No, I wasn't. It was cold and I had to pull my shawl tighter."

Never before had I seen anyone look at me with pity in their eyes. "Countess, you don't have your shawl."

"I must have dropped it on the way here. I tell you I had it!"

She looked down. "Your shoes, Countess," she said gently. "They're not wet."

"What do you mean?"

"If you were walking outside, they would be soaked with dew."

I stared stupidly at my slippers. I knew I had been in the garden. I remembered hearing the owl, I remembered feeling cold. But my slippers, which should have been stained with wetness, were dry.

"Wait right here, Countess. I'm going to get something for you to drink." She pulled a robe around her and left the room. I sat on the edge of her bed, too confused to explain what had happened. She came back with a bottle and glass. "Drink this."

I tried to lift the glass to my lips, but my hands were shaking so much the liquid spilled. Jeannine lifted the glass to my mouth.

"Take sips, Countess," she said. It was brandy, and it burned my throat as it went down. I coughed. "Take another sip."

It burned my throat again. "I don't want any more." She took the glass and set it on her table.

"Will you stay with me tonight, Jeannine?" I said, clutching her hand.

"Of course. I'll use the sofa in your sitting room. I'll stay there as long as you want."

227

She held my hand on the way back to my room and put me to bed. It was dawn before I finally fell asleep.

Later that morning Jeannine brought a breakfast tray in. "Your shawl was in the library," she said. "One of the maids found it."

"But I wasn't in the library last night. And I remembered something, Jeannine. I stayed on the gravel path in the garden, and I was on the stones by the count's window. I wasn't on the grass, that's why my slippers weren't wet."

"Countess," she said gently, "Mme Vacher told me M. Martel had left for one of the count's other chateaus before you went to bed last night."

"I saw him, Jeannine. And I heard his voice, too. He must have changed his mind."

"His bed wasn't slept in last night."

"Then he left later, after I saw him."

She paused and the said, "Mme Vacher said the count has been concerned about your health and wants you to rest more."

"I don't need rest, I need someone to believe me."

She bit her lip and I saw tears in her eyes. She couldn't be right. I knew I had seen him. My hands starting shaking again and I couldn't steady them.

The next day I sent the white pigeon home early in the morning.

It wasn't market day, but people were out in the village when I went through in the carriage. The blacksmith was at the door of his barn, talking with a farmer. The butcher shop had a few women waiting for meat. I saw Jacqui and waved to her. But Thomas's shop was closed tight, with none of the debris that used to be piled outside.

I swept up the cottage path, paved now with large, flat stones. A sturdy new bench sat under the front window and the door had new hinges on it. The workmen from the chateau were taking good care of my family. That was what the count had promised, and it should have made me feel better. It didn't.

228

Renard jumped out of the carriage and bounded to my side. "Remember your manners, Renard. We never had a dog inside here. You're not something they're used to."

He licked my hand.

The door swung open and Anne came out to hug me. "A little bird told me you were coming today," she said as we went through the door. "Maman and I are going to have some tea and I put out a cup for you."

I saw four cups on the table. "Who else is coming?"

"Adam, as soon as he can get away from the mill."

"How is he?" I asked.

"The mill is doing well. His father hurt his knee a few weeks ago, and it's hard for him to work now. He comes to the mill less and less, so Adam is busy."

"That's good," I said. "Not that his father got hurt, but that he's busy."

Anne laughed. "I knew that's what you meant. I saw Jacqui yesterday and told her you're planning on having a ball at the chateau."

"The count hasn't spoken of his trip again," I said. "I'm sure he's still going, though."

"I don't think she cares how long she has to wait. Just the thought of another party made her happy."

"Good." I studied Anne's face. "You look well." Actually, she looked more than well. She was radiant.

"We've decided to marry in two months instead of waiting longer," Anne said. "Adam sold the emeralds the count gave to me, I hope you don't mind. He's sure he was cheated, but we got so much for them! We were able to buy some land near the mill, and Adam started building a cottage already. We're rebuilding part of the mill, too, and putting on a new waterwheel. It won't all be finished by the wedding, but I don't care. Oh, Marie, I'm so happy. I'll finally be his wife. It's too good to be true." She hugged me.

"I'm glad you sold your jewelry, Anne," I said. "It's all wonderful news." Anne was never excited like this. I felt cheated next to her joy.

We went in and I sat at the table. "I need to talk with you before Maman comes in," I said. But before I could say more,

229

Maman came in the door. She had on an old dress and dirty boots and looked cross.

She kissed me. "Marie, I'm glad you're here. Can you have the previous workers sent down from the chateau? These boys don't know how to plow. I had to show them. Show them! Out there in the fields!"

I laughed. "You'd only get more new ones to train. The count sent the other boys to a different chateau."

She sighed. "Then I suppose these know well enough now. How are you, Marie? I haven't spoken to you for weeks. You leave the church so quickly when I see you there on Sundays. At least I know you're well when I see you there."

"I'm sorry, Maman. He always does that, I don't know why. Even when I complain and he tells me, 'Next week we can stay,' we never do. He always says he has to get back to the chateau for a meeting."

"Who would want to meet with him on a Sunday?"

"M. Martel or Father Gregory. M. Martel's always around and Father Gregory's there more than I realized. He hides from me. If I come into a room where he's sitting, he won't speak until I notice him. Sometimes I wonder how often I walk right by him and never know he's there."

"He still blinks all the time, have you noticed?" said Anne.

"Yes, and he always wipes his hands on his robes," I said. "He does it before he takes my hand and after he touches me, too. I've been tempted to ask him if he'd like some soap."

Anne giggled, but Maman frowned. "Don't speak poorly about a man of God."

"It's hard to think of him as one, Maman," said Anne.

"It's disrespectful. How are other things at the chateau?"

"The same," I said.

"You sound unhappy," Maman said. "Is there something wrong?"

"It isn't what I thought it would be."

"You need your friends," said Anne. "You should come here more often. Next time we'll have Jacqui over."

230

"He doesn't want me to come. He doesn't even want me to keep Renard." His tail thumped on the floor when he heard his name.

"But Renard saved you!" Maman said.

"Renard growls at him."

"Why?" asked Anne. I shrugged.

"What a dog thinks isn't important," said Maman. "How are you feeling since your fall?"

"I'm fine now, Maman. And did Anne tell you? The count is going on a trip and he said I can have a party while he's gone with all my friends from the village."

"That will be fun." Maman patted my hand. "When is his trip?"

"I think he's leaving soon since I'm better from the fall. Anne, maybe you can help me plan it."

"That would be fun," Anne replied.

"Good. Let's go to the fields," I said to her. "I want to feel dirt in my hands and look over Papa's land."

"Marie!" Maman said. "Going to the fields is for the hired men, not a countess. Even Anne doesn't go there anymore."

"You don't?" I asked her in surprise.

"No, she doesn't," said Maman. "We have the workers from the chateau now. I'm thinking of asking the count to provide harpsichord lessons for her. He offered them once."

"Maman, I told you I'm not going to take lessons," said Anne. "And I'm not at the fields because I'm helping Adam at the mill."

Maman sniffed and took a sip of tea.

"I hate my lessons," I said. "I've played for the count and Father Gregory, and I wasn't any good either time."

"I'm sure you'll get better," said Maman. "It takes practice."

"Practice doesn't help," I said. "And they make me nervous. I make more mistakes when they're watching me."

Anne rose from the table. "Never mind. Let's go to the fields if you'd like. We won't be long, Maman."

Maman sighed but I kissed her and went out the door with Anne, Renard right behind us.

We went down part of the path to the fields, then Anne sat on a stone wall. "The chateau workers are there. Do you want to talk first?"

231

I sat down.

"What is it, Marie?"

"I'm afraid of him. I'm afraid of Martel, too. And the count isn't happy with me anymore. Everything scares me. I see things and hear things that don't make sense."

She didn't say anything, she just took my hand.

"You're not surprised?" I asked her.

"No, not really, not after what you said on my birthday. What else has happened?"

"The black pigeon. It got out of the cage and Renard found it buried. Its neck was wrung. Someone killed it, Anne. And when I brought Jeannine back to show her where it was buried, it was gone." I put my head down in my hands. "They think I'm losing my mind."

"Who does?"

"The count, Jeannine, the servants. I've been walking outside at night because I can't sleep. I ran into a gypsy who knew Papa, and he warned me."

"What did he say?"

"That there's evil at the chateau, and I shouldn't trust anyone." I gave a little sob. "Maybe I *am* imagining things. I saw Father Samuel's crucifix in the cellar and the chain looked broken, like when my necklace was pulled off my neck. But that can't be right, no one would do that to a priest. And when I went back, it wasn't there."

"What has the count said to you? Has he told you he's going to hurt you?"

"No, nothing like that. When he was angry with me about Renard, though, he said I was going to be sorry. He said it softly, like he didn't want me to hear, and he looked so angry."

"When people are angry, they say things they don't mean. Once you said you hoped lightning would come down and split me in half like a tree, remember?"

"Did I? Oh yes, I remember that. It was after you told on me and Thomas for something. Well, I didn't really want it to happen, you know that."

232

"That's what I mean," Anne said. "I don't trust him, but the count knows he can't do anything to you with the whole village at the foot of the hill."

I took a deep breath. "No, he couldn't hurt me with you nearby."

"And I don't think you're losing your mind. I think some things happened that scared you, and that makes you think ordinary things are threatening. But they're not and you're fine, Marie."

We sat for a while and I swung my feet, just as I had before I was a countess. It was comforting, sitting on the wall with her as if I'd never left.

"You've made it much better, you really have." I kissed her cheek.

"Good. I wish I had another black pigeon for you, but he was my only one. At least you have the white one. Do you still want to go to the fields?"

"Yes, I do. I miss them."

She pulled me up and we went the rest of the way to our fields. We waved to the chateau workers and then rested by the wall under the trees. It was a lovely morning, sitting with Anne in the shade, smelling the fields around me again and digging my fingers into the soil. Everything seemed so normal here. Renard nosed through the field, made friends with the workers, and then sat with us. I never wanted to leave.

I stayed most of the day, first in the field and then in the cottage. Before Renard and I left, Anne promised she'd come up as soon as the count went on his trip. And Maman told me, finally, that she'd visit after the count returned.

I went back to the chateau feeling happier than I had in months. The count noticed immediately.

"I see a visit with your Maman has helped you," he said that evening.

"Yes," I answered. "I spoke with Anne about the ball."

"What ball?" he said.

"I'm going to have some friends from the village here for a party when you go on your trip. We talked about it before."

233

"Did we? That will keep you busy," he said, and then turned to Martel. They didn't speak to me the rest of the meal. It was quite a contrast to the day with Anne and Maman. I excused myself early and went up to my rooms.

But I wandered back down again several hours later. Jeannine, asleep in the next room, was snoring. It was too early for me to sleep so I decided to get a book from the library.

When I passed the dining room, I saw someone sitting at the table. It was Martel. He was alone in the room and his head was cradled in his arms on the table.

I paused in the doorway and watched him. He heaved a deep sigh, but didn't lift his head. I backed away from the room into the hall. At first I was glad he was unhappy, but then I could hear my papa's voice. "Kindness, Marie. There is always something you can do to be kind."

I went to the kitchen. Even though dinner had been cleaned up and breakfast dishes laid out, there were two girls sewing at the table, the same two who had been there when I went in with Jeannine. "Heat up some water and take tea in to M. Martel," I said. "He's in the dining room."

I left them busy heating water and making up a tray and went to the library for my book. I had been reading there for a while when I was surprised by the sound of Martel clearing his throat.

"Yes?" I said.

"Thank you for the tea, Countess."

"You're welcome."

He paused, looking uncomfortable. "May I come in, just for a moment?"

"If you wish."

He came in and stood by the couch, some papers in his hand. I put down my book. "Yes, M. Martel?"

"Have you ever thought of leaving the chateau, Countess?"

"Why would you suggest such a thing?" I said in surprise. He looked at me intently, then leaned forward as if to say more.

But then we heard someone's footstep. He glanced at the doorway and then straightened up. "Ah, good evening, Count. I have the papers you wanted."

"Up late, my dear?" the count said to me.

234

"I've found the book I wanted and I'm just leaving." Whatever Martel was going to tell me was lost. He handed the papers to the count as I brushed by them and said, "Goodnight, gentlemen."

Later when I was lying in bed I wondered if Martel had been trying to warn me of something. The comfort I had felt earlier in the day with Anne was gone. When I finally fell asleep, I dreamed of being chased through corridors with doors that wouldn't open.

Chapter Thirty-One

I was sure the servants were treating me differently. They seemed concerned, as if I was sick. Jeannine was, too, she always had a worried look. She brought me tea and told me to rest several times a day. "Too many things going on," she said now whenever she knew I was uneasy or anxious. "You should rest."

I decided to talk to Henri. He had seen the crucifix, he would know I wasn't making it up. I found him in his office. "Henri, may I speak with you?"

"Of course, Countess."

"You saw something shining between the barrels when we were in the wine cellar, didn't you?"

"I'm sorry, Countess, I don't recall seeing anything."

"Are you sure?"

"You may have seen something, Countess, but you were between me and the barrels. If there was something there, I could not have seen it."

"Have you been back down since we were there?"

"Yes, Countess, several times."

"And nothing was different?"

"No, Countess."

"Was there a bottle on the floor near the barrels?"

"No, Countess. All was in order."

"You didn't see anything between the barrels or a bottle on the floor?"

"No, Countess." He answered each question patiently. I thanked him and left.

Jeannine was in the bedroom, cleaning my jewels. She *had* to believe me; she was my only ally in the chateau.

"I need to talk with you," I said.

She put down the jewels and folded her hands. "Yes, Countess?"

"I just spoke to Henri. He said he didn't see anything between the barrels, where I saw the crucifix, and he said there wasn't a bottle left on the floor. But I left that bottle there. I had it in my hand when I knelt down. I remember putting it in the dirt by the barrel. And I know I saw the crucifix. It glittered in Henri's lamplight."

"But nothing was there when you went back."

"No, but someone could have gone there and taken it." I buried my head in my hands. "Oh, Jeannine, I don't know what to think any more. I can't have imagined all that. And everyone thinks I'm dreaming these things."

"Countess," said Jeannine, and I felt her warm, soothing hand on my back, "you haven't been sleeping well, and you always look tired."

"But what if I'm right? Even if I'm misreading everything and seeing danger where there isn't any, these things really are happening. Anne believes me. Can't you?"

Her hand stopped. "Well, maybe someone else went in and picked up the bottle before Henri saw it."

I lifted my head. "And they took the crucifix?"

"I suppose they could have."

I sighed and sat on the edge of my bed. I could tell she didn't really believe me. Renard came over and laid his head on my lap. I patted his head and his tail wagged. Life was so simple for him. "Want to go out, boy?" I said. "I'll stop thinking about all this and we'll play."

We went outside with Renard, but even while I was throwing his ball for him I could see a worried look in Jeannine's eyes when she glanced over at me.

237

"Shall we take a tray of tea up to the tower room?" Jeannine asked two days later.

"That's a lovely idea. We haven't been there for a while."

She got a tray from the kitchen and we stole quickly through the halls. When we entered the tower and pulled the door closed behind us, I put my hand on her arm.

"Wait, don't go up the stairs yet. Look over there, on the floor. There's more dirt, see?"

She put the tray down and we went over to the wall. "Someone's been in that hole," she said, touching the dust with her toe. "Maybe they took the box."

"We're going to find out," I said, tugging on the stone. When it came out of the wall, I put it down on the floor and reached into the hole.

"The box is still here," I said, getting my fingers around it and lifting it out. "Let's see what they took."

But they hadn't taken anything, they'd added something. When I opened the box, Father Samuel's crucifix lay on top, its chain broken.

The box fell out of my shaking hands and Jeannine's arms went around me. "I knew it was in the cellar," I said, my voice hoarse, "and now someone's put it in here."

"Oh, Countess," she whispered. "I'm so sorry I haven't believed you."

We stood there, holding each other, until we grew chilled from the dampness of the stone tower around us. "Let's go to my rooms," I said, "after we put everything back."

Jeannine gathered up the spilled contents and put the box back the hole. We replaced the stone, she picked up the tray, and we went back to my sitting room. I threw some logs on the fire and we both pulled chairs close to the hearth. "Who put it there? Martel, the count?"

"Perhaps it's one of the servants, playing a trick," Jeannine said.

"Who?"

She frowned. "I don't know. Maybe it's just all coincidence. It was different people – someone found the bottle and put it back,

238

maybe an animal got the pigeon that was buried – it wasn't just one person doing all this."

"There's still the crucifix."

"Yes, but maybe there's a reasonable explanation for that, too."

"Just knowing I'm not imagining things makes it easier to bear," I said. "You have no idea how frightening it's been, wondering if I've lost my mind."

She knelt by my chair. "Countess, how can you ever forgive me? I'll believe everything you say, truly I will, from now on. And I'll tell Mme Vacher, she'll believe you, too."

"No, don't tell anyone yet. I'll talk with Anne first. You know I'm right, that's enough for now."

I leaned forward and kissed her cheek. If I couldn't have Anne with me, Jeannine was a wonderful substitute.

I woke later that night. I couldn't stop my thoughts from tumbling around. The more I tried to sleep the more anxious I felt. Every time I tried to grasp what was frightening me, it slipped away. I had to walk.

I took Renard with me. He seemed to know something was wrong and stayed by my side. We walked around the edge of the garden, then up the garden steps behind the chateau. This time I made sure my slippers got wet.

From across the stone walkway I saw the count in the small salon holding something in his hand. I went closer to the window. In the fire and candlelight, I could see he was holding a woman's portrait. It was a small sketch of the large portrait hanging in the parlor, the one of his first wife.

Then I saw his face. He was weeping. I forgot about my anxious thoughts as compassion for him overwhelmed me. I knew I could comfort him.

But as I raised my hand to open the French doors and step through, he threw the portrait into the fire and watched it curl up and burn. Then he turned, his face twisted with rage, and swept his arm across a table. A glass and an empty plate shattered on the floor as I snatched my hand away from the latch.

239

My heart raced and I heard Renard give a low growl. "No, boy," I whispered, and stepped back into the darkness. We ran to the side door I had left open, went up a back staircase, and slid past Jeannine, still snoring.

Renard slept in my bed that night.

At breakfast I hardly spoke. The count didn't seem to notice. After the coffee was served, he leaned forward and said, "I'm going on my trip tomorrow. I'll be away for several weeks, and I'll be giving you all my keys this time. I've never left all of them with you before." He smiled at me then, more warmly than he had in weeks, and was attentive to me the rest of the meal. I didn't enjoy conversing with him, but I was glad for a peaceful meal after what I had seen the night before.

"Maybe I'll have Anne up tomorrow to help plan the party."

"What party?"

Why couldn't he remember this? "I told you about it. I'm going to have it while you're gone, remember? You said you thought it would be good for me."

"Ah, yes, to keep you busy."

Martel slid into his seat. I hadn't even heard him enter the room. "Perhaps the countess can go on a trip instead, to another of your chateaus. I would be happy to make the arrangements. I could take her there myself."

"No." The curtness of the count's voice surprised me, although I was glad he didn't want me to travel with Martel. "Not this time," he said more gently. "She can have a visit from her sister."

Martel took a sip from his glass. "I'm sure your sister would be happy to stay here with you."

"There's no need for her to stay," said the count, "unless, of course, the countess wishes it."

I didn't answer. I wanted Anne to stay the entire time but I knew she wouldn't.

I told Jeannine he was leaving when I went back upstairs. "I'm glad it will be for several weeks," I said. "It will give me time to

240

sort out all that's been happening. I can tell Anne everything, and the three of us will figure it out."

"I'm sure she'll know what to do," said Jeannine with certainty, and with that I put it from my mind.

I was on my way downstairs from my room that afternoon when I stopped to look at the colors dancing on the steps around me. The sun came through the stained glass window at the landing, throwing jewels of light all over the stairs and hall. I had never looked at the design in the window closely, it was just a jumble of color to me. This time, though, I climbed back up the stairs and studied it.

I spread out my arms; it went from fingertip to fingertip. It started about two feet from the landing and soared above my head. It was rectangular with a pattern inside made of red, blue, green, purple, and yellow glass. It made me think of a rainbow.

I realized it was a picture of a scroll. There were figures in each corner of angels pulling back the four edges of the scroll. The patterns, I saw now, were radiating from a little figure painted in the center.

I looked closely. It was a small naked Eve holding an apple, a serpent twined around her feet.

I heard someone clear their throat and turned to see Father Gregory studying the window. "One cannot even tell it was shattered. Such good work the glassmaker did." He nodded with satisfaction.

"I don't like looking at it," I said. "All I can think of is the poor girl who went through it."

M. Martel and the count were ascending the stairs as I spoke. "Yes, such a terrible accident," said Martel as the count looked sadly at the window.

"I have never understood," said Father Gregory as he reached out and touched the window, "how she could have fallen through. The glass is quite strong. She had to hit it very hard, almost as if she was trying to break it."

The count glanced at Martel, who took Father Gregory's shoulders and turned him away from the window. "She tripped,"

241

he said. "So tragic. Shall we go to the count's room, Father Gregory?"

"Yes, yes, of course," he said, and allowed Martel to steer him up the stairs. He seemed like a chess piece again, a stupid, expendable pawn that the rook was manipulating, with the king following behind.

I went downstairs and Martel came into the salon a short while later. To my surprise, he walked right over to where I was sitting on the sofa and sat down.

"Countess, I would like you to consider what I have to say."

"Yes, M. Martel?"

"I believe it would be wise for you to travel somewhere for a time. Perhaps you could even experience another country. You could take your Maman and sister and the chateau could make arrangements for your family's farm to be watched in your absence."

"Why are you saying this?"

He glanced at the door. "My name was not always Martel, Countess. Before I came here, I was known as Fontaine."

"I don't know anyone by that name," I responded coldly, wishing he would leave.

"No, but you know the one I had before that. I am Paul Moreau, your father's cousin."

Shock raced through me. Martel was our cousin? This couldn't be true.

"How did you end up here?" I whispered.

He spread out his hands. "A lifetime of foolish decisions."

"You made things worse for my father and mother when they wanted to marry."

He shrugged. "That is not my problem, Countess. I was on my way to see your father when I came here. I had been caught in some difficulties, and thought perhaps he could help me. But I found the count and no longer needed your father. And once I was here, I could see he couldn't have helped me anyway.

"My position with the count has been one of comfort, and I have no wish to leave. You, however, may want to do so."

"Why?"

242

"Let's just say the count doesn't lay all of his cards on the table."

"Are you telling me it's not safe for me to stay here?"

"I would never say that, Countess. I am merely suggesting travel to broaden your world." With that he rose, bowed, and left the room.

As I watched him leave I thought I saw movement at the other door, and looked just in time to see the edge of a shadow disappear.

Someone had been listening.

Chapter Thirty-Two

"Here are the keys," my husband said early the next morning, drawing them out from his jacket after the servants cleared away the dishes. "There is a new one on the ring, I haven't left it with you before. It opens a small door under the old tower stairs." He leaned forward, his eyes glittering. "You are not to use it, do you understand? It's the golden one. It is a forbidden key. If you choose to disobey me, I promise you will live to regret it."

"You told me you didn't have a golden key."

He pushed the keys over to me. He was smiling, but his eyes looked odd – almost fiery with excitement. "Of course I do. It's on the ring."

I didn't argue. "You must be looking forward to your trip," I said as I took the key ring.

He ignored my comment and pointed to the key. "That one," he said. "It must stay with you, but you are not to use it."

I looked down at the keys. Almost hidden among the darker ones was a small, bright, golden key. My eyes were drawn to it and I couldn't help touching it.

"Remember what I said." He smiled as he left the table.

I played with the key ring for a minute or two, listening to the heavy clunking of the large keys and the sweet, tinkling sound of the small golden one. When the maid came back, I stood up and put them in my pocket.

The key ring seemed heavier than it had been when I'd carried the keys before. By the time I reached my rooms I was tired of feeling them in my pocket as I walked. I decided to leave them in my room and put them in the table drawer by my chair.

Later that morning when the count left, he kissed me affectionately and told me he'd miss me. I waved as the carriage pulled away and went back into the chateau, feeling a weight lift from my shoulders.

By early afternoon, Jeannine and I had finished planning the ball before Anne even arrived to help. "We'll open the main ballroom," I said to Jeannine. "I'll have new candles placed in the chandeliers and put the fanciest chairs in the chateau along the walls."

"Will you have your guests stay the night?" asked Jeannine.

"No, I don't think so," I replied. "They all have chores and if I take them away too long, they won't be able to come back again."

"For another ball?"

"Why not?"

"Would the count mind?"

I shrugged. "He'll be gone for several weeks, and I don't think he cares what I do."

"Oh, Countess," she said, understanding more than I intended. She took my hand. "I'm so sorry."

"It doesn't matter," I said, but my eyes stung. Jeannine put her arm around me. "I don't know why I'm crying. It's a relief that he's not here. I'm so tense now when he's with me, it's awful. He hates me, Jeannine."

"He doesn't hate you, Countess."

"Yes, it's true. I see it in his eyes whenever he looks at me. I see it all the time now." I brushed my tears away, but they didn't stop. Then I hiccupped.

"Well," said Jeannine matter-of-factly, "he isn't here now. And you're planning a party, and your sister's coming up, so don't cry. What night do you want to have it?"

I dried my eyes with the handkerchief she handed me. "Tomorrow?"

"Do you think that gives enough time to get everything ready?"

"The day after?"

Jeannine nodded. "I think that's perfect. You can send the invitations out tomorrow morning, that would give everyone time to get ready, and we'll have time to prepare here."

"Oh, Jeannine, this will be fun!" I sent for Mme Vacher, drew up the invitation list, and we began writing them out.

"We may be able to get these down to the village today, if you would like," said Mme Vacher.

"That would be even better," I said. "It will give them more time to look forward to it. Don't forget to tell them what the invitation says. Most of them can't read."

"We should pick out your dress," said Jeannine. "Do you know what you want to wear?"

"Maybe the green velvet one. And Jeannine, you and Raoul can come!"

Jeannine was aghast. "Oh, no Countess, we can't do that."

"Why not?"

"We mustn't mix with you and your friends."

"No one is high born, Jeannine, not even me."

"But Countess, we're just village people."

"So is everyone else."

"But you are the countess and we're the staff. We must treat you with the respect of your station. We can't mingle with your guests. It isn't done."

No matter what I said she was adamant, and so was Mme Vacher. None of the servants would come, they said.

"Then I know what I'll do," I said, growing excited again. "There's a second ballroom, the smaller one on the other side of the chateau. You'll have a ball there."

Jeannine shook her head. "We couldn't do that, Countess, not when you're having a ball that night. We need to be serving you."

"Then you'll have it the next night. There won't be a conflict with mine and I'll be too tired from my party to need very much from anyone. It's perfect! You can wear any dress of mine you like, we're close to the same size. Raoul would be there," I said slyly, "and he'll see how lovely you look."

Mme Vacher looked interested but Jeannine wavered. "I don't think the count would wish it."

246

"Why wouldn't he? You won't disturb him, he's not here. And it will keep his staff happy. I wish it and I'm the countess. Mme Vacher, can you make invitations for that, too?"

"I don't think invitations for the staff will be necessary, Countess," she said.

"Whatever you think, I'll leave it up to you. And all the servants are invited, including you. And guests."

"Thank you, Countess," said Mme Vacher. Her eyes shone. "Such a thing has never happened here, not in my time."

"Then it's long overdue," I said. I felt powerful again, as I had when I challenged the count about Renard. If I had known what lay ahead, I would have felt only fear.

It didn't take long for Jeannine to hand out the invitations in the village. "Everyone said they were coming," she told me.

"Good," I said. "We've sent word to the musicians for both of the evenings. Mme Vacher told me when they know it's at the count's chateau they'll come, even on such short notice."

By evening all the servants knew about both my ball and theirs. The next day the chateau became a beehive of activity. Servants were busy everywhere, cleaning, moving furniture, and decorating the ballrooms.

The main ballroom floor shone. The chandeliers were lowered and polished. Long white candles were placed in the holders. Rows of chairs appeared, upholstered in velvet and brocade, with gold painted legs and frames. Rugs lay in front of them. Beautiful filigreed lamps stood along the edges of the room. The servants uncovered a harpsichord and set up chairs for the musicians.

"There is another harpsichord in the smaller ballroom, too," Mme Vacher told me.

"And another in the music room. Why are there so many?" I asked.

"I think in days past, they were used for both entertaining and the personal pleasure of the family," she said. "I've heard the count's mother was quite accomplished, but they were only here for a short while. They left for another chateau before their son was born."

247

I dismissed her and she left. Then I checked on the smaller ballroom. That one, too, was starting to sparkle.

Late in the afternoon I wandered into the kitchen. The cooks were busy baking and preparing mounds of food. We would start the ball with a dinner. Cakes and pies already lined the baking counter, soup simmered in a huge pot on the fire, and rows of vegetables waited to be cut up. The meat wasn't out yet, but there would be pheasant and venison at the table.

Jeannine was so busy helping with the preparations I hardly saw her. I spent the rest of the day watching the progress, my excitement mounting along with the staff's. The parties would be glorious, both of them.

The next day dawned brilliantly bright and warm. Birds sang from the gardens and the forest beyond as I leaned out my window and breathed in the soft air. The day could not have been more perfect.

"We'll send the carriages out late this afternoon to get the guests. That way they can rest here before dinner," I told Jeannine when she came in.

"Yes, Countess. Would you like your sister here earlier?"

"Oh, that would be nice. And is my mother coming?"

"I don't think so, Countess." Jeannine opened my wardrobe. "She said yesterday it was a young people's party, and she would come up for dinner when the count returned."

"Well, I'm glad she said that much." I chose the dress I wanted to wear for the day.

She pulled it from the wardrobe and shook out the skirt. "It will be nice when your maman visits you, Countess. I know you've wanted her here."

I agreed and then spent the rest of the morning checking the preparations and talking with Mme Vacher.

"Everything is running smoothly, Countess," she assured me when I asked again in the early afternoon. "The musicians have already arrived and are setting up their area. We have given them rooms in the servants' wing to accommodate them the next two nights."

Anne arrived shortly after that. Jeannine had been right, Maman wasn't with her. "She said her time will come later," Anne

248

told me as we were going in. "And there's something else, Marie," she said softly. "Thomas sent word that he's coming back, and he needs to talk with you."

"Thomas?" I stopped on the steps and stared at Anne. "He's coming here? To see me?"

"Shh, I don't think he wants the count to know."

"He's not here."

"His servants are. Let's go to your room." We went inside and up the staircase.

The perfect day had come crashing down at the thought of Thomas. I missed him so much I could hardly breathe. "Why is he coming?"

Anne shut the door. "To tell us something he's found out. I'm sorry, I didn't think about how much it would upset you."

She sat down on the sofa with me and I searched her face. "What does he need to tell me?"

"I don't know. I should have waited to tell you. It doesn't matter right now, he's not here yet. I'll let you know as soon as he shows up in the village."

It felt as if a huge hole opened in my chest. I had worked so hard at not caring about Thomas. "Anne, how can I meet with him? I'm married."

"He doesn't want to see you for anything improper. If you don't want to see him, you don't have to. He can tell me whatever it is and I'll tell you."

"Don't want to see him? The problem is I *do* want to see him!"

"We'll work it out, Marie. I won't let you do anything wrong and neither will he. We have a party ahead of us. Don't let this ruin it. Everyone is looking forward to coming and seeing you. Show me the ballroom, I haven't seen it."

I nodded. "And the smaller one, I'll show you that, too. The servants will have a ball there tomorrow night."

"I heard. That was a wonderful idea. Yes, show me that one, too."

We went downstairs and I tried to be excited again. But it was hard to push away the yearning to be sitting on my old stool, watching Thomas work in his shop.

249

Everyone arrived for the ball and went upstairs to rest. When the bell rang they came down for dinner, excited and talkative.

I was at the head of the long table where the count usually sat. Anne and Adam were to my right and Jacqui sat on my left. With other guests seated down the sides, the dining table finally seemed comfortably full. There was a servant behind each chair, ready to get whatever we wanted. Plates piled high with food appeared constantly.

It was a fun time, with everyone talking and laughing. I felt as if I was one of them again instead of a countess. And even though I was upset knowing Thomas was on his way, the spirit of the party was so joyous I couldn't stay sad.

When Henri came to tell me he needed to get more wine from the wine cellar and his key was missing, I pulled out the large key ring from my pocket. "Where is yours?" I asked him.

"The count asked for my keys just before he left. He must have taken it off the ring for some reason and forgotten to put it back. It will be found, Countess." He took the one he needed and placed the ring on the table by my hand before he disappeared through the door.

"Look at all those keys," said Jacqui, her eyes big. "Is there one for every single room?"

"I think so," I said. "It's certainly heavy enough."

"What's that one for?" She pointed at the small gold key.

"One of the rooms," I said.

"Why is it gold? Why isn't it like the others?"

"I don't know. Wait until you see the ballroom. It's like a fairy tale."

It worked. She forgot the key and turned to the boy next to her. "Are you going to dance all night?"

"As long as the music lasts," he answered.

But the distraction of the coming ball didn't work for long. After a few minutes she looked at the key again. "Which room is it for?"

"A little room in the tower," I said, growing annoyed.

"A tower room? That sounds exciting! Can you show us?"

"No, I can't. The count has told me not to use the key."

"Have you ever been in it?" she asked.

"No."

Now Anne was listening. "You haven't?"

"No. It's a room under the stairs."

Anne looked at the key, curious. "There's a room under the stairs?"

"Yes," I answered, wishing I could stop the discussion.

"You're really not allowed to go there?" said Jacqui.

"No, and I don't know why, so don't ask."

"Doesn't it make you wonder what's in it?" she said.

"Well, it does, but I can't find out, so I *try* not to think about it." I glared at both of them and they turned away.

I kept glancing down at the key. It glinted in the candlelight, so much brighter than the other ones. How big was the lock? It was such a small key, surely the lock wasn't very large. Maybe I could go see it later. Looking at the lock wasn't the same as using the key, that would be all right.

It was a relief when Henri returned, put the wine cellar key back on the ring, and I put the key ring safely back into my pocket.

But I couldn't stop thinking about the golden key. It seemed to be calling me.

The ballroom glittered and shone when we entered. The musicians were already playing and once we were all in, Anne and Adam started the first dance. I hadn't realized until then that I didn't have a partner. I stood by the chairs, wondering what to do.

Adam came to my rescue at the second dance and led me out onto the floor.

But it was different than the balls we had during the week at the count's other chateau. I wasn't being wooed. I was alone. Everyone else had someone attentive at their side. As the evening progressed the boys were gracious and often asked me, but then someone else had to stand or sit by.

And then, halfway through the evening when everyone but me was dancing, a hand went under my elbow.

"I would be pleased, Countess, if you would dance with me."

251

When I heard the voice, my stomach churned. It was Martel. "That is not necessary," I said coldly, but to my surprise he propelled me onto the floor.

"The count will be pleased to hear of your hostess skills," he said.

"What the count thinks of me is no concern of yours," I said.

"Ah, you're wrong, Countess. It is very much my concern, and something I would like to talk about with you."

He was too close. "I don't wish to talk with you. I have guests, M. Martel. Excuse me." I broke away and walked toward a chair. When I passed Anne, I whispered, "I need you." She and Adam stopped dancing and followed me. I looked back and saw Martel disappear through a door.

"Does this mean the count is back?" Adam said when I told them.

"I don't think so," I answered.

"What did he say to you?" Adam asked.

"Nothing, really. I walked away."

"Are you sure the count won't be angry with you for having a ball while he's gone, Marie?" said Anne.

"I don't know why he would. He knows all about it." But I wasn't sure about anything with him anymore.

Martel didn't return, and the rest of the evening passed in a blur of happy faces, lovely music, and my own foreboding feeling. Perhaps I shouldn't have cut him off. I should have listened to what he wanted to say.

Everyone left quite late. After I had climbed the stairs to my room, Jeannine came in to help me undress. "It was a lovely ball, Countess," she said.

"Except for Martel showing up," I replied.

"He's here?"

"Yes, didn't you see him?"

"No. I'll let Mme Vacher know."

She left the room and returned several minutes later. "No one has seen him, and Mme Vacher had his room checked. He's not there. You're sure it was him?"

"Of course, Jeannine, he tried to dance with me. I wish I knew where he went."

252

"He must have left, Countess. The servants always know where he is." That was true, she'd said before he was very demanding with them. He couldn't still be here.

But it was hard to fall asleep that night. And the last image in my thoughts was a small golden key.

Chapter Thirty-Three

The morning of the servant's ball was gray and drizzly. I wished Anne had stayed. I knew Jeannine would be preoccupied and wouldn't be very good company.

"I'm glad the staff is already here for the ball," I said to Jeannine as she brushed my hair. "It wouldn't be very nice to go outside all dressed up when it's raining and muddy. I hope your guests can still come."

"It doesn't look like it will last," she said, glancing out the window. "See, it's brightening already over the trees." She laid out my dress for the day. "What will you do today, Countess?"

"Recover from last night. Sleeping late won't be enough. I think I'll read for a while, and then maybe take a nap. I'm looking forward to a quiet day."

I was silent while she helped me dress. When she finished fastening the back of my gown, I saw the count's large key ring on the bed side table. As I lifted it, the golden key flashed in the light. I stared at it for a moment and then shoved the key ring deep into my pocket. It felt heavier than the day before and I tried to ignore it.

Jeannine's eyes shone as she picked up my brush again. "May I really wear one of your dresses tonight?"

"Of course. And shoes, too, if you'd like."

Her eyes got even bigger. "This is too much to believe, Countess! To wear such beautiful things!"

"That's what friends are for," I said. "And you've been a loyal friend the whole time I've been here. I wish I could do more for you. I want you to be so beautiful Raoul won't be able to keep his eyes off of you."

Jeannine blushed and laughed. She went to the wardrobe and chose a cream-colored silk dress and matching shoes. "You'll be breathtaking," I told her as she held it up in the mirror.

A knock sounded on the door and a maid entered with a note. "This just came up from the village, Countess," she said.

I opened it and read it through.

"May I go now, Countess?" Jeannine asked.

"Yes, Jeannine."

She left the room holding the dress high. I was alone. I looked back at my sister's small, neat penmanship and read it again.

Marie,

He sent word he will arrive by tomorrow at the latest. He said he must talk to you here. He signed in code. I will come up later today.

Anne.'

In code. When we were young, Thomas and I used to spell our name backwards on something as a warning to the other one that trouble was coming, usually because someone was unhappy with one of our pranks. Anne was the only other person we told.

He knew something. And he was warning me to be careful.

I folded Anne's note and put it in the drawer by my chair. Should I tell Jeannine? I stood up, undecided. I couldn't tell her, I didn't know enough yet.

I'd wait for Anne. Jeannine was too excited about the ball anyway, and I didn't want to spoil it for her.

I looked over at Renard's rug. It was empty. He was probably down in the kitchen, begging scraps from the cook. Or perhaps feasting on unattended food someone left out. He'd claimed more than one roast since he came here.

I went downstairs and peeked into the large ballroom. It looked dismantled and barren. The chairs were gone, the rugs rolled up or missing, and the musicians had moved all their things to the smaller ballroom for tonight.

I wandered through the halls to the other side of the chateau and looked into the smaller ballroom. It was a miniature version

255

of last night. Rugs and chairs lined these walls now. At the end was a table for refreshments, since they weren't having a meal. Candles in the chandelier waited to be lit. No one was around. The staff had gotten everything ready and left to finish their duties elsewhere in the house before their big night. The chateau seemed deserted.

I went back up to my rooms to wait for Anne. Every step I took, I felt the key ring. When I reached my sitting room and sat down in the chair, I pulled it out of my pocket and looked at the gleaming, golden key.

It was so pretty, the bright gold flashing among the other dark, worn keys. Why would that room have such a lovely key? It should be the key to a beautiful room, not some forgotten one in an old tower. Was the lock old, like the other locks in the chateau, or was it bright and shiny like the key? Why could I not use it? I was the mistress of the house; surely there wasn't anything I shouldn't see.

I had a quick flash of Mme Vacher reading from the countess's journal:

"'I found the key... Why would he forbid me to use it?... What can harm me? I'm going to unlock the door.'"

Was this the same key? She had used it, but she didn't write about what she found. Perhaps she was going there when she fell and never saw what was in the room.

The golden key shone brilliantly and the urge to use it was growing stronger. It seemed to call to me. I touched it. Then suddenly I wanted to put it away, somewhere I wouldn't see it. I opened the drawer by my chair and dropped the keys in next to Anne's note.

Except Anne's note wasn't there anymore.

I stared at the drawer, empty except for the keys. I took them out, searching the back corners of the drawer for the note. The drawer was empty.

I don't know how long I sat there, staring at the drawer as if her note would appear. Then I looked under the table, under the chair, around the pillows and covers. I searched the table and chair half a dozen times, going over and over the same spots.

I knew, even as I grew more frantic, I wasn't going to find it. I think I would have lost my mind if Jeannine hadn't walked in.

256

"What's wrong, Countess?"

I was on the floor, looking under the chair again. "Anne's note, it's gone."

"What note?"

"The note that came up from the village when you were leaving my room. Anne sent it to me." I pulled myself up. "It was a warning from Thomas."

"A warning?" She closed the door behind her and came to my chair.

"I put it in here, right here, and it's gone," I said.

She looked into the empty drawer. "Are you sure?" She pulled it out all the way, just as I had, and looked in the back corners.

"Yes, I think so. I've looked everywhere. It's gone."

"Are you remembering it right? You're very upset now."

"Oh, I don't know any more, Jeannine," I wailed. "I *think* I put it there. Where else would it be?"

"Your pocket."

I thrust my hand into the folds of my skirt. "No, it's not there."

"Could it have fallen out?"

"I hope not. I don't know where it would be. I walked all over the chateau. It could be anywhere. And I don't want someone else to find it."

"What did it say?"

I sat down on the chair. "Anne said Thomas was coming home and wanted to talk with us at Maman's. And she said she was coming up later today."

"There now, Countess, that sounds fine. Even if someone found it, there's nothing wrong with it."

I found myself calming down. "You're right, Jeannine. I was sure, though, I had put it in the drawer."

"No one would come into your rooms and go through your things," Jeannine said as she sat down near me.

I thought of Martel, but he wasn't here. "Yes, I must have dropped it somewhere." Whatever had happened, it was gone now. I shut the drawer and tried not to think about it. "I'm glad you came in, Jeannine."

She looked uncomfortable.

"What is it?"

257

"You've been so generous, Countess, with the dress and the shoes..." she trailed off and looked at me painfully.

"Is there something else you want, Jeannine?"

"It's just the neckline dips, Countess, and I have no necklace."

"I should have thought of that," I said, getting up from the chair. "And earrings, too. Let's find something grand for you to wear."

We spent the next half hour sorting through my jewelry and found a necklace, earrings, and a bracelet, too, for her to wear. She was so excited she could barely thank me before she whisked out of the room.

When she left I dropped down on my chair again, suddenly exhausted. I almost nodded off to sleep waiting for Anne to arrive. This side of the chateau was completely quiet. Even though the servant's ball must have started, I couldn't hear anything.

Something drew my eyes back to the key ring on the table. As I stared at the golden key, I grew more and more awake. I lifted up the ring. The golden key was mesmerizing. It would slip so easily into a lock. Almost without thinking, I wrestled it off the key ring.

It lay in my palm, little more than half the width of my hand. How big was the lock? Surely it wouldn't hurt to look.

My fingers closed around the key and I moved swiftly through the empty hall, stumbling once on the stairs. The key seemed to pulse in my hand. I could almost hear it whisper, "Hurry, hurry."

I went past the large, empty ballroom and down the hallways. There were no servants around. My steps on the stone floor echoed in the old hallway as the tower door came into view.

I pushed it open. The door must be just around the curved wall. My hand touched the cool, rough stones as I stepped, now cautious, around the huge hulk of the tower stairway. I thought of the secret room above me, the retreat of the previous countess and now mine, too. That countess had died. All of them had died. All of them but me.

I shivered and stopped right next to where the box was hidden in the wall. I stood as if rooted to the floor fully five minutes, unable to move forward or backward.

258

But the key's warmth in my hand seemed to pull me toward the door. I gave in to it, went the next few steps, and the door came into view.

It was small and wooden, flush with the stone wall. An iron handle beckoned me to open it, the way barred only by a small, golden lock.

My hand shook as I lifted the key. The count's voice rang in my ears as I remembered what he said: "You are not to use it, do you understand? It is a forbidden key. If you disobey me, I promise you will live to regret it."

My hand paused. What could it mean, that threat? My heart pounded in the silence. I knew I should heed the warning. There had been something eager in his eyes as he handed his keys to me, as if he enjoyed taunting me. I felt a stab of fear, and then defiance flooded through me.

I would show him I wasn't afraid – not of him, and not of a foolish curse. I slipped the key into the lock and turned it.

The lock clicked and the door moved slightly. It was my last chance to turn back. I hesitated, my hand still shaking.

Then I pushed the door open and stepped into the room.

Chapter Thirty-Four

In the darkness it was the heavy metallic smell I noticed at first. I knew that smell. It took me back to the butcher's shop in the village.

Then my eyes adjusted to the dimness from the one high window that let in light. Straight ahead of me was the curving stone wall of the tower. Almost immediately my eyes were drawn to long, hanging objects on the wall to my right.

It couldn't be. It wasn't possible. I was in a nightmare.

Placed in a neat row there were four young women hanging from hooks in the stone wall, their throats slit, blood still dripping down from the gaping wounds onto their gowns, onto the floor. I knew right away it was his wives. The one who loved mirrors was still incredibly beautiful, her raven hair falling across part of her face. And the last one was small, dainty, and blonde. The lonely German girl.

Even as shock raced through my body, my mind couldn't embrace it. How could they still be bleeding? How could they not have rotted? Each one looked as if she could step down and speak to me, except for the horrible open wound sliced across her throat. And the hook that had been rammed through her back.

And then I saw a fifth hook, gleaming in the dimness, and I knew it was meant for me.

I screamed then, loud and ragged and long. I felt so oddly detached it seemed it was coming from someone else's throat.

I turned away and saw another body on the other side of the room. This one wasn't on a hook. It was crumpled in the corner, and it was a man.

"Father Samuel!"

I ran to him, crouched down, and turned him to his side. His head lolled back. His throat, also, gaped open. I screamed again and staggered back to the center of the room, not knowing which way to look.

That was when I realized I had been standing in a pool of blood and it was leeching up my gown.

When I saw the blood on my skirts I shuddered so violently that the key, which I was still clutching, flew from my hand. It landed near the wall of corpses.

I stared at where it lay, submerged in blood under the first body. How could I get it without going near them? Another scream started in my throat and I put my hand over my mouth, forcing myself to stay quiet. Feeling sick, I took those awful steps to the wall, reached down in front of the corpse, and fished the key out of her blood. A drop fell from her throat and landed on my sleeve.

When I saw my hand dripping with blood I felt dizzy and started to sway. But I couldn't faint, not in that room. I fought it off, lifted my skirts, and stepped through the puddles to the door. I managed to think clearly enough to remove my shoes so I wouldn't leave bloody footprints. Then I closed and locked the door and ran back to the main part of the chateau, holding the key and the hem of my gown with one hand, my shoes clutched in the other. The house was still deserted.

I ran up to my rooms, opened the door, and almost screamed again.

Anne sat on the coach, her smile disappearing as soon as she saw me. "What's happened, Marie? You're hurt!"

I shook my head, closed the door, and fell to the floor.

She ran to me. "Marie!" She put her arms around me and helped me up. "You're covered in blood!"

I tried to answer her, but had no voice.

"What happened?"

261

"The key," I finally said. "I used it. I opened the door. They're all dead, Anne. They're all dead, and Father Samuel, too. I've seen them. He's killed them all, and I'm next. Their throats are slashed and they're bleeding –"

"Who are you talking about? Where's Father Samuel?"

"In the tower room, and he was killed, too, Anne. The count's wives – they're dead. He killed them all. And there's a hook for me, Anne, he's going to kill me too." I groaned and covered my face with my bloody hands. "I can't stop seeing them."

"Marie, calm down, you're not making sense. We've been in that room. Nothing's there. His wives have all been buried, they're in tombs in the chapel."

"No, they're not, they're hanging from hooks in a room under the stairs and they're still bleeding. The count killed them. Look, this is their blood! I'm not imagining it, see? And the key – I dropped it in their blood."

She looked at my gown and my hands and the key. "Marie, they've been dead too long."

"I know." I shuddered. "But it was still coming out of their throats, as if it had just happened. Like when the butcher is bleeding a cow. Their blood is still fresh on the floor, too. Look at my gown."

She took my arm. "First we're going to clean you up. Then I'm going to find out what's going on."

"No, Anne! You can't go there, it's too awful –"

There was a knock. I stared at Anne, shaking as she turned and went to the door.

"Who is it?" she said.

"It is M. Martel my dear, just making sure everything is all right. I thought I heard the countess speaking in distressed tones. Is there anything I can do for her?"

Anne held onto the knob. "No thank you, M. Martel. We're fine. We're resting right now."

"Very well. Let me know if there is anything at all –"

"I will, thank you."

"I'll be nearby."

We heard his footsteps go down the hallway. Anne locked the door. "He tried to open it," she said as she came back to me.

262

My heart was racing. "He was listening!"

"Yes, I think he was."

"How much did he hear?"

"I don't know. Let's wash you up and get this blood off."

She brought the washbasin and pitcher over and helped me get out of my dress and underclothes. "Burn them," I said, and she threw the clothes in a heap by the fireplace.

"First we clean you, then we burn that," she said, and helped me wash my hands in the basin. The water turned dark pink. I looked away, feeling sick again.

Anne handed me clean underclothes and I tried to pull them on. I was so weak she had to help me.

"The key," I said. I had dropped it into the water, and it lay on the bottom. I rinsed the blood off and took it out of the water. "I have to put this back on the key ring," I said, "or he'll know I've been there." I put it down on the table.

"Marie, look at the key."

As we watched, dark bloodstains reappeared on it.

I plunged it back into the basin, rubbing and rubbing. But when I took it out the stains were still there. They grew darker as the water dripped off.

"It's cursed," I whispered, shivering with an unnatural chill.

"We'll use cleaning sand," Anne said, rummaging through a cabinet. "Here."

She gave me a pouch. I poured out some sand and scoured the key with it. When that didn't work, she found a small brush and again I used the sand, scrubbing it into the key with the brush.

The stains reappeared just as clearly on the golden key as they had been when I first picked it up out of the blood.

"It's bewitched," she said, watching the stain reappear after I scrubbed it yet again. "It's not going to come off, Marie. What are we going to do?"

"He'll know." I dropped the key onto the table and buried my face in my hands. "He'll know I went in there and saw what he's done, and he'll kill me. I'm next. That's why there was another hook in the wall. It's for me."

"No, it's not. He's not going to kill you," said Anne. "We'll leave. We'll go back down to the village and tell Maman, and the

263

men will come up here after him. He'll be the one who's killed, not you."

I lifted my head. Of course. We would walk down the steps and through the door and I could even have the carriage take us to Maman's.

"I'll finish getting dressed and we'll go right away," I said, pulling out a plain dress from my wardrobe. I put it on, pulled off all my jewelry, and slipped on the most comfortable shoes I had.

Anne unlocked the door and pulled it open. M. Martel was right on the other side and I started shaking as soon as I saw him.

"Can I help you, ladies?"

"We're going for a walk," Anne said.

"We just got word that the count will be home this afternoon," he said, "and he wants to see the countess right away. He's asked me to make sure you are available. So I'm afraid you won't be able to take a walk, Countess."

He caught us off guard, or he never would have been able to do what he did. He pushed us back into the room, whisked the key from the lock, pulled the door shut, and locked it from the outside.

"I'm sure you don't mind visiting in your room until he calls for you," he said. We heard him walk down the hallway, talking softly to someone.

"He knows," I said hopelessly. "We're trapped. Anne, you never should have come here. Now he'll kill you, too."

"Who was he talking to?"

"Father Gregory's the only other person who comes here."

"Where's Jeannine?"

"They're all on the other side of the chateau."

"Their ball?"

"Yes."

Anne went to the window and leaned out. "No one's in sight. What if we call?"

"They won't hear."

Then she looked at the cage on the table. "We can send the pigeon!"

"The black one's gone, Anne. Someone killed it, remember? It wasn't my imagination."

264

"I didn't tell you why I came." She sat me down on the sofa. "Thomas is already here. He wants to confront the count about something but he's waiting for Adam. He said they'll come up together."

The thought of Thomas nearby gave me strength. I went to the white pigeon's cage. He turned his head and looked at me with one eye.

"We'll send a message. We can dip him in ink and make it black."

"He'll preen it off his feathers," Anne said, "and it'll poison him."

I peered at him through the cage bars. "He can't preen his head. I'll put patches on. Maybe someone will realize what it means." I took the ink bottle and poured some ink onto a rag. Gently, I wiped his head and a bit of his neck. Streaks of black ink stained his feathers. "That will have to do." I pulled him from the cage and brought him to the window. He cocked his head and eyed the sky.

I opened my hands and held him out; he launched out and flew toward the forest. "Fly home," I whispered, watching him soar above the first few trees.

"He's headed toward the village," Anne said as he disappeared. "He'll get home, Marie."

"Even if he does, someone has to find him, understand what it means, and come up. They'll never get here in time." Once again, I plunged into despair.

"Adam and Thomas will figure it out." She came back from the window. "And he'll get home in a few minutes."

"They need to be here now."

"They'll get here soon," she said, "and Martel can't turn both of them away. They'd know something was wrong and they'd come in to get us. There's still hope."

"What do we do?"

She took my hand. "We wait."

It wasn't long before we heard footsteps out in the hallway again. I was resigned to dying like a rabbit that had been cornered by a fox. It was only when I thought of Anne getting hurt that I felt a stirring inside to fight back.

265

We heard Martel speaking to someone in the hallway, and there was a rap on the door.

"Marie?" It was the count.

Anne nudged me. "Yes?" I replied, my voice wavering.

"May I come in?"

"If you don't mind, Count de Roesch, my sister is not feeling very well at the moment," Anne said, her voice strong and assertive. "If she could greet you later, when she is feeling better, I think that would be best for her. I wouldn't want her to become ill."

The count sounded amused when he answered. "That would be fine, Lady Anne. You are a most attentive sister. Father Gregory will be concerned, too. He's downstairs, watching for you."

The count chuckled and we heard them walking away. We heard Martel say, "I meant it when I said I won't help you with this one. The village is too close. Let me take them both away. There are places I could —"

"No." We hardly breathed, straining to hear. "Even if they get out," the count continued, his voice fading as they went down the hall, "I can take care of them. Gregory will keep them over here. He was useful after all."

"They must have gone into the count's room," I said, then thought of the connecting door to his room. I ran to it, quietly slid the bolt through the lock, and went back.

"You were right, it was Father Gregory with Martel earlier," said Anne.

"What are we going to do?" I said. "Stay locked in here until Thomas and Adam come? We won't hear them. They might not even get in."

Anne looked thoughtful. "That's true, Marie. Now that the count's here, he, Father Gregory, and Martel can keep them from coming through the door. Can we get to the servants' ball?"

"With Father Gregory downstairs? They're waiting for us to try something. I'm sure he's guarding the way to that side of the chateau."

"And if we try to run from the chateau, they'll catch us before we get to the village," she said. "Where can we go where we'd see

266

the road? Somewhere high. We can watch for Adam and Thomas and send a signal."

"The tower."

"Do you really want to go back there?"

"No."

"I didn't think so." She paused. "But that's the last place they'd think we'd hide. You may have come up with the very best spot in the chateau. If we can't get to the servants, we'll go there."

"But we're locked in, Anne. How are we going to get out?"

"Is the connecting door locked on his side?"

"Not usually."

"They know by now that you've locked it on your side. And they know we're afraid so they wouldn't think we'd go into his rooms. We'll wait until they leave there, and if they didn't lock their side, go out that way."

It sounded simple, but the thought of going into the count's room made me feel light-headed again. "What if they don't leave?"

"They won't stay in his bedroom. They've got us trapped, and they're not going to do anything until the servants' ball is well underway. My guess is they'll make sure we can't get out our door and run to any of the servants. They'll come back later, when the music is loud and no one will hear anything."

I shuddered. "I don't want to go in his room. Why don't we break through our door?"

"Without them knowing? We can't."

I reached for the key ring. "I have to put the key back on."

"But it's stained."

"Maybe if he asks for it and I hand it to him as if nothing's wrong, he won't notice," I said as I worked the golden key back on the ring. Anne snorted and leaned back against the sofa, closing her eyes.

What was I thinking? The stains still screamed out, even with the key almost hidden among the other ones. I put the key ring into my pocket. I didn't want to see the accursed thing.

Half an hour later we were creeping through the count's bedroom and into the empty hallway. We could hear his voice as he and Martel talked in another room close to the main staircase. I prayed they would stay in the room and not see us.

267

We fled soundlessly through the hall and down the side staircase. "Let's go to the servant's ball," I said. But the bulky shape of Father Gregory blocked the end of the hall.

"We'll make him move," I said, and started toward him. Then I saw he was slowly spinning.

Anne's hand clapped over my mouth just before a scream came out. A rope was around his neck and his feet were several inches above the floor.

"They killed him," she said, and then we heard a shout upstairs.

We turned around and raced to the old tower.

Anne pushed open the heavy door. "We made it," she whispered, and stepped through. I followed her and then thought of what was on the other side of the curved stone wall. Everything started to go black.

"Not here, Marie," Anne said, holding me up.

Then we heard someone coming. And it was when we were hopelessly trapped that I grew strong.

"Get upstairs, Anne, and fly something out the window. Thomas will know it means to hurry."

She turned, but it was too late. The door to the tower, which in our haste we hadn't latched, slowly opened.

And Renard came around the door.

I started laughing with relief. I laughed so hard I had to sit down. Renard shoved his nose into my face and whined.

"Marie, you're hysterical. Calm down."

I couldn't. I wiped tears away as my high-pitched laughter went on and on, finally frightening even me. I buried my face in Renard's fur and grew quiet.

"Where have you been, boy?" I said to him.

He licked my face, then stopped and smelled the air. His hackles rose and he looked at the wall behind me.

"He knows what's in there," Anne said. "I'm glad he's here, he can come with us."

But he looked over his shoulder, barked, and ran back through the door.

"Where's he gone?" I said. He had saved me once before, why didn't he do it now?

268

Then I heard a snarl and the count's voice shouting an oath. "Renard's bitten him!" I said.

There was a loud yelp and then silence. He'd killed Renard.

Rage welled up inside of me. He'd killed my dog and he was coming to murder Anne and me. All of my fear left. I was angry, and it made me feel strong and invincible.

"Get up the stairs, Anne," I said calmly, "and fly that banner for Thomas. I'll stay here and keep him away."

"But Marie —"

"No, Anne, go."

She ran up the tower stairs and I waited for my husband.

Chapter Thirty-Five

The first shock was his beard was bright blue. The second, that he was smiling. "Marie, my dear, how fortunate to find you here. I'm glad you're feeling better. Has Anne left you?"

"Yes," I said, watching him carefully.

"My lovely Countess, I must ask you to return my keys," he said, and held out his hand.

"I don't have them."

"That's not true, Marie. Give me the keys."

Reaching into my pocket, I pulled them out and flung them to the floor. "There they are."

He bent over and picked them up, still smiling. "And what is this?" He pulled out the golden key, still stained with the blood of his wives.

I didn't answer him. Instead, I stared at his blue beard and thought of the day Thomas spoke of the curse at my market stall, a lifetime ago.

"It seems you have found my secret, Marie. You know, of course, what that means." He waited for me to answer. I looked at his eager smile and hoped Renard had bitten him hard.

"Nothing to say, my dear Countess?" It wasn't until his hand went to his waist that I could see, hanging partly behind him, a long, curved sword. "You will be joining my other wives. Surely you saw your hook? I made certain it was there for you to find. I knew you would disobey me, you see, and I knew I would have to kill you." His fingers touched the sword and his eyes gleamed.

"What, no begging? It's so enjoyable, to hear begging. Come, my dear, don't you want to try for a few more minutes of life? Perhaps some miracle will happen, you're thinking. Or do you want to go quietly, as my first one did? That was no fun at all. My third one begged the most. She was so desperate to live. I let her die slowly, just so I could hear her pleading longer. Won't you be like her, my dear Marie? It would please me greatly to hear you beg."

He paused for a moment, his eyes bright with anticipation. "You found the box, didn't you? I knew you did. I think I'll take your earrings, or perhaps your ring." He looked more closely at me. "No, you're not wearing any jewelry, and after all the jewels I gave you. Ah – I see a pearl comb in your hair. I'll use that. I want something of yours to put in my special box. It will help me remember this moment of ours."

I felt sick.

"Let's go into their room," he said pleasantly. "There's no need to clean up when I do it in there. Come, my dear."

He took a step toward me, his hand on the hilt of his sword now. His beard blazed even bluer. I was tense, ready to run, but I had nowhere to go. He was blocking the door out of the tower, the steps led up to where Anne was hiding, and behind me was the room where he'd kill me.

Then, far away, I heard a bark. Renard wasn't dead. It gave me hope.

I would never win by strength, but perhaps I could outsmart him. What I needed was time. He took another step.

"Surely you wouldn't deny a dying person the right to prayer," I said with coolness.

He stopped, surprised. "Prayer? Do you think that will save you?"

"That is not what I said. A dying person has a right to prayer, don't you agree?"

He frowned. "Perhaps."

"Or would you rather face their Maker having not let them pray?"

His hand came down from the sword. "I would not deny a faithful person their right to pray," he said, his voice growing tight.

271

I had angered him, but he was afraid to argue. Even he was wary of God.

His beard flamed even brighter blue in his anger. I could hardly take my eyes off it.

"I will lock you in here, Countess, and return in fifteen minutes. That will be time enough."

He left, pulling the tower door shut, and I heard a key turn in the lock. I waited for his footsteps, but he didn't walk away. He was listening.

I crept part of the way up the tower steps. "Anne, do you see anything? Are they coming?"

"There's nothing, Marie. Where is he?"

"Just outside the door," I said softly. "He's given me fifteen minutes to pray before I die. Do you see anything?"

"Yes! I see a cloud of dust! Oh – it's just goats."

The count pounded on the door. "Are you ready?"

I flew back down the stairs. "It hasn't been fifteen minutes, my husband."

He didn't open the door and I went back up the steps. "Anne, do you see anything?"

"No. Wait – yes, Marie, I do! It's horsemen – it's them! They're coming!"

"How far?"

"A long way still. I'm signaling them – they're coming faster, they've seen it."

He pounded on the door again. "It is time, my wife. Your prayers are over." I didn't move. The door smashed open. "Where are you?"

"Here, I'm here."

"Come down!"

"I will, I'm coming." I turned back and spoke softly up the stairs. "How close are they, Anne?"

"They're almost here. Oh, Marie, just a few more minutes. You can't go down now. Come up here, we'll lock the door."

"Then he'll kill you, too, Anne."

"I'm coming up!" he shouted.

"Marie, come up now!" cried Anne.

"No, I'm going to get him away from you. As soon as we're gone, go as fast as you can to Thomas and Adam."

"No, Marie!"

But she was too late. I flew down the stairs and crashed right into the count. My momentum made him stagger back. It was only a second before he regained his balance, but that was all I needed. I ran past him through the door and into the chateau, racing down the hall with him right behind me.

I saw Jeannine at the end of the hall. "Countess!" she cried. "Father Gregory –"

"Run to the front and let Thomas in," I shouted, then turned and ran through the ballroom and outside onto the terrace.

That's where he caught me.

He pinned me against the stone balustrade as he caught his breath. "Did you really think you could escape? First you will die slowly," he said as he held me with one arm and pulled his sword out with the other, "feeling every drop of your life leaving. And then they will die." He gathered my hair in his hand and pulled my head back. I closed my eyes and felt his hot breath on my face.

Oddly enough, my mind went through a mental list as he brought the sword to my throat. Anne was getting away. Jeannine was running to the front. Renard was still somewhere. And Thomas was coming.

His blade was against my throat as I thought of Thomas, and I realized how much I wanted to live. He pressed on it as he drew it across and I could feel my skin begin to split.

Then the chateau seemed to shudder as I heard the great wooden front doors smash open and Thomas called my name.

"He'll never let you live," I whispered.

He faltered and the blade stopped. He was listening. This was my chance. I lifted my foot and slammed it down as hard as I could on his boot. He howled in pain, and the sword was gone from my throat.

I looked up in time to see a body fly through the air and land on top of him. It was Jeannine, and she was a madwoman. She scrabbled at the count's face with her fingernails and tore at his blue beard. "You won't hurt the countess, they'll kill you, they

273

will," she shouted, and he beat at her, trying to keep her away from his face.

His sword had fallen when she hit him, and I picked it up. It was heavy and I couldn't angle it correctly to stab him with the curved blade.

He saw me struggling with it and laughed, then shoved Jeannine off of him and leaped to his feet. He reached for the sword. I tried to swipe his hand but hit the stones instead. The vibrations jerked the sword from my hands and it clattered to the ground.

He reached for the sword again, but just before he grasped it he looked up, turned, and ran across the terrace. Then two men swept by me.

It was Thomas and Adam.

I watched while Adam held him at the steps and Thomas rammed a sword through his stomach. He dropped to the stones and they left him. Thomas caught me up in his arms. "Marie, my love, we were afraid we'd be too late."

I looked over at the count. To my horror he opened his eyes. Then his hand slowly reached for a dagger in his belt. I stepped back from Thomas, pulled the dagger away from the count, and shoved it into his chest. Then I went back to Thomas and buried my face in his shirt.

But he still wasn't dead. I heard him make a noise and then a sword clattered on the stones. Later they told me it was Adam's stroke, slashing right across his throat, that finally killed him.

274

Chapter Thirty-Six

Thomas ripped off a piece of his shirt and held it to my bleeding throat. We'd hardly caught our breaths when we heard a roar from the side of the chateau.

"The tower," said Jeannine. "It sounds like it's falling!"

"Anne's in there!" I cried, and Adam ran back into the chateau. Thomas, Jeannine and I came more slowly. If Anne had died, I didn't want to know. I couldn't bear the horror of losing her after all that had just occurred.

But she had done what I'd told her. As soon as the count ran after me, she left the tower and ran for the front of the chateau.

When we got outside, Adam and Anne were watching the tower. Most of it had already collapsed and the stones that were left were swaying and falling.

Thomas, his strong arm around me, noticed the fire first. "Look at the moat. It's aflame." Where long ago there had been water, tongues of fire licked up around the circular wall. We stood and watched the tower collapsing into a fire which no one had started. I shuddered. Stefan had been right. The walls had known too much, and they were coming down.

Then Renard ran up and sat by my feet. "He came for me," said Jeannine. "He barked and pulled on my dress, and I knew something was wrong." I leaned over and kissed Renard's head.

The servants came out of the chateau, all dressed for their ball. They stood in stunned silence, looking at the fire and the remains

275

of the tower. Jeannine went over and told them what had happened.

When the fire died down the room under the stairs still stood, untouched. The stones had no burn marks. Even the wooden door was there. But the lock was gone.

"That's where they are?" Thomas asked.

I nodded. He and Adam went to the door and pushed it open. When they came out, they pulled the door shut behind them, shaking their heads.

"Were they there?"

"Yes, Marie. We took them down and laid them out," said Adam. "We'll bury them properly in the village graveyard."

"Did you see Father Samuel?"

"Him, too," he said. "I'd like to see what that new priest has to say about this. He knows more than he's led us to think."

"He's dead," said Anne. "He's hanging inside, at the end of the hallway."

I leaned against Thomas. He put his arms around me and pulled me closer. "What matters most of all is you're not in that room," he said, and kissed my forehead.

We buried his wives and Father Samuel in the graveyard under the tree near my father, five fresh graves with flowers planted at the headstones. I grieved for them, each of the wives becoming a countess as I had, all dreaming of a changed life in the chateau on the hill only to find horror and death in the end. I tried not to think of their last minutes. I had come too close to mine.

I wept the most for the fifth grave, Father Samuel, so gentle and caring. He must have discovered what was happening. I think the count murdering our Father Samuel made me hate him most of all.

The servants found Martel dead in the study, his throat slashed so deeply it almost severed his head from his neck. The count must have killed Martel right before he came for me.

They found Father Gregory, or whoever he was, hanging in the hallway. He wasn't a priest after all. Thomas had gone all the way to the city to ask about him. They wouldn't listen to him at

276

first, thinking he was only an ignorant village man, but he persisted. When they finally checked, there was no such person in any of the church records.

"We should have known," said Anne when he told us. "He never knew how to do things like Father Samuel did."

"How did you know we needed you at the chateau?" I asked Thomas.

"Your dove," he said. "The Widow DuBois saw it fly up into the dovecote, and she came inside and told us. She said it didn't look right. We saw the black you put on it, and when she told us what that meant, we came."

"God bless Widow DuBois," said Anne. "What would we do without her?"

The village men buried the count, the last of his family, and the false priest in unmarked graves far away from the village. They wanted to bury my father's cousin there, too, but I stopped them. "As wicked as he was," I told them, "he tried to warn me. And he was part of my father's family." So they dug his grave in the churchyard, and I sent word to his family that he had received a proper burial.

Thomas and Adam made sure the tower was completely gone. Even the foundation stones were dug up and carted off to the river. I left the chateau and went back to our cottage, a wealthy widow after selling his other chateaus and lands, but I felt empty inside.

Mme Vacher and Henri ran the chateau in my absence. I had the colored window on the staircase landing dismantled, the glass destroyed. In its place went a paneled wooden wall with, at the very top, clear arched windows to let in the light. And underneath the windows Mme Vacher hung a beautiful painting of Germany's mountains covered with snow.

The one bright spot up on the hill was the betrothal of Jeannine and Raoul, a perfect match. As a wedding gift, I had a cottage built for them along the trail where we found Renard.

The Widow DuBois came over every day. She and Maman grew closer, and Maman talked of having her move in with us. "That would be perfect," said Anne, and when Adam and Anne got married, Maman told her she was welcome to live there.

277

"I will some day," she said, and I knew she was giving me more time to be with Maman.

Thomas waited patiently while I healed, opening his shop again and letting me visit whenever I wanted. I went often, talking with him like I used to do, sitting high up on my stool. I stayed for hours watching him work.

But my favorite times were when he finished early and we took long, slow walks through the village and out to Papa's fields, checking on the crops and sometimes picking something for supper. It felt so right, standing in the fields with him next to me, but I didn't know how to tell him.

One morning after bringing him a freshly baked loaf of bread I climbed up on my stool and sat, swinging my feet and watching him work. "What exactly were you going to tell me?" I asked. "About Father Gregory, I know you found out he was false. What else?"

He kept working. "No one outside our village seemed to know that he'd had four wives. And at both his other chateaus, several village girls had disappeared and never been found."

Then he stood up and looked at me. "I knew he was going to kill you. Just watching him, I knew he had killed his wives, and when I heard about the other girls I knew he'd killed them, too. I was going to take you away, Marie, no matter what anyone said."

He bent down over the wheel again. "That's why I left. I knew, but I had to find proof so you would listen when I came for you. Father Gregory being false, no record of his wives, other girls disappearing – everything I found out about him was wrong."

"I thought it was Martel who was evil for the longest time," I told him. "He even looked wicked, with his pointed beard." I watched Thomas for a few minutes. "Where did the count grow up?"

"He lived at his other chateaus before he came to ours. I think his parents must have known this place was cursed and kept him away from it."

"Then why did he come back?"

Thomas shrugged. "Maybe to be near the tower. Maybe he had to get away from the chateaus where he'd killed other girls. I don't care. You're safe, and that's all that matters to me."

278

That day at the shop, watching the morning sun touch his hair as he worked on the wheel, I knew I could never love anyone but him.

"I'm sorry, Thomas."

He looked up. "For what, Countess?"

"I'm not a countess anymore, I'm just Marie. And I'm sorry for everything. What I did was so stupid."

"Which part?" He smiled at me, and I loved him so much it was overwhelming.

"I knew that first night I'd married the wrong man."

"So did I."

"I cried all the way up to the chateau."

He pulled me to him and kissed me, a long, warm kiss, more loving than any I'd had before. Then he kissed my cheek and my nose and my forehead and said, "Marry me, Marie? I'll do my best to make you happy, I promise."

"It depends," I said, and he pulled back in surprise.

"On what?"

"Two things," I said.

He smiled. "Are you bargaining with me?"

"Yes. Want to hear what it is?"

He nodded.

"First, you have to hire someone to help you in your shop. That way I'll have a husband who shows up for dinner."

"Done," he said, kissing the tip of my nose.

"And second, we have to live at the chateau."

"The chateau?" he said in surprise. "I thought you wanted to live in the village."

"I do. But the chateau needs someone to live in it. And the village needs someone living there. I've changed, Thomas. I understand now some of the things Papa used to say to me. It's hard to explain. I know it sounds strange, and I'll understand if you can't marry me." I tried to be strong, but my voice faltered. "It's all right if you don't want me anymore."

He pulled me back to him. "I'll try again. Marie, will you marry me?"

"Yes," I said, smiling at him. This time I was marrying for love and a promise. And this time I knew it would last.

279

Author's Note

Forbidden Key is a retelling of two French fairy tales woven together. The first is *Bluebeard*, an early gothic story considered a fairy tale because of the magical key. The second is *The White Dove*, a variant of *Bluebeard*. Gaslighting was added to the plot, which is trying to make a victim question their sanity in order to manipulate them. The term originated from a play which was made into a 1944 MGM movie, *Gaslight*, starring Charles Boyer and Ingrid Bergman.

Although this is a French fairy tale, some of the names and titles are in English since that is the language of most of my readers.

Roesch is the family name of my grandmother. She would have been delighted to know it was used for the villain. That side of her family was originally from France.

Also by Joan Friday:

My Sister, My Soul: An Arabian Nights Tale
The story of Dunyazad and her sister Scheherazade who told the tales of the Arabian Nights in the palace of King Ryar.

The Plans of Morgiana: An Arabian Nights Tale
How could a cave cause so much trouble? Morgiana learns the surprising cost of belonging in the tale of Ali Baba, told by his slave Morgiana.

Made in the USA
Las Vegas, NV
23 November 2023